DEVOTION

ALEX SINCLAIR

BLOODHOUND
— BOOKS —

To my girls

PROLOGUE

KATHERINE - NOW

Someone is watching me. I can feel it on my skin. I take a moment in the darkness of therain-soaked night to sense their presence from a distance. It's not until I slowly turn my head and allow my wideeyes to adjust to the black that I see them standing in the open doorway to the room I'm staying in. I always keep the door shut.

In the middle of the frame, a hooded figure looms, brandishing a knife in one gloved hand, the kind I've seen people use when they go hunting. It's him. I know it.

I try to move an inch, but every muscle in my body seizes. Frozen and bathed in the moonlight glimmering off the side of the sharp blade, my breath stutters. Can he tell if I'm awake? Does he realize that I see him there? What am I supposed to do? My heart pounds with a dull agony in my chest as I remain crippled with indecision.

He doesn't move, but I understand this isn't a trick of the eyes or a cruel joke my brain is playing on me. This is happening. I am about to enter the situation we spend our entire lives seeking to avoid: fight or flight.

As if proving to govern the world around me, I break

through the fear immobilizing my body and reach for the bedside lamp. My shaking hand fumbles with the base until I find the switch. I push it in, hearing the click penetrate the quiet night air. No light fills the void. The shadows hold their control. I press the button again.

Nothing.

That's when I realize the bright alarm clock that also sits on the bedside table is dead. The power is out. Or he's cut it.

One thought overwhelms me before I can make sense of anything else: Ava. I throw out both hands and pat around the mattress, trying to find my five-year-old daughter who should be snuggled up right beside me. I moved her in here when I went to bed.

She wasn't sleeping with me because of imagined monsters dwelling under her mattress. I made her sleep in my room so I knew she would be safe from him, but she's not here. And now I'm about to discover that some beasts are all too real.

"Ava," I call in a harsh whisper. I can't speak any louder. Not with this panic muting my vocal cords while he gawks at me and hovers a short distance away from my bed in the night.

There's no response. I try again, a little stronger. "Ava. Where are you?"

No answer.

He doesn't move. Instead, he twists the knife and rolls it about, as if eager to find something to cut and slice open with its sharp edge.

I have one last play at my disposal before I make the choice I am dreading more than anything else. I slap at my bedside stand and feel for my cell, hoping to discover it and enable its flashlight. Scanning the entire table with the palm of my hand proves fruitless. There's nothing but a glass of water, the lamp, and the dead alarm clock.

A soft chuckle pierces the room in the form of a sharp rasp

of breath that comes from the doorway. Is this a game to him? Has it been all along? That's when I acknowledge how long he has planned this. He took note where Ava would be. I have to move.

I fall out of bed and recover as fast as I can before I run for the window in the opposite direction, getting my fight-or-flight answer. A thick curtain only three quarters closed stands in my way to freedom. There's no other escape out of this room apart from the blocked doorway.

As I claw at the window, I look back at my intruder and see him walk toward me, taking his time. The knife flows and dances through the air. An invisible force takes over me again, grabbing hold as I accept who is watching me with mocking eyes.

This is no hallucination. I am not losing my mind. My husband is here, and he will finally kill me if I don't escape.

1

KATHERINE - BEFORE

A lot of crazy things can happen in a short amount of time. For me, life is a blur of monotonous routine where one day rolls into the next. But in the space of less than two weeks, I got engaged and married.

It feels good to be home. I've lived in Battery Beach, Oregon, most of my thirty-four years. I left the small coastal city when I turned eighteen to attend college and see how the outside world worked, but the town called me back after only ten years, drawing me in with its simple beauty. This time, I was only gone for a short while for my honeymoon.

Things never seem to change in Battery Beach as I stare out the window of my husband Corey's Nissan Maxima as we drive to work together. My five-year-old daughter Ava sits in the back, singing away to herself as usual. It still sounds so odd to say the word 'husband' in my head considering Corey and I only got married less than a week ago.

Even stranger is thinking about my new surname. I've been Katherine Armstrong for my entire life. It will take some time to get used to calling myself Mrs. Katherine Grayson. I would have kept my maiden name, but I knew sticking to tradition was important to Corey.

We're returning from a whirlwind honeymoon to head back to our local K-5 school where we work as teachers. I have the pleasure of teaching a class of first-grade kids while Corey handles the fifth graders. Ava also attends kindergarten at our school, making our lives so much easier.

It's crazy to think eleven days ago Corey and I weren't even engaged and were unsure what the future held. We'd only just moved into our new rental when Corey popped the question. I said yes without thinking.

Corey isn't Ava's father, so neither of us wanted to bother with some expensive wedding. Instead, we grabbed two friends and rushed down to the courthouse that day and got married. We then had to beg our principal to get any time off so we could celebrate our nuptials with an impromptu trip to Vegas. My closest friend in the world, Annette, volunteered to take care of Ava while we were away. I owe Annette for helping us out at such short notice.

It all happened in a crazy blur, but I'm happy we got married. Never has a decision seemed so scary at first, but I'm glad I pushed through. Many people would call us nuts for taking such a huge step so quickly, but they don't understand how much we love each other. Plus, Corey and Ava have become like father and daughter. What more could I ask for?

Corey and I have only been together for six months, but when you realize you want to be with someone for the rest of your life, you have no choice but to dive into that commitment headfirst.

We arrive at work a tad earlier than usual to settle back into the swing of things. The sign for Battery Beach Elementary School stands proud and tall as it always has, fighting against the close-by ocean air, inviting us in. We walk across the grounds and drop Ava off at before-school care prior to her all-day kindergarten class. She attends school four days per week from nine till three. On the fifth day, she goes to a local daycare. It's a lot for a five-year-old, but we believe she can handle it.

I love my job, probably a little too much. First-grade children are at that magical age where they are keen to learn about the world while still holding respect for any authoritative adults they have in their lives. They remind me of Ava more than I realize. I don't understand how Corey handles the fifth graders. They'd eat me alive within the first hour of class despite them only being ten to eleven years old.

We reach the main building. I stop for a moment to breathe and contain my excitement for when I see everybody. We announced our marriage over Facebook like it was another post. People were shocked and full of questions. With our honeymoon to sort out, we didn't have time to answer them and accept any congratulations that were coming our way. I'm sure there were some lectures and warnings from a select few, but it was too late for any of that. We got married. Done and dusted.

As we walk inside the entrance to the school, I'm surprised not to see Annette behind the Perspex barrier of the front office. She works as an administrative assistant to the small school's principal and comes in a full hour earlier than Corey and me. In fact, none of the office staff are present which is odd, given it's now eight thirty. The students and parents will file in shortly.

"We must have scared them all off," Corey jokes.

I react with mere confusion as we continue down the corridor to the faculty lounge. Maybe there are a few teachers floating around that can tell us why the office is devoid of life. If not, I don't know what's happened in the short time we've been away.

2

KATHERINE

When Corey and I step through the open entrance to the faculty lounge, a group of people greet us by shouting 'surprise.' All the teachers and office staff fill the small space. A banner hangs above on the far wall that says, 'Congratulations Mr. & Mrs. Grayson!'

"Oh my god," I blurt as my hands fly to my mouth in shock. My eyes begin to water as I take it all in.

Annette is front and center of the grand gesture. She walks forward and gives me a tight hug, whispering further salutations into my ear.

"Thank you so much," I say, knowing Annette would have been the one to make this all happen. Sure I get along with most people in the school, but I've known Annette since we were kids. She, like many of the locals around town, has lived in Battery Beach her whole life.

Annette waves me off. "What, this? Piece of cake. Took no time at all to organize these guys," she says with a chuckle. We both understand how difficult it is to get anyone in the school to agree on how things should be run when we have our meetings. How Annette pulled this off seems impossible.

"Thank you again. We really appreciate this a lot, don't we?" I ask Corey.

He steps forward and thanks Annette with a smile. She gives him a quick hug and congratulates us again.

"We do appreciate it," Corey says. "This all happened so fast, it's nice to know people care."

"Of course they do," Annette says. "You and Kat are part of the BBES family. Now, enough of this gratitude. I need to see the rock you bought for your wife." Annette's hands fall down to my left hand and studies the diamond ring Corey purchased for me in Vegas. I insisted upon him getting me something modest and affordable, but he wouldn't listen.

Corey and I continue to take what congratulations we can squeeze in until time forces the staff to dissipate and go to their assigned rooms before all hell breaks loose. The school doesn't rest. At least not until the summer break.

I say goodbye to Annette and Corey then head to my classroom to enjoy a day of fun with my students. They'd managed to not send my temporary replacement running and worked through most of their planned material. Some children have lots of questions for me regarding my sudden wedding. I suppose most of their parents got married before they were born. There were also plenty whose parents had divorced and moved on to other relationships. Those children had no questions and remained quiet. My new name is the biggest pill to swallow with most of the kids still calling me Miss Armstrong.

Time passed by so quickly. I couldn't tell if that was a good thing or not given how tired I am. We got back from Vegas late last night on a flight into Portland so we could enjoy every minute of our short honeymoon. We only picked up Ava early this morning. I've been high on adrenaline all day. Now I'm crashing.

There is one fun task I need to complete before our trip home together with Corey.

I return to the staffroom with Ava holding my hand. The 'congratulations' banner had been taken down and given to me at lunchtime. I asked if I could keep it, not realizing how much I love seeing Mr. and Mrs. Grayson written in any format.

I head over to my appointed mail slot to check for my daily surprise. Professionally, the staff hardly use the aging system anymore with email and the school's network. But every day, I find a handwritten note placed in my slot from a certain special someone.

Corey is a hopeless romantic. Each day, he writes me a little love note and places it in my mail slot. I figure most of his material gets plagiarized from the web, but I appreciate and love the effort he goes to.

When I reach inside the waist-length slot, I find nothing but the cold aluminum surface of an empty space. I squat down and take a proper look to check if I'm getting confused with a neighbor's spot. I have my hands in the right place, seeing the label from my old surname, Armstrong. It reminds me I need to make up more than a dozen labels for my classroom and update all of my records online now that I am a Grayson.

I rise and step back from the columns of mail slots to see if Corey's note has fallen to the ground. It must be here. For the last three months, he hasn't missed a day, never once failing to write me a note that told me how much he cares for and loves me. I feel a pit in my stomach. Is the romance over now that we are hitched? This has to be a mistake.

"Mommy?" Ava says.

"Yeah, sweetie?"

"Where's your note from Corey?"

My cell interrupts me with a pulse in my pocket before I can answer. I already know it will be a text from Corey, so I pull my phone out and read a message saying he is ready and waiting for us at the car.

"Mommy?" Ava presses.

"I'm not sure, baby. I guess he was too busy today. Let's not worry about it, though."

Ava nods and continues waiting patiently for me.

I shuffle away from my empty mail slot and make my way past Annette in the office. I don't want to chat to her without a note from Corey. It's stupid, I realize, but I can't do it. Instead, I wave goodbye with a smile and thank her again before I head out to Corey's car with Ava. All the while, only one thought runs through my brain: why didn't Corey leave me a note?

3

The love notes. I hate these stupid pointless scraps of paper. For months they drove me to the point of madness until I could no longer stand it. They had to stop. So for once, Katherine won't get one of her precious love letters in her mail slot. I know it will make her fear the worst, but maybe she needs a good dose of reality for a change.

Does she honestly think she is this important? Does she feel she's so special she deserves a message that holds her high above the rest of the world, delivered to her daily? Well, it's over. I didn't offer her a choice in the matter, nor did she utter a word about it. I wasn't sure if she would complain or not, but now I don't expect her to say a thing. How weak. I might bring the notes back into the mix tomorrow to observe what happens. Surely, she'll mention something about it then.

It wasn't always this way. I didn't always detest Katherine so much that I would purposely make her unhappy. But a lot can change in six months. People evolve. Lives shift direction. A person you once thought you understood shows you their true self. What happens next is not on me. That's on her and is already written, embedded into history ahead of time.

The honeymoon wasn't easy. Vegas and back in five days. It pushed me to breaking point. Five days might be a flash in the sky to some, but it felt like a lifetime.

The trip did, however, confirm everything I already knew about Katherine. It showed me how selfish and thoughtless a person she really is. I didn't know what else I was expecting.

I hope she's ready for anything because today will be her first true day of being a wife. What's coming next will test her and show me what she's made of, and what she's capable of withstanding. After all, she wanted to get married.

She stood before the judge that day and made a commitment, one that shouldn't be thrown around so openly in a courthouse of all places. I never hoped for things to go down this path. Still, I complied with my end of the arrangement, completed what the law required of me, signed what the judge told me to. It's what Katherine wanted. I merely agreed to the event like a mindless drone. It makes me wonder if Katherine knew what she was getting herself into by saying yes. I guess time will tell.

The 'congratulations' banner today made me feel sick the second I laid eyes on it, but I had to smile and play my part the way she expected me to. What was there to even congratulate? Two people agreed to be bound by the law and little else. Nothing had really changed. In today's age of divorce, a commitment such as marriage is almost meaningless. That's how little stock I put into the proceedings. But I could see on her face how much she valued the idea. She felt special and above the others in the room while we stood there. I had to pretend to be happy about the whole thing and toe the line.

Well, I've got news for my dear Katherine. I will teach her that marriage is not something to underestimate. She will learn what it means to be Mrs. Katherine Grayson.

4

KATHERINE

I'm an idiot. Before Ava and I reach Corey's car, I realize my keys are missing. And these aren't the ones you want to misplace. They're not for my house or sedan, but the keys I need to unlock my classroom and everything within it. I'll be in all kinds of trouble if I can't locate them and will be on the hook for a fee to have them replaced.

After emptying my bag for the third time to check if the keys got caught somewhere in the lining, I drag Ava to my room trying to retrace my steps. I had the damn things only a few minutes ago when I locked the door, didn't I? My daily routine flashes through my head as I recall doing everything today slightly incorrect. We were only gone for five days, but the excitement of our honeymoon pulled my mind too far away from the real world. I guess Corey and I celebrated hard in Vegas to make up for our basic nuptials.

Don't get me wrong. I loved our spur-of-the-moment cere-mony, but I always thought I'd have that special wedding I grew up dreaming about. Corey seemed so eager that I went along with the proposal without thinking. As if that wasn't enough to blow my mind, he pressed hard to charge down to the courthouse and marry me. Really, I could have taken some time to plan out something amazing, but it was probably for the best we never did. I doubt we could have afforded the day I was fantasizing about.

I don't recall locking my classroom door now that I think about it. What I remember is an overwhelming desire to see Corey. Did I let thoughts of our honeymoon distract me like a moth when a porch light got flicked on for the night? I missed my husband, despite seeing him at recess when he dropped in for a brief visit. I'd even sent a few quick texts to him whenever I could, breaking the principal's most annoying rule.

Ava and I reach my classroom and find no keys fallen along the way. I must have left them inside the room like a moron. My head shakes as I open the unlocked door, resisting the urge to cuss under my breath. My daughter need not hear it.

"What are we doing, Mommy?" Ava asks, her voice half in complaint. She gets tired and somewhat cranky at this time of day until she's home with a snack watching her favorite animated shows. I can relate to the thought.

"Silly Mommy forgot her keys. We'll just have a quick look inside to see where I left them. It won't take a minute, I promise."

"Okay," she says, elongating the word as she drags her feet while we walk in. You'd think I was asking for a kidney the way her shoulders had drooped.

"Sit down in a chair and I'll quickly locate them." I direct Ava to the nearest seat with my index finger and get to work searching the usual places I throw my keys each morning. Rummaging through my desk, I find it amazing how it only took me today to mess up my workspace again. I had the area spotless for once before we left. Now, it's a pigsty.

I stand, hands on hips, after having searched in and around my workstation. Ava sits at one of the tables, swinging her legs back and forth with her fingers gripping the sides of the chair.

Boredom has kicked in fast as she makes noises with her mouth while her neck struggles to hold her head up. I can't help but snicker at how cute she looks with her blonde pigtails and green eyes.

My attention shifts to the clock on the wall, reminding me that Corey is waiting. I debate sending him a text as I go through my desk again in vain to produce nothing but frustration. Where could they be? Did one of the kids have them? The class acted up the second I took a day off, which wasn't often. I run through the list of potential suspects in my head and pray none of them have taken my keys home in their bag.

"Mommy?" Ava asks.

"Yeah, honey?"

"Did you find your keys?"

"No, sweetheart. But it's time to go. We don't want to keep Corey waiting, do we?"

Ava smiles at the mere mention of Corey. The two get on like a house on fire. I'm so lucky.

"Let's move," I say, matching her smile as I extend out a hand to guide her off the chair. It's crazy to think that she'll soon be ready to leave the kindergarten and start first grade. My little girl is growing up too fast. I won't be teaching her if I can help it, wanting to avoid any classroom favoritism.

It feels like only yesterday when she started to walk and talk as I raised her all on my own. Things took a dark turn when I had Ava, but somehow, we pushed through that time. Then Corey came along. Not only did he win over my heart, but he made sure he got to know Ava, treating her as if she were his own flesh and blood.

We hurry across the school grounds with cloudy weather threatening overhead. I have no choice but to report my lost keys to the office, so I figure Annette might help me out with a spare until I find my own. She could save me a lot of embarrassment.

I've put the lack of a love note to the depths of my mind and feel better able to hold a conversation in the office without thinking about it.

This is not the best first day back given I'm missing two important items. I can only hope Annette helps me make things right again.

5

KATHERINE

As Ava and I reach the office, my cell buzzes in my bag. I don't always feel the vibration in my hand, but it must be sitting in the right spot for a change. I pull it out and see a text from Corey asking again where we are. My thumb attempts to draft a reply as we approach Annette, but she calls out to me before I can get any words down.

"How are you?" she asks when we reach the glass divider Annette is standing behind. "How was your first day back?"

"Good," I say. "Exciting and draining all at once. I swear we never left. Vegas feels like a distant memory."

"Oh, come on, Kat. I'll bet there are some unforgettable memories in there, huh?" she says, flicking her brows up.

The corner of my mouth scrunches into a coy smile I can't contain as I try not to blush. Among other reasons, I hope Ava doesn't understand the conversation taking place. "Maybe I'll tell you over some coffee this weekend."

"Maybe? How about definitely? It's the only thing that'll get me through this slow week."

"Okay. You've twisted my arm," I say, not wanting to discuss my honeymoon. If I'm lucky, Annette might forget in a few days.

"And how are you, Ava? Happy that Mommy and Corey are back?"

"Yeah," she says through a huge grin as she nibbles her index finger while swinging from my grip.

It's so amazing that I have Annette around to help with babysitting when I need it. She made our honeymoon happen when she agreed to watch Ava the entire time. I pat Ava's head with a light hand at her innocent response to Annette. "So anyway, I hate to be a pain, but I have to ask you for a huge favor."

"Yes?" Annette asks, leaning closer.

I close my eyes for two seconds and flash them open. "I've lost my keys."

"What?" she whispers, half glancing over her shoulder. "Seriously?"

I nod, lips taut.

"Crap," Annette lets slip. She keeps her voice quiet. "There's the spare master set I can give you, but you have to find the original as soon as you can. The school will have no choice but to have the locks changed over if you can't locate them. With the budget cuts going around, Barry won't be too happy about it."

Barry Snyder is our principal. A reasonable man most days. But recent pressure pushed down on him from his superiors regarding the school's finances has put him on edge.

"Understood. I'll take the spare set until I can turn the room upside down."

Annette slides them over to me as if we are doing some kind of drug deal.

"Thank you," I say as I scoop them up. "I owe you big time. First you look after Ava for me. Now this. You're too good to me."

"Anytime. You know I've got your back. You'd better get out of here. Best not to keep that husband of yours waiting around."

Husband. I love hearing the word. It still sounds alien. A

huge grin plasters my face. "Thank you again," I say as we leave. I give Annette a small wave while Ava tells her goodbye.

"Oh, and don't worry about locking up. I'll ask the janitor to do it."

"You're the best."

"I know, I know. You can make it up to me with a tall cup of coffee this weekend," Annette shouts as we go through the office doors.

With the spare master in hand, I rush out to the parking lot where Corey has been waiting. When he hears about me losing my keys, he'll have a good laugh. He knows how unorganized I can be.

We arrive at the car. I load up Ava and speak to him from the back seat as I buckle her in. "Sorry we're late. I've lost my classroom keys like an idiot. I had to—"

"Where were you?" he barks.

I snap my eyes to his in the rearview mirror. His brows narrow in with focus as I sense tension in his body.

"I was about to tell you that—"

"Just get in the car. I've been waiting long enough to drive home."

"Okay," I say, almost frozen by his tone.

"What's wrong with Corey, Mommy?" Ava asks.

I glance to the mirror again to see his expression soften as he addresses Ava. "I'm sorry," he says. "I've had the worst day is all, sweetheart. I shouldn't have spoken like that to your mommy."

I want to say something, but I don't, figuring we're both tired and grumpy from having to rush back to work from a nice vacation. I finish with Ava and move around to the front passenger seat and climb in. I keep my gaze fixed on Corey as he starts the car and drives out of the school's parking lot.

. . .

"Is everything okay?" I ask him as we drive through town.

"I'm fine," he says. "It's been one of those days, you know. I'm sorry I spoke to you like that. Let's go home and forget all about it. What do you say, Ava? How about some chocolate ice cream for dessert?"

"Yes, please!" Ava shouts.

"So tell me about the keys," he says.

I glance away from his smile with downcast eyes. Corey tells me when something is bothering him. What is he keeping from me?

Katherine fell for it. She believed that her haphazard classroom management made her lose her school keys. How gullible can you get? As stupid as she is at the best of times, even I know she would never do such a thing, but she accepted the fact without question.

It didn't take much for me to swipe them from her open bag today due to how careless she is with her belongings. How she hasn't been mugged yet astounds me. I could have done the deed in front of her as we had our morning coffee, given the way she leaves her keys sitting at the top of her handbag for anyone to snatch. Now that I have them, the fun can begin.

With some doubt running around inside her head, I will use those lost keys to open up a few opportunities. She won't believe what I have planned for her next. She'll think her life is falling apart, that the world has somehow changed overnight. I'll play my part to perfection.

Katherine has been careless from the moment I first met her. Only a few months ago, she lost her cell when we went out for drinks one night. She'd barely had a glass of wine, yet she still misplaced her expensive new iPhone within fifteen minutes of our arrival, ruining our fun the way only she can. I had no choice but to offer to pay for a replacement. Of course she said no, always trying to present herself as the mature adult. I could tell though underneath her thin skin she was ready to insist the world come to a screaming halt because of her own stupidity.

The look on her face will be priceless when she suddenly finds those keys. I can imagine the slight twitch she'll have in her eyes as her small brain attempts to piece things together. Confusion will take over and soon meld into anger. If only I could record the whole thing without her noticing.

No doubt Ava will interrupt the precious moment with some demand. I can't stand that little brat, but Katherine thinks I love her as if she were my own daughter. Every time I interact with that kid, I'm forced to pretend I give a damn about her well-being. She's the last person on this planet I ever think about. Why should I give any consideration to a child whose parents were stupid enough to fall pregnant when they could barely take care of their own pathetic lives? She's not my damn problem, but that devil continually gets thrust upon me. Still, I smile and laugh when I'm supposed to, constantly aware that Katherine is watching and judging my every interaction like an obsessed social worker.

So far, my plan is on track. Katherine can't help being predictable, so it won't be hard for me to reach my end goal without so much as one hiccup as long as I stay focused. But before I achieve everything I need to accomplish, I will have a little fun driving Mrs. Grayson to the brink of insanity.

W e roll into the driveway of our new rental. Before we got married, Corey and I decided we needed a bigger place to live so we could pull all of his things out of storage and save some money. Part of me thinks the move might have inspired his sudden desire to propose to me without discussing the idea first. Sure, we already lived together, but the minute Corey wanted to remove his belongings from storage was the moment he'd taken this relationship to the next level.

It wouldn't have been an easy decision to make given the extra commitment Ava brings alongside me. I know caring for someone else's child isn't a hassle most people want to bother with, but Corey has put in the hard work with Ava. He makes her feel loved. Sure, occasionally I notice the situation getting to him when he'd rather be alone with me, but he's only human.

Corey kills the engine and sighs.

"Are you sure everything's okay, honey?" I ask. I don't want to be a pain, but I can see something's on his mind.

"It's nothing."

"Come on. You can tell me. That's what wives are for."

He shifts to me with his usual loving smile, the one I fell in love with six months ago. But it soon turns sour. "The same old thing as ever: a parent complaining. I don't know why, but I thought being away from the school even for a few days might have allowed some change to sweep in. Of course not. If anything, it's given them more ammunition."

I shake my head in support. "What happened?"

"What always does. I give a kid a grade, he takes it home to show his parents, they lose their minds and yell at me over the sheer possibility that their child is less than perfect. Little do they realize how many lies their son has sprinkled over that terrible mark I've handed out. If I dare argue with Mom and Dad, they'll run to the principal and threaten all kinds of legal action. Then, before I know it, I'll be forced to reverse the grade and destroy all authority I might have held over the damn twerp to begin with."

"Hey, it's okay," I say as I rub his arm. "Did this all happen today?"

"No. My old school before I moved here. So far, I'm at the stage where this kid's parents are questioning the mark I gave out before we left. It's only a matter of time before they escalate the problem though." He slams the steering wheel with a fist.

I flinch and pull my arm away from him as if I was patting a dog who's suddenly bared its teeth. I've never seen this side of Corey.

"I'm sorry," he says after opening his hand. "I didn't mean to—"

"It's fine. Let's just get inside. I'll make you some dinner while you take a nice hot shower to unwind. What do you say?"

"You don't have to do that. You've worked hard today. Probably harder than me."

"I'm happy to do it. I know it's your turn to cook, but you need a break. Plus, I had a good day." I hate lying to him.

"But what about your keys? That can't be an easy thing to deal with."

"They're keys that'll wind up in some silly place on my desk at school. Guarantee it." I climb out of the sedan and walk to Ava. I pull the handle on her door to let her out. The child lock prevents her from opening it herself. Once I help her down from her seat to the driveway, I twist to spot Corey still sitting in the car like he's caught in a daydream. There's more going on inside that head than some threatening parents with too much time on their hands. I can see it.

"Come on," I say as I tap on the glass of his window. "Let's forget about school and relax." I give him the best smile possible after the whirlwind of a day I've had.

Corey reciprocates and climbs out of the car. "I'll be inside in a second. I just need to look for something in the garage."

Most of our unpacked moving boxes are in there. "Okay. I'll be inside making you some dinner. Once you're done out here, go take a shower."

"All right. Fine. I'll do what I'm told," he says, raising his arms in defeat.

"Did you want me to bring your bag in?"

"Thanks," he replies, handing it over as he heads toward the garage.

Grabbing Corey's laptop bag, I walk Ava in and set her up in front of the TV with some snacks and a few of her favorite toys. I know I won't ever win mother of the year, but I need to keep her occupied so I can make us all some dinner. Nothing pushes a bad day to the back of your head better than a full stomach, and I happen to be a decent cook. At least I think I am.

Corey comes inside by the time I've got half a chicken Cobb salad prepared. The meal is one of his favorites and a breeze to whip up. I hear the shower run while Ava continues to stare at some kids' show on the TV that has a solid line of purchasable toys supporting it. I swear the creators add new characters every other week so they can throw another toy onto the shelves at Walmart. Still, I can't deny it makes her happy.

Putting my cynicism aside, I spot Corey coming out of our bedroom redressed, rubbing his short hair to make sure it's dry.

"Smells wonderful," he says toward the sizzling chicken on the frying pan.

I move over to him and wrap my arms around his body for a firm hug. He squeezes me back after a moment.

"What was that for?" he asks.

"I wanted to cheer you up. We all know how some of these parents can be. I don't think it matters what grade you teach or how long you've been in this industry. Some people will never give you the respect you deserve."

Corey agrees as we break off our embrace. He heads for the refrigerator and pulls out a beer, popping the cap a second later. I thought he was getting the drink out ready for dinner, but he takes a long swig. It's unlike him to have any alcohol before we eat. I say nothing, figuring he needs to relax and forget about work.

"So where do you think your keys are?" he asks, jutting his beer at me.

"Oh, it doesn't matter. They'll turn up. And if they don't, I'll have to beg the school not to send me a bill for the replacement locks and new keys. Annette would vouch for me."

Corey chuckles. "I'm positive she would take the blame if you asked her to."

I know Corey's only joking, but there isn't much Annette and I wouldn't do for each other. We've been friends forever. So long now I've lost count.

"That reminds me," Corey says. "I got a funny email from one of the guys I wanted to show you. Here, it's on my cell." He heads over to his laptop bag and unzips the main section. A jangling of metal falls out almost immediately. Two sets of school keys sit on the kitchen table.

"Are those my school keys beside yours?" I ask as my brows pull in tight on my forehead.

"What the hell?" Corey blurts. "I don't know how they got there."

"It's okay. You must have grabbed them by mistake somehow."

"How?"

I squeeze my right elbow with my left hand. "Maybe when you dropped in during recess, you picked them up by accident and put them in your pocket."

"What? Come on. I'm not that stupid."

"I wasn't saying you—"

"Do you really think I'd do something like that?" Corey asks, cutting me off. His nostrils flare up along with his rapid breathing. Yet despite his anger, he looks guilty. Why can't he admit it was an accident?

I shake my head. "No, of course not." I throw a weak smile in his direction, hoping I sound genuine. I doubt my desperate message is getting across as I wonder why he's reacting this way. I wasn't accusing him of anything. All he has to do is own up to his mistake.

"I wouldn't, all right?"

"But—"

Ava sneaks up on our argument and tugs at my pant leg. "Mommy?"

"Yes, sweetie?" I ask, pulling my eyes from Corey's intense stare.

"Is dinner ready yet? I'm still hungry."

Corey walks away before I can give my daughter an answer

or say another word to him. I gaze down at Ava and smile with a face my parents only ever used when they were trying to cover up a fight. "A few minutes longer, baby. Okay? Go back to your show."

Ava runs off without a care in the world and leaves me alone in the kitchen as confusion pins me to the floor.

What's wrong with the man I just married?

8

I can't wait for tomorrow. The look on Katherine's face today was perfect. Little does she know it's only the beginning of what's to come. I wasn't sure if things would ever reach this point, if I'd commit to this plan or take off one day without an explanation, but here I am, ready to do what is necessary. There were many times when I thought it was wrong to fantasize the way I have about Katherine, wishing ill upon her life, but now I have clarity.

Katherine deserves the fallout the coming storm will bring. Some days I wonder if she's conscious or not of the past or her part in what happened, but I doubt it would have stopped her from doing what she did. I know the real Katherine and not the fake one the rest of the world has had thrown in its face. Her true nature hides behind an ignorant mask that presents her as nothing but an innocent pushover. She knew what she was doing that day, and I can't let another minute go by without punishment. Actions have consequences.

I thought about how best to make her suffer. A swift resolution didn't seem enough. After mulling it over for many nights, I decided a slow burn would be the strongest approach. I want her to feel real pain first and slowly lose herself piece by piece. She will beg for it to stop once I'm through with her. And before she ever realizes the truth, I'll have her regretting the second she became Mrs. Grayson. As for Ava, the system can deal with her. There's no chance in hell that little brat will become my problem.

The game has begun. Soon Katherine will understand true pain. She will appreciate the compounding intensity each new minute brings me whenever I see her living without consequence. The clock is ticking over her head, and the poor dear has no clue what's coming these next few weeks.

It's almost too easy.

9

KATHERINE

The next morning, Corey and I drive to school in silence while Ava sings more songs to herself in the back seat. Her voice is off-key and cute as hell. Every word she gets wrong or skips allows me to delay the inevitable in my mind: I can't stop her from growing up. It's happening faster than I can handle. I only have myself to blame for any wasted moments passing me by when she was a toddler. I was too wrapped up with her father's absence to realize I should have been focusing on what was best for her. Instead, I spent most of my time being mentally checked out.

I know Ava's only five, but I can't shake the feeling that I squandered away the early years of her life dealing with her father, Peter. Even before Ava came along, he used to make everything about himself. He would have never understood the core concept of parenting: the child comes first. Instead of being with his family, Peter disappeared one month prior to Ava's birth so he could continue drinking, gambling, and doing God knows what else. It was his only way to deal with the unwanted household he felt he'd had thrust upon him.

I did what I could to raise Ava while her father abandoned

me with no funds. The pain he scarred my soul with only made me believe that Ava and I weren't good enough for him. The truth was the opposite, but I would never see that until later.

When Peter took off in the middle of the night before Ava came to be, he stole the last chunk of money I had and got out of town. He would have burned through that cash fast, so there was never any point in trying to pursue him for child support. He'd never pay.

All I can do now for Ava is make up for any lost time her dad caused and appreciate every new moment as if they are our last.

Having Corey around only helps me to give Ava everything she deserves in life, and not just financially but emotionally. Finally, I'm proud to say there is a man in her world deserving of her attention. Corey is such a good father figure for my little girl. I know deep in my heart that she sees him as her dad. The lowlife scumbag who knocked me up will never be worthy of the title.

Corey's sedan bounces over the slight bump at the entrance of the school's parking lot. We find a decent spot reserved for staff, reducing the distance I need to walk Ava to her before-school care.

"I'll take her," Corey offers as we both climb out the front at the same time.

"It's fine," I reply, unsure if he is trying to make up for last night. We haven't spoken a word about it and have kept any communication to a bare minimum. It was unlike us to go to bed with an argument hanging over our heads. Corey would always try to talk things through no matter what. I once preferred to be left alone for at least a day, but I've gotten used to the way he promptly deals with any issues we have.

"No, I'm happy to take her," Corey says. "Catch up with Annette so you can drop off the spare key."

"Good idea," I say, choosing diplomacy over further argument. I squat to Ava and give her a big kiss and cuddle, enjoying the giggle on her face as I tickle her under the chin. "Have a wonderful day, honey. I'll be by after school to pick you up, okay."

"Bye, Mommy," she says, waving me off.

Corey walks her away from me without saying a word. He always kisses me goodbye and wishes me a nice day.

Was our fight really that bad?

10

KATHERINE

I walk toward the main building through the cold morning air to drop the spare keys in to Annette. She'll be thrilled to see that I found the set that belongs to my classroom. I should have texted her about it last night, but the confusion with Corey got me so upset. We didn't have the best first day back as a married couple. Tonight will be different as we have plans to head out to dinner with a reservation Corey made the minute we reached town. At least I hope we still do.

Pushing open the door to the office, a soft breeze of warm air wraps itself around my body, inviting me in. The heating in the main building has always been the school's best feature, extending to the faculty lounge. It's one of the few perks we teachers have. Our classrooms, however, run on a separate system that never seems to keep up with the weather.

"Hey, Kat," Annette calls out to me with her head down in some paperwork. It's after eight and she's already deep into her work. I always take a good hour to get into things each day no matter how keen the students might be to learn. Thank God we don't start as early as some elementary schools in Oregon. The thought only reminds me there's coffee with my name on it in the faculty lounge. The school doesn't provide us with the best cup of brew you'll ever have, but it's free.

I step up to Annette with a smile and pull the spare keys from my coat pocket. She glances up from her paperwork and smiles. "Does this mean you found your keys?"

"Yep. Bit of a silly story between Corey and I, but the important thing is there's no need to spend hundreds of dollars fixing the problem."

"That's a relief, but I would have saved your butt." She leans forward and lowers her voice. "Between you and me, Barry is a pushover if you catch him on a good day."

Before I thank Annette for helping me out, a fellow first-grade teacher from my team walks in from the corridor that backs onto the office. My mouth closes whenever Susan Black is around. I don't hate Susan or anything so petty, it's just that she is a stickler for the rules.

Pushing retirement age, Susan has been at BBES longer than anyone else—the principal included. There is a running joke that they had assembled her alongside the school when they built the facility many decades ago. All kidding aside, Susan is as serious as they come, and not much slips by her.

"Miss Tibbs. Mrs. Grayson," she says, greeting us with zero warmth.

"Hello, Susan. How are you today?" I ask her, not wanting to hear about her mood. Without a doubt she had arrived a few hours earlier, not having anything better to do.

"Don't ask. I've been pouring over the first-grade planners for next week and I can see you've made several mistakes that need addressing."

"Oh, is that—?"

"When can you meet so we can fix this?" Susan asks, cutting me off. There's no checking to see if I've agreed to meet up. She's telling me what's happening as if someone appointed her to be

my mentor teacher. I try to think on my feet, but nothing comes
to mind.

"I'm free at lunchtime," Susan says. "We'll meet in your classroom. I'll see you then."

"Okay," I reply as Susan bustles away on to her next victim.
"Great. There goes my break out the window. I'll be lucky if
she doesn't dig into the rest of the year's planners. Who
knows what made her do a sudden audit on next week's
lessons?"

"Forget her," Annette says. "It's Friday. School finishes early.
We should grab a coffee after work at the mall. I'm dying to hear
about Vegas, and Saturday is too far off."

The idea sounds fun apart from me having to talk about the
honeymoon. Then Ava comes to mind. "I could go for a few
hours, but I should check if Corey's okay to watch Ava. Corey
and I are supposed to be going out for dinner later, but I'm not
sure if that's still on."

"Why?" Annette asks, her forehead creasing.

The corner of my mouth screws up as I look away.

"You two had a fight, didn't you?"

"Yeah. Our first argument as a married couple. Probably one
of the worst, too. It's not like us to get so crabby at each other so
quickly either."

Annette gives me a weak smile. "I'm sure it's nothing. You
know what, let's bring Ava along. No need to bug Corey. Besides,
her Aunty Annette can buy her a nice outfit."

"You don't have to do that. Corey won't mind."

"I won't mind what?" he asks as he comes through the front
door to the office.

My mouth freezes, half open. I feel like someone has caught
me in the middle of doing something wrong.

Corey reaches the desk as we both stare at him. The look on
his face asks a second time.

"I was wondering if I could steal your wife for a few hours before your hot date tonight," Annette says.

Corey purses his lips and focuses on me. "Not a problem. I'll pick up Ava so you can both head out after school."

"Are you sure? We don't mind taking her with us, seeing as it's an early finish," I say.

He holds his gaze on me for a few moments longer than is necessary. "Not a problem. You two go have fun. Just be home in time to put Ava to bed. You know how funny she gets when other people try to do it."

"I will. Thanks, honey."

Corey smiles and heads toward the faculty lounge.

"Thank you, Corey," Annette calls out as he leaves. She faces me with a grin and says, "Hey, that reminds me."

I spot something in my mail slot before Annette finishes her thought. "One second." I turn my head round to see one of Corey's notes sitting where I swore it wasn't the day before. "Corey, wait."

He stops partway up the corridor. "What is it? I'm dying for a coffee here."

I shuffle toward the note on autopilot with my mouth half open. "Is that one of your love notes?" I ask, pointing at the folded pink piece of paper.

Corey walks back, huffing a sigh under his breath. "Yep. I placed it there yesterday. Why?"

"It wasn't there. I swear it."

Corey's hands fold across his chest. "I don't know what else to tell you. I put the thing in your slot yesterday. You mustn't have seen it."

"No, I checked this before we left. There was nothing there."

"That's my fault," Annette says. "I relocated your mail slot and the note so they'd be next to Corey's. When I came in this morning, I realized you hadn't seen it so I moved it back to your old spot. Sorry for the confusion."

"No, it's fine," I say. "I'm a little sensitive today is all." I turn to Corey. "Sorry, honey. I didn't mean to accuse you of anything."

"That's okay," Corey says. "I was a tad defensive myself." He opens his arms and draws me in for a hug. I accept, feeling like an idiot at the same time.

"Phew," Annette says. "Glad I didn't cause you guys to fight."

Corey waves her off with a smile. "Don't worry about it. I'm sure we would have worked it out before security needed to be called. Anyway, I better be going." He turns to me with a much calmer face. "I'll see you later."

"Bye," I say as I wave my hand.

"Later, Annette."

Corey disappears down the corridor as I approach Annette, embarrassed. "I'm such a moron. I don't know why I always have to assume the worst."

"Forget it. Just get through the day and we'll go have that coffee. Plus, we can find something sexy for you to wear tonight. Corey will forget all about any fight you had."

I chuckle as I shy away, wishing she wouldn't talk about such a topic.

"You know he thinks the world of you. It's all right there in that letter you still haven't read."

"Yeah, I guess," I reply not wanting to read Corey's love letter. Somehow, they've lost all meaning now that we've had a fight over them. I open the note for show and read a poem Corey has inserted my name into.

I flash a grin at Annette, wishing I could start this day over.

11

I can't believe how furious Katherine got over the note. I knew the new location would make her lose her mind, but not as efficiently as it did. Without a doubt, she'll ask to have the letters put to rest as she finally realizes how pathetic the process is.

What sort of individual can honestly expect to have such a fuss made over them every single day? It's exhausting and childish. She's not sixteen. But then again Katherine is about as naïve a person as they come. To top things off, her sensitivity has always been a commanding force in her life thanks to her ex, Peter. It takes no one long to see how little Katherine can handle. Messing with her is going to be easier than I expected. The complication with the note will only fill her head with more self-doubt and anxiety than she already has.

From the moment we first spoke, Katherine came across to me as someone I could walk all over and mold into the person I wanted her to be, provided I chose my words correctly. How little effort I would have to make to take advantage of such a feeble mind. Her backbone is made of glass and shatters at the first sign of conflict. I see it at the school so often it has become an embarrassing joke. It's why she always has to have other people ask easy questions on her behalf. A request for someone to watch Ava for a few hours shouldn't be such a difficult task. Pathetic.

It's the choices Katherine makes when she thinks no one is watching that truly astound me. Only then does her real self come out from hiding.

Tonight I'm stepping up the game.

Dinner will be a true test of her failing will. She thought things were all perfect on the honeymoon. The romantic meals, the sightseeing, the endless sessions spent in bed all made her feel invincible, that her world could only get better, not worse for a change. That time is in the past. Expired. Merely the calm before the storm for what I have planned. I hope Katherine enjoyed her break away from reality, because she won't ever find such ignorant bliss again.

Seeing her reunite with Ava after spending a few hours at the mall reminds me of her biggest weakness. That child is a huge vulnerability to be exploited. People never seem to realize how weak children can make them. But Ava is too easy a target to use for now. No, I need this to be a challenge. I want to break Katherine by twisting her mind again and again until something snaps.

An outsider looking in might wonder what Katherine has done to deserve such punishment. I don't like to think about it, though. The pain only becomes all too real, pulling my focus away from where it's needed, converting my anger into a crippling sadness I have no control over. I've spent too many nights staring up at the ceiling with thoughts of what Katherine did, only having to face the world the next day and pretend everything is okay.

I won't slip back into the darkness. Not until Katherine knows what it's like to suffer.

12

KATHERINE

The mall was a blast, just what I needed to forget about the silly note business. I think I'll tell Corey not to worry about writing them anymore now that we're married. It was selfish of me to expect that much effort from him each day. It's not like I was doing the same for him.

I get myself ready for dinner with enough time for my mom to help me put Ava down for the night. My little sweetheart doesn't handle being taken to bed by anyone else. Even Corey has trouble, no matter how many attempts he makes or the number of stories he reads her. I see the frustration on his face every time she tells him she only wants Mommy to tuck her in. To add more insult to injury, she won't go to sleep until I've kissed her goodnight. Hopefully, it's just a phase.

Corey takes me out to one of our favorite restaurants in town, The Wayfinder. With an ocean view of Battery Beach coupled with the sounds of waves crashing on the shore, I remember what I love about this coastal town. I don't think I could ever leave it again, especially now that things are settling down.

I take a seat in our reserved timber booth by a window overlooking one of the iconic cliff stacks that fill the area. The tide has come in, allowing three-foot waves to break over the edges of the rocks the way it has for longer than I can fathom.

Corey sits down opposite me as I hold my gaze outside. "I couldn't believe how lucky we were to get this reservation. This restaurant books out fast for a small town."

"It's easy to see why," I say as I bring my focus back indoors. "I've lost count how many times I've come here over the years."

In moments like these, I remember that Corey isn't a local of Battery Beach. Sure, I left for a time, but I was born and raised here. He's only lived in the area for a little over six months after taking a job at the school. He used to live and work in Portland, but something urged him to pack up his things and move out to the coast.

After I first met Corey at school, I had this feeling inside me whenever I spoke to him. That sensation developed into something far stronger after enough time had passed.

The next six months were a fast-paced blur. We dated, became exclusive, and moved in together in less than three months. Sure, it was quick, but it all felt right. Corey not only showed love for me in such a short time but also for Ava. There's no quicker way to my heart than through my daughter's. Three months later Corey and I are married, have moved into a bigger place, and are celebrating with a fancy dinner after arriving back home from our perfect honeymoon. Things are amazing. At least I think they are.

The argument we had feels like it was hiding something that's been bothering Corey. He couldn't have exploded over such a small disagreement, could he? All I can do is put a smile on my face and show him how much I love him and hope that he realizes I'll always be here to support him through anything.

We order our food after having a bottle of the house wine brought to our table. I go with the crab cakes for a starter and the grilled filet mignon with vegetables for a main. Corey picks his favorite: oysters and a thirty-four-ounce rib-eye steak. The meal will cost more than we should spend at the moment. I guess we're still on a honeymoon high and not concerned about finances.

The wine gets us talking again like we hadn't argued yesterday, putting me at ease. Our starters make their way out during the busy service and go down smooth. As I see our waitress return with our mains, confusion dots my forehead.

"The rib-eye steak," she says.

Corey raises a hand.

"And you must have ordered the salmon," she says, placing down a plate full of food I didn't order.

"Um, sorry. I asked for the grilled filet mignon with vegetables."

The young girl's eyes grow concerned as she reaches for her order ticket. She scans our meal. "I'm sorry, ma'am, it says here that you ordered the salmon. See?" She shows me the docket.

"I didn't order that. I would never order salmon. I can't stand it, sorry." I look to Corey for support. "Honey? You remember, right?"

He shakes his head and shrugs at us both. "I honestly don't recall."

I sigh, unable to hide my frustration. "Okay, but you know I hate salmon of all things."

"Of course, sweetheart, but maybe you accidentally ordered the meal. It's written clearly on the docket. I can't imagine anyone would mix it up with grilled filet mignon."

"What are you saying?"

"That you're tired. You made a mistake. Why not try have salmon this one time?"

"Are you serious?" I ask as my eyes lock in on Corey's.

"Look, there's no need to cause a scene—"

"I'm not trying to, but this is ridiculous."

"Ma'am," the waitress says as her hands clutch at her apron. "I can put in a request for the chef to make you the grilled filet mignon instead if you'd like."

With my stare locked on to Corey's, I see the answer he wants me to give the girl. I close my eyes for a moment then face her. With a whisper, I say, "No, that won't be necessary. I'll eat the salmon."

"Are you sure?" she asks. "I can bring you a free bottle of house red."

I wave her off before I change my mind and apologize for the interruption. Corey doesn't say a word and cuts up his steak.

Why the hell didn't he back me up?

13

Dinner was perfect. A thick bustle of conversation combined with the clinking of cutlery against plates and bowls set the stage in The Wayfinder. The optimal ambience could only be matched by the continuous rise and fall of the ocean water over the rocks and sand outside.

The disgust on Katherine's face when the wrong food came out was impossible to ignore. Her reaction couldn't have been rehearsed better if it were part of a Broadway play. The woman is always so soft spoken, so delicate with her words and responses. I was near dumbfounded by the way she addressed the waitress. Of course, the young girl who took the order played her role well, going to the effort of showing Katherine what had been written on the docket, suggesting such a mistake was unthinkable. She earned her bonus fifty dollars tonight.

It makes me wonder what about this little experiment of mine got Katherine so riled up. Did she really hate salmon that much, or was there something deeper there pushing her one step closer to doubting her every thought?

Each day I see Katherine presenting herself as this perfect person who never lets a single thing bother her. The people pleaser is always happy to help. It makes me sick. I know the real her and what she's capable of. She's no pushover. When she wants something, Katherine's not afraid to take it no matter the cost.

My victory this evening may seem insignificant to most, but I implanted a seed deep within Katherine's brain that won't come unstuck anytime soon. Things could have gone any number of ways, but in the end, I couldn't have asked for a better outcome.

I'm ahead of myself with my plan. I only meant tonight to be a probe to understand how Katherine handles doubt in a public setting. And not just any public setting but her favorite restaurant. There, in a place where she thought she could relax and unwind from the stresses of life, came a test of her resolve. She failed. And more spectacularly than I ever anticipated.

Piece by piece, I will tear Katherine down until there's nothing left but a pathetic excuse for a human being. I won't have to lay a finger on her body to bring her to complete and utter submission.

On the drive home, a comfortable silence fills the car. The coastal route seems fitting given the evening's events. I can't help but enjoy the sneer on my face as it creeps through and gives me a slight chuckle at the image of Katherine struggling to comprehend what had happened. How could the world be against her? How could her mind slip in such a way? Impossible, right? Wrong.

Before long, I'm going to show her the meaning of insanity.

14

KATHERINE

Dinner fell apart so quickly. I thought Corey and I were having a good time. I'd even assumed he'd forgotten everything from the previous day and wanted to move on from our silly little disagreements. Clearly, he hadn't. If he wasn't still angry at me in the back of his mind, he would have supported me at the restaurant. Instead, he made me look like a petty child who didn't want to eat her food.

Nevertheless, I can't understand what happened when we ordered. I know in my heart that I didn't say salmon or point to it on the menu. Why the hell would I order something I can barely stand the taste of? Don't get me wrong, I'll eat the stuff when I need to. You grow used to eating fish when you live in this area. But I wouldn't go to an expensive restaurant and request a meal that sounds nothing like grilled filet mignon.

That girl had it in for me. She must have jotted down the incorrect item when she took our order. Sure, I never saw what she wrote on the notepad, but I can guarantee she wasn't paying attention when I spoke. The worst part was the way she doubled down on her argument. I've worked in the food service industry before and never would I have spoken to a customer in such a way. It almost felt like someone was forcing her to disagree with me. It makes no sense.

Corey and I arrive home without a word. These silent car trips are starting to annoy me, especially on a night with only the two of us. We were supposed to be patching things up and celebrating our return into town as a married couple. Instead, this is what's happened. I can't believe it.

Corey puts on an act the second we come through the front door and find my mother sitting in the living room watching TV. It's all smiles and laughs as we sit down at opposite ends of the space and get an event-free report regarding Ava's care for the night.

"How was dinner?" Mom asks.

I stretch my fake smile to its limits. "Perfect as ever. They were busy, though."

"I can imagine. Despite the cost, that place will always be popular. And it's not just with us locals, it's these tourists driving up and down the west coast every other day taking up seats. I'll bet you had a hard time getting that reservation, Corey."

"Mom," I interrupt, trying to give her the hint that no one cares about her crazy thoughts on visitors. She doesn't seem to understand that a town like Battery Beach needs them to survive.

"No, it's okay," Corey says. "I did have to book in the minute we got back. I was lucky we could get a seat, really. The table we had was all they had left, and it was by the window."

"You're kidding," Mom says.

Corey shakes his head.

"You won't pull that off again, I can tell you that much." Mom changes the channel on the TV as a commercial comes on. It's an annoying habit she's developed over the years from my late father. The second an advertisement hits the screen, she surfs around until she finds something else. Even if that other show is halfway through airing, she'll watch it. Corey and I have shown her a hundred times how to skip through the ads or better yet how to stream her favorite shows, but she won't listen. She's reached that stage in her mind where nothing new can be learned.

I had the same struggles with Mom when Ava came along. Mom would show me the old way of doing things doctors and midwives had since eradicated. She didn't want to hear that the world had evolved, or that they had improved the methods used to raise children. One could say it's an age thing, but the older people I know aren't as opposed to learning new things. I'm unlucky, I guess.

"I'll go check on Ava," I say.

"Why?" Mom asks. "She's fine. No need to bother the young girl. Let her sleep."

"I'll be a minute, okay?"

"Suit yourself," Mom says, waving me off.

I glance to Corey and see he has already lost any attention for me down into his smartphone. He normally would be up on his feet with me, defending my decision to check on Ava. But there he is, ignoring me, fueling the argument to continue.

I shake my head as I leave and walk from the living room down the corridor to Ava's bedroom. It backs onto the master and always will. I need to know she's close in case something ever happens to her. I love my little munchkin too much to let harm befall her. If she got hurt because I was too far away to act, I could never forgive myself.

Seeing her plain white door, I can't help but think of the signs and decorations we are yet to cover this one in to give her room some personality. As best you can in a rental. We did what we could at the last place, hanging posters wherever possible. I always want Ava to feel like any house we live in is ours even if it belongs to someone else. One day, I'll buy her our dream home.

I twist open her door with care and poke my head in a crack. I hear her soft breathing within, matching the rise and fall of her lungs. Ava's arms are splayed out the way only little kids can sleep. Her blankets are a mess from her tossing and turning, and her worn stuffed giraffe has fallen to the floor. I pick up Jeffry and snuggle him into Ava's arms. I'll never understand why she named him that. A smile forms on her lips as she takes comfort in feeling Jeffry's gentle synthetic fur against her skin.

I finish tucking Ava in and give her a warm kiss on the forehead. No matter what kind of day I've had, she always cheers me up by lying there and being her own sweet innocent self. Only a child can manage such a feat.

"Mommy?" Ava asks with one eye open.

"It's okay, honey. Go back to sleep. I didn't mean to wake you."

"Can I have some water, please?"

"Of course." I slowly rise and head for the bathroom, taking Ava's empty mug with me. When I walk into the room and switch on the light, I almost drop the cup when I spot Corey standing in the doorway to our bedroom.

"You scared me. What are you doing here in the dark?"

"I was seeing if you needed help, but it appears you've got things covered. Besides, it's not like she'll want me to go in there and comfort her back to sleep."

I place my hands on my hips. "Come on. Don't be like that. She loves you."

"I don't think so."

"She does. You know it. This bedtime thing is only because it's always been just the two of us for the most part. It's a habit."

"I understand, but I guess I wonder why you keep going in there and waking her up. Wouldn't that only make this habit last longer than it should?"

I feel my forehead tighten up as I struggle to find anything to say back to him. "I was only tucking her in. She gets cold in the night if I don't."

"That's fine, but you always sit in there longer than you need to until she wakes up. Maybe it's time to let her work out how to get through the night on her own. She is five."

"What would you know?" I snap. "You've never had kids." My hand flies to my mouth. I regret my choice of words.

Corey's nostrils flare as he exhales a lungful of anger while holding his gaze. Before I can say anything, he shoves past me.

"Corey, wait," I call after him, but he doesn't stop. I don't follow and instead listen to him gather up his keys to leave.

Another perfect night.

15

After seeing Katherine's behavior tonight, I can't help but think about how this all came to be. Thoughts enter my head of how swiftly she allows such big decisions in her life to occur. The wedding is the perfect example, given how fast the whole thing happened. It was a snap commitment made to her with little regard, but I guess it was no surprise the way she fell in line with the romantic notion. From day one, she was a willing participant who only wanted to please.

It didn't take long for Katherine to move herself and her daughter into a house with a man she'd only known for a short time. Her accepting a marriage proposal is not a surprise. There seems to be a layer of desperation surrounding Katherine at all times. I've tried to work out again and again why she is so eager to force her life into line years after her ex has been out of the picture. It's as if she is on the run from more than her past. And it can't only be because of Ava. There's more there I'm not seeing.

It's so easy to see the fault in ourselves with a lengthy bit of retrospect, but Katherine is the mystery I'll never work out. How she can live with herself knowing what she did, all the while assuming I don't know the truth, is something I can't ignore. She plays the innocent card so well the damn thing is worn at the edges, but I will show the world she isn't who she portrays herself to be. Her true colors will shine before I dole out the punishment she deserves.

The argument from the restaurant continued into the night like a viral infection. I didn't expect it would fester into something worth fighting about. Katherine pulled out the big guns whether she intended to, cutting deep with so few words. I guess Ava will forever be a sensitive topic of discussion. It's almost too easy.

I wonder how Katherine can justify her outburst. Will she admit fault and take the full blame the way she usually does, or will she attempt to fight back? It seems the more she's pushed with certain issues, the bigger a response received.

Her behavior confuses me in these moments. During this ordeal, she has tried to be the perfect partner—the ideal candidate for a strong marriage. Yet now that I am testing her, I'm seeing her push back. Is there a backbone hidden away in her body only reserved for the hardest of times? If so, I'll find out what it takes to snap her resolve in two.

In less than twenty-four hours, Katherine will ask herself something she once thought to be impossible. It will dive deep into her brain and burrow down hard, making her scrutinize every aspect of the man she's married. But will she do anything about it?

16

KATHERINE

After Corey left, I spent an hour on the phone with Annette, telling her everything, as usual, letting her reassure me that all will be fine. It half works.

Corey didn't come home for another few hours. I don't ask him where he has been when he slides into bed and cuddles up to me. I feel lucky he even still wants to be in the same house as me after the horrible thing I said.

I turn to him and apologize for the no-children comment as best I can. He dismisses me and says it's fine, that we both said stupid things and that we should move on. I agree and let him continue to hold me, vowing not to fight over such matters again.

After an hour of curling up to him in silence, I fall asleep.

The next day, I try to unpack a few more items from the boxes we have strewn about the house. I give up after a short while, opting to relax and spend time with Ava and Corey instead.

Being the first Saturday of the month, we decide to visit the flea market held in the school's parking lot. We never go looking to buy anything but enjoy digging through people's old belongings. Ava in particular loves finding worn household items she's never seen before so she can ask what they are.

The morning is cold as expected as a rush of wind carries a cool ocean mist over from the beach. I squeeze my body tight with my thick jacket, keeping a keen eye on Ava as she rushes from one stall to the next. Corey's elbow interlocks with mine as we stroll along. The smell of ground coffee beans in the distance lures me to a small row of food trucks.

"How about I grab you a latte," Corey says, reading my mind.

"You're the best," I reply. I could say Corey's being overly nice to make up for our recent arguments, but he's always like this because he's a good man. I need to resist saying anything stupid again. Then this marriage might stand a chance.

I want to forget the past and focus on the future. It's important that I be the best wife and mother I can not only for Corey and Ava's sake, but to show everyone I know that this hasn't all been a rushed mistake.

"Mommy, Mommy," Ava shouts out. "Look at this. What is it?" She holds up a small meat grinder. I walk over to her and attempt to explain what the tool is without sounding like an idiot. Ava rotates the rusty handle while the seller stares at us from a foldout chair a few feet away. With both hands in her jacket pockets and a frown on her face, she wills us to leave.

"Let's put that back, shall we?" I say to Ava before I give the lady in her late fifties a smile. Her stall is laden with random items I'm confident she bought from antique stores, thinking she could make a few bucks. I doubt she ever used such a tool in the kitchen.

Corey finds us and hands over a latte as we continue down the row of stops.

"That was fast," I say.

"I know. I caught a break in the lines. What's her problem?"

Corey asks, subtly pointing toward the grumpy lady Ava and I moved away from.

"The usual. She thought Ava would damage her worthless junk."

Corey chuckles behind his coffee cup as the woman stares at our small family from a distance. "Let's move on before she throws one of those rusted frying pans our way."

It's good to see Corey smiling again and back to his normal bubbly self. I feel like we can reclaim what's left of the weekend and start the next week off happy. Maybe our fighting was something newlyweds go through. After the shock of getting married, followed by the fantasy of a honeymoon, returning to reality hit harder than we realized.

We spend the rest of our time wandering the stalls, sipping our coffees, while Ava enjoys her rummaging. She eventually finds a stuffed toy elephant she begs us to buy. Corey and I both know it will become old news within a week, but it's worth spending those few dollars to see her beautiful smile.

As one, we stroll back to the car with Ava's new friend making up the fourth member of our group. Corey opens the doors and stops.

"Something wrong?" I ask.

"Nothing. I saw a cool coffee mug before I thought about buying. I might go and get it if that's okay with you?"

"Of course. Go for it. We'll wait for you here."

Corey gives me his signature grin and a kiss on the cheek. I absorb the love beaming from his eyes the way it should and feel like my old self again. Ava prods me in the stomach with her elephant and makes a trumpet noise. I chase after her at a playful speed and threaten to tickle her.

After a minute of entertaining Ava, I load her into the car and brush her hair out of her face. I move to the front passenger side of Corey's sedan and climb in. Once I settle into place, I twist around and talk to my daughter to fill the time. "Did you have fun?"

"Yeah," she says, nodding in one big exaggerated motion.

"That's good, sweetie. Happy to hear it."

"Where's Corey?"

It's strange hearing a child call an adult by their first name when you're a teacher. I wonder if she'll ever come to think of him as her daddy.

"He's buying a funny coffee mug for school. He should be here any second, baby."

Ava doesn't seem to care about my answer as she plays with her elephant, so I turn around. I pull out my cell and browse Facebook while I wait. An amusing post catches my eye, so I tag Corey in it only to hear his phone beep right next to me in the center console. He's always forgetting to take it with him. I see my post alert sitting on his lock screen, waiting to be read. Sometimes it feels strange to 'tag' my husband in something I want him to see when I could show it to him in person. I guess this new impersonal way we socialize is how things are done now.

Before I pull my eyes away from Corey's cell, it beeps again as a text comes onto his screen, pushing my Facebook notification down. Normally, I wouldn't think much of him receiving a text, but I realize it's from an unknown number.

I take a peek around and don't find Corey nearby. I know I shouldn't be sneaking a look at his cell, but I can't help myself. I pick up his phone and see the message come up again. My heart nearly falls out of my chest when I read the words on his phone. So much so, I check it twice.

I'm so glad you're back from the honeymoon. Give me a call ;)

Never has a winking eye sent such a sharp pain through my body. I accidentally touch the text notification, unlocking Corey's phone. He has no passcode or fingerprint option enabled, so the messaging app opens right up, sending out tiny packets of information into the world to the sender, telling them that someone has read their words.

"Shit." The cell drops from my fingertips and clatters about in the center console.

Ava does an exaggerated gasp. "Mommy said a bad word."

"I'm sorry, sweetie. I didn't mean to." I turn to Ava as my hand fumbles around for Corey's cell. The device finds its way back into my hands, unlocked to the message sent by an unknown person.

Figuring I've done the damage by reading the text, I try to scroll up to see what else has been shared between Corey and this mystery person, but I find nothing. Not a single word.

Who the hell sent this text?

17

Katherine has no respect for privacy. She never has. I know she won't be able to resist reading that text the instant it alerts the world of its existence. The important question I have now is what will she do once she reads it?

I can imagine her face as her mind attempts to rationalize what's in front of her. Her forehead will wrinkle as she rereads the text ten times over, hoping to stop creeping doubt from entering and settling a sickening image into her brain.

My husband couldn't possibly be cheating on me, could he? That question must be flying through Katherine's mind in circles with no answer to reassure her fragile being that her worst fear hasn't come true. And I know she won't think of the message as some innocent line from a friend or coworker. Why would the sender be unknown? This seamless idea works on so many levels.

I check the burner phone in my hand and see that someone has read the text less than a minute after I sent it. Now is the perfect time to sneak up to the car and enjoy the look on Katherine's face without her knowing.

Pushing through one moron after the next at this cesspool of a flea market, I walk around the back of a few food trucks. The people in this town seem so happy to waste their hard-earned money buying crappy pre-made food served in cardboard that has been slopped from a bucket. As long as the truck has a pun name and an interesting enough vibe, they will give cash to the operators hand over fist.

I use the side of a gourmet hotdog food truck to sneak my head around its end at the parking lot. Katherine and Ava sit alone, waiting. Ava is preoccupied with her new stuffed animal she didn't deserve. I never got random toys bought for me when I was a kid. This little brat will grow up expecting the world. I focus on Katherine in the front seat and see her frozen in place with a look of devastation plastered across her eyes.

I let out a chuckle as a huge grin stretches out my lips. There's a cell in her hand that doesn't belong to her. Her pupils dance left then right again and again as if she is reading a novel in fast-forward.

"Excuse me. You can't be back there," calls out a voice.

Spinning round, I spot one of the hotdog workers staring at me from the open door of their truck. Without saying a word, I walk by him and out into the flea market. I glance over my shoulder as the guy lets me see his outstretched arms begging me to explain myself. I ignore him and continue blending into the crowd, not needing to waste a single moment explaining myself to some jackass.

The image of Katherine's face flashes into my mind, fueling the grin I can't seem to control. How powerful a few words can be. How cataclysmic an impact a semicolon and a closing parenthesis have when combined to form a winking smiley face. I could send a second text and push the dark thoughts clouding her brain deeper in, but I want Katherine paralyzed with uncertainty.

It's more crippling not knowing one way or another if her

husband is being unfaithful. Doubt is so powerful it can turn a person into an indecisive mess in a short amount of time. Rather than splintering her world into tiny pieces, I want to watch it break in two.

Katherine's reaction is going to determine the next stage of my plan. How will she handle her new problem?

18

KATHERINE

I deleted the text before Corey returned. I had no choice. He would have found it eventually and discovered I had read a private message on his phone. The text was new and unknown to him, so I figured the best idea was to wipe it from existence.

To keep my story straight, I also deleted the tag from Facebook so he wouldn't wonder why he didn't get a notification on his cell when he finally saw the post. I couldn't have him suspecting that I'd touched his phone. The next thought I have as Corey drives us home is whether he was expecting the message today. And who the hell sent it?

I need to know what the text means more than anything else if I want this marriage to last more than a few days. A million possibilities rattle around in my head, making too much noise. One crazy idea attempts to compete with another as I do what I can to silence the chatter.

I could scream, but Corey is sitting next to me without so much as a guilty twitch on his face. Was he expecting the text? Or is this all a simple misunderstanding? *Give me a call ;)*

Should I just come out and tell him what happened? I kind of destroyed that opportunity when I deleted the message. I'm so stupid. Why do I always pick the worst solution for a problem? I swear I'm cursed.

Maybe the text went to the wrong number. It was from an unknown sender. Maybe it's a cruel coincidence that the person spoke about Corey having returned from a honeymoon. It wouldn't be the first time in my life that such a strange thing gave me crazy assumptions to worry about.

Ava sings to her elephant in the back seat, breaking my unfocused thoughts. I can't help but worry for her if there's any truth behind that text. Could she handle Corey going away and no longer being a part of her world if this all goes south?

I shudder, unsure why I'm even thinking about such possibilities. I still don't know a damn thing about this text.

"Everything okay?" Corey asks. "You seem tense."

A forced smile finds its way to my face as I answer him. "I'm fine. Just feeling a bit off for some reason. Don't stress about me."

"How about we get some burgers for a late lunch on the way home? Would that help?"

"Yah! Burgers!" Ava shouts, making the choice for me.

"We don't have to do that," I say.

"Seems like Ava's already decided for us," Corey says with a chuckle.

"Burgers it is." I stop my false protest. It's clear something is bothering me from my body language alone. I can't let on that I have a problem sitting on my chest, weighing me down, until I recognize what it is I'm dealing with.

Could I be overreacting to a few basic words? Am I searching for problems that don't exist because deep down I feel unworthy of this marriage? I can't tell anymore. All I understand is that I need to pull myself together before I ruin this day.

"What burger are you going to have, Ava?" Corey asks.

"Um, I don't know. What can I get?"

Corey lists off some options to Ava as I drown out their

conversation. I have to focus and not compromise what we have here as a family over a stupid text. Corey wouldn't cheat on me. I know him. He's a gentle soul who values and respects Ava and I too much to treat us in such a way. I have to remind myself of this anytime that winking smiley face enters my mind.

Before I can piece together the fractured thoughts in my head, we arrive home with burgers and fries ready to eat. I don't even remember stopping off to get them. I was too busy being stuck in a world I had hoped I'd walked away from. Surely, I haven't fallen back into the past. When I glance to Corey, I see Ava's dad take over his face.

Peter was about the worst human being a person could ever stand to be around. He treated me like garbage on a good day. No one had less respect for me in their life. In Peter's eyes, I was his property, until I fell pregnant with Ava.

He freaked out the second I told him about the baby. I had hoped it might have settled him down and made him focus on steadying himself into a career over the string of jobs he could never hold down.

It always seemed to be someone else's fault whenever Peter got fired or quit without notice. The world was against him and I was too stupid to see that. Every time this happened, he took it out on me. Not physically, but mentally. He berated me, tore me down, and made sure I knew that I wasn't worthy of being loved.

For the longest time I believed him. I thought he had to be right. Why would anyone want to be with me? He was nice enough to take on the burden that was being my boyfriend. Throw in the pregnancy on top of everything else and we had the makings for nothing but a dramatic and explosive outcome.

Some days it still gets to me that Peter is Ava's dad. Don't get me wrong, I love her more than anything in this world, but I wish his disturbed DNA wasn't in her body. All I can do is raise her to be a kind person and surround her with loving people.

She deserves so much more than the likes of the deadbeat father she's never met.

"Are you coming?" Corey asks me.

I glance up with an open mouth to find Corey and Ava staring at me outside of the car, halfway to the front door.

After a few seconds, I remember we're home.

"Come on. We want to eat our food before it gets cold," he says.

"Sorry?" I look down to discover the paper bags in my lap with no memory of them ever landing there. I didn't even notice the heat pouring through to my skin. With a quick shake of my head, I unbuckle my seat belt and climb out of the car.

We walk inside as one, minutes away from eating a meal as a family. I realize as Corey shuts the door and engages the lock that I need to forget about the text and give him the benefit of the doubt. I'm reading too much into something that isn't there, allowing my past to compromise my future.

Corey wouldn't cheat on me. At least I don't think he would.

19

K atherine hasn't said a word to me yet. It's been at least three hours. If the message was an issue, she'd have unloaded her anger upon me by now. What in the hell is she waiting for?

I can only assume one thing has happened in the last few days to cause Katherine to swallow this devastating piece of information and pretend like she never found the text: she's falling in line the way she did with her ex.

From everything I know about Peter, Katherine once put up with nothing but abuse from the man in almost every form it came in. He was unfaithful and unreliable. She told me how he would take off randomly and not show up home again for three, four, sometimes ten days. He'd smell of beer, cigarettes, and cheap motels. Katherine said she never asked him what he'd been up to. She was happy he showed up at all.

Katherine's past almost makes me feel sorry for her until I remember the pain. Her screwed-up background does not excuse what she did to me. Not in a million years. Instead, I'm using every little crazy thing Peter did to mess with her now. Before long, she will start to see her ex everywhere she goes.

Still, it's hard to fathom that Katherine may have already given up and become the same submissive loser she once was in such a short amount of time. Is this what happens when marriage is thrown into the mix? Did a pair of wedding bands have that much impact on a person's life?

I guess I shouldn't be all that surprised. Katherine is a pushover in almost every situation. I've seen it inside and outside of work. Face to face, she does whatever anyone tells her. Ava is going to walk all over her when she's older.

I doubt Katherine will find the courage to say anything now. She's not waiting for the right moment to speak. She's decided to keep quiet and has sunk into line, awaiting her next instruction like the obedient wife she's fast become.

I know what needs to happen now. I must put this new dynamic to the test with Katherine's past at the forefront of my every action. I will find out exactly how far Katherine has fallen into the dark void she has only recently clawed her way out of. And if she finds the courage to climb out again, I'll be there to kick her back down.

20

KATHERINE

I wake up early on Sunday morning to see a text from Annette. I read it and feel my eyes go wide as I remember that I'm supposed to be meeting her for breakfast to catch up. We'd both decided our quick shop on Friday afternoon wasn't enough time spent together. And my late-night call was too one sided.

"Crap," I mutter. Corey is still asleep next to me. It's seven and he'll want to sleep in as much as he can before school starts again tomorrow. To make things worse, I forgot to tell him about watching Ava while I went out for breakfast with Annette.

I send a lengthy message to Annette explaining my stupidity. She replies instantly saying she hasn't left yet.

"Thank God," I let out as I scramble to get myself ready without waking Corey. While throwing some clothes on, I text Annette again to say I'll rush to meet her at the café by eight at the latest. Only thirty minutes late isn't too bad.

The only reason we planned on meeting so early was so Annette could head out to Portland straight after to visit her mother. It's a good hour and a half drive each way without traffic, so we had no option but to catch up several hours before we normally would.

I don't mind helping Annette out, but I realize based on how deep Corey is sleeping that I have no alternative but to bring Ava with me. Given how long it will take me to get myself and Ava ready, eight is going to push our luck.

After a quick struggle to slap my clothes and makeup on, I handwrite a note and leave it for Corey on my side of the bed. Hopefully, he sees it before freaking out, wondering where we are.

I close the door to our bedroom in slow motion and cross over to Ava's room. As I open her door, I find her mattress empty, already knowing where she will be: watching TV.

Corey and I let Ava get herself up and watch TV on the weekends as long as she's quiet. I know it's lazy, but it's the only way we can have a decent sleep in. Otherwise, Ava would have been jumping on our bed as early as six, eager to play.

While I'm in Ava's room, I gather some clothes and her brush, hoping to get her ready fast. I don't want to miss this catch-up with Annette. These past few days have taken their toll on me with Corey. Our arguments and that worrying text weigh heavy on my mind. The latter more so than the former. I'm not sure what I'll say to Annette about the message I found. I went over the words again and again in my head last night until I fell asleep from exhaustion. Whatever I spill to her, I need to think about my relationship with Corey first and not jump to conclusions.

I find Ava in the living room, watching a kids' show while playing with the family iPad. I've told her off time and time again, demanding that she either watches the TV or plays with the tablet, not both. Of course, I'm nothing but a hypocrite considering Corey and I both have the same bad habit running our lives when we sit down in front of the TV with our smartphones.

"Ava, honey. We need to get you ready. We're going to meet up with Auntie Annette for breakfast." Annette isn't Ava's real aunt, but she's family to me.

"But, Mommy. I want to watch cartoons."

I put my hands on my hips. "Is that so, because it looks like you're playing that puppy game on the iPad and not really watching the TV."

"But, Mommy—"

"But nothing. We have to get ready. Auntie Annette is waiting, so it's time to move your butt."

Ava rolls her head and huffs at me. "Fine."

My daughter can be such a cooperative sweetheart when she wants to be. Other times she is like this and argues with every request that comes out of my mouth. She falls in line and helps me with her clothes while I adjust things and brush her hair from a wild mess to something presentable.

"Thank you," I say, partway through the process. "If you're well behaved, I'll buy you a nice treat at breakfast."

"Yah!" she shouts.

I cringe, realizing I didn't tell Ava about Corey still being asleep. My eyes slowly move to the corridor and wait for him to come out with a confused look across his brow, but the door to our room remains closed.

After some sloppy mothering, I get us both ready. We hop in my car and head into town after eight. We won't be too late. Plus Annette knows what I'm like.

We reach the Battery Beach café ten minutes later and find a good parking spot for a Sunday morning. The establishment is one of the most popular cafés in the area with its beautiful location a short distance from the water. It's at the opposite end to the cliff stacks, but still has an enticing view of the ocean.

"Hello, Ava," Annette says the second we walk inside. She's saved us a table in amongst the busy breakfast service. The café is far prettier on the interior than out with burgundy feature walls that run up to a brass-covered ceiling.

Ava runs up and gives Annette a quick hug before climbing onto one of the wicker-styled chairs the café seems to love. She pulls herself into position at the glass-topped stone table and immediately grabs the menu. We all know she'll order the waffles and a chocolate milkshake.

"How have you been?" Annette asks. Her eyes fall to Ava. "Was Corey busy?"

"Sorry. I know you wanted to 'catch up' on the honeymoon, but I didn't want to disturb him. Anyway, I bought Ava's iPad along. So we can still chat, if you understand what I mean." Again I feel like the world's worst mom, but I'm only trying to keep everyone happy.

Annette chuckles. "That's okay. It'll be fun to speak in code. I'm sure I'll get it all out of you."

I smile, hoping she doesn't. I don't want to talk about the honeymoon any more than I want to confess to Annette about the text. Plus, I shouldn't say anything negative about Corey in front of Ava until I know more.

Annette and I order breakfast and fall headfirst into a conversation about school within minutes. It's hard to avoid the topic given we are best friends who work in the same building. I love the bonus information she gives me from the administration side of things at BBES. I also think she loves getting a teacher's perspective on the impact of our principal Barry's decisions. It's almost like having an inside source to the inner circle of the school.

As a teacher, it's hard to not believe the system can be

against you with the amount of crap we get thrown at us daily. As time goes on, it only becomes harder and harder to do our jobs. Roadblocks in the form of angry parents and red tape only reduce our ability as educators to teach the children.

I shake the depressing thought and try to concentrate on the positives as Annette finishes telling me a funny story about Barry. I'm glad the focus is not on Corey and my time away at Vegas.

"So, tell me everything. I want to know how much fun you got up to on your honeymoon." Annette crosses her arms over the table as she leans forward, too keen to hear all about my sex life. I reveal as little as possible, hoping Ava's presence is enough of a deterrent to force a change of the topic. Even if Ava weren't here, I wouldn't feel comfortable getting into the nitty gritty of the trip, even though I normally tell Annette everything.

After a few hours of breakfast go by, Ava cracks at the seams with boredom. Even though she's playing games on an iPad while sitting in a cozy space consuming her favorite food, she still wants to leave. I swear my daughter does this on purpose.

"Okay, we better get going," I say as I pack Ava up and clean her face.

"Where are you off to?" Annette asks.

"Just home. I thought about heading to the shops, but I can tell I won't make it very far." Ava ignores my words as she waits for us to get up and leave.

"Good. I might follow you to your place before I head to Portland."

"How come?" I ask.

"I need to have a chat to your husband. He hasn't responded to my text."

I nearly fall out of my chair in front of the busy café. Did Annette say what I think she said? She can't be telling me that Corey hasn't responded to the damning text I found on his cell.

"What's wrong?" Annette asks, grabbing my elbow lightly.

"Uh, nothing. What text, sorry?"

"One I sent around nine last night. I hope it didn't disturb him. Anyway, I was trying to get his opinion on a gift for a certain someone's birthday that's coming up this week."

"Oh, right," I say, relieved while looking like a stunned idiot at the same time. I don't know why I would think Annette would send Corey a flirtatious text and follow up with me when he didn't respond. She stares at me, waiting for a response. "You know what he's like. He fell asleep early last night. He's probably only waking up now. He loves to sleep in."

"Lazy, lazy. You should get him up at the crack of dawn to do chores around the house," Annette says with a chuckle. "Anyway, I might have a quick chat with him, if you don't mind."

"Of course not. I'll call him now in case he's still asleep." I fumble for my cell as I guide Ava up and out of her chair.

Annette pays the bill and leaves a generous tip. I squish my phone into my cheek as it calls Corey's while I scramble to find some cash in my purse to cover mine and Ava's meals.

Annette shakes her palm. "No, no. This is on me. Consider it a bonus wedding gift."

"You don't have to do that."

"It's already done. You can pay me back later when we catch up alone at school tomorrow. I'll get those juicy details off you."

I shake my head with a forced giggle. "You're terrible."

"Hello." Corey says, sounding half groggy.

"Good morning, sunshine," I say, mocking his voice. "Just thought I should call you, so you make yourself presentable before Annette drops in."

"Sorry, what?" he asks, confusion filling his voice.

I explain that there should be a text from Annette waiting for him on his cell to justify the sudden interruption to his lazy Sunday morning.

"Oh, right," he says, understanding. "I'll see you all soon."

When Ava and I get home, we knock on the front door as we walk inside the house to make sure Corey knows of our arrival. Annette pulls up a minute later in her car.

"Sorry, honey," I say as I kiss him on the cheek.

"No problem. I was awake. Well, stirring at least."

I smile at him as Ava runs over to her toys and plays as if she was on the brink of dying from the tedium of breakfast.

"Knock, knock," Annette says as she lets herself in.

"Hi, Annette," Corey says. "Sorry I didn't see your text last night. I'm pretty sure I was asleep by eight."

She shakes her head and tuts at him with a smile. "Eight o'clock? You should have been taking your wife out on a hot date. Don't tell me now you guys are married the romance is gone."

"No, he's always been an old man in a young teacher's body," I say.

We all laugh, Corey doing his best not to show his embarrassment. "It was a big week. I couldn't help myself."

"Sure, sure," Annette says. "Now, if you can keep your eyes open for five minutes, I need to chat with you about an idea I had for your wife's birthday."

"It's her birthday?" Corey asks, pretending he's forgotten.

"Ha ha," I say as they leave the room. I'm not into birthdays and never expect people to buy me anything. Annette, however, is into them to a point of obsession. She loves to find the perfect gift, so I know it will upset her if I don't let her get me something.

I sit down on the sofa near Ava and stroke her soft hair while she plays, oblivious to the world. Some days I wish I could zone out the way she does.

Annette and Corey come back into the room, each giving me a coy look as if they can't hide their sneaky behavior from me. I instantly feel guilty for thinking the other text was from Annette. She would never do that to me. I still don't understand who sent that weird message to Corey's cell and can only hope it was an innocent mistake. It has to be.

"I hope that helps you," Corey says loudly to Annette, making sure I hear.

"Oh, it has. Big time."

I stare at them both with squinted eyes as I cross my arms, playing my part. "What are you two up to?"

"None of your business," Annette says. "You'll have to wait to find out. Besides, I really need to get going if I want to make it to my mom's place by lunchtime."

"Okay then. I suppose we'll see you at work. Have a nice rest of your weekend. Thanks again for breakfast."

We wave Annette off and fall into the sofa to relax.

"That's all the excitement I can handle for one day," Corey says with a chuckle.

"Is that so? I guess those boxes you agreed to unpack in the garage will sort themselves out."

He sighs and allows his shoulders to drop. "I promised you that, didn't I?"

"Yep. No escaping it either. We've put off unpacking for too long."

"Yes, I know," Corey says, leaning back with his hands behind his head.

"Come on," I say as I pat his legs. "I'll help you. Make the job go twice as fast. Ava's occupied so we should do something productive for a change." I stand and offer Corey a hand to motivate him up from his comfortable position. He climbs out of the sofa onto his feet like it's a big deal to do so.

"I'll get changed and meet you out there, okay?"

"Sounds wonderful," he says, not hiding his sarcasm one bit.

Corey is normally eager to help around the house. He does, however, fall into these lazy moods over the weekend. I understand the importance of taking a break, but sometimes there's work that needs doing.

I head into our bedroom and change into some sweatpants from my nice outfit, ready to do some dirty work. Corey already has some old jeans and his college sweatshirt on so there is no need for him to dress down any further.

As I walk through the living room, heading for the front door, I tell Ava to keep playing and that we'll be out in the garage if she needs us. It's detached from the house and is serving as storage for all of our junk. I was hoping to move into this new place and have things organized from day one but our sudden wedding and trip to Vegas messed up any chance of that happening.

Ava barely registers my words as she continues coloring in a book full of princesses at her small kids' table while her giraffe sits in the opposite chair. I smile at the cute scene before me, unable to help myself as I walk out the door.

Outside, the morning sunbeams filter in through the surrounding trees, filling me with the energy I'll need to work through this task. It's such a perfect day. As I reach the open side entry to the garage, I find Corey already getting into some boxes. He appears to be keen to get this job over with so he can rush back to the sofa. I don't care. Whatever gets the work done.

I stop in the doorway when I spot something flash in his hand. I almost need to look twice as I discover a decent wad of cash clutched in his left fist. Not seeing me, he claws open a box and stuffs the money deep inside. Ducking away, I make sure he doesn't see me. I feel my heart thud through my body and pound against the wall of the garage I'm pressed against.

Why is he hiding money from me?

22

K atherine spotted the money quicker than I expected. Its discovery will no doubt generate an instant trust issue considering the huge gambling problem her ex had.

The careless hiding of cash around the house will spawn all kinds of thoughts in Katherine's head. She won't know what to think and will send herself spiraling down into a chaotic void of confusion.

I wonder if she'll say anything. Will she demand an explanation to her findings, or will she keep her knowledge under wraps the way she did with the text? It still boggles my mind to consider that she hasn't said a thing about that message. What does it take to push her trust to breaking point?

Katherine will never guess what the money is truly for. And when she finds out, her expression will bring me far too much delight. The truth will crush her spirits as she realizes how terrible a wife she really is.

I'm working a longstanding mistrust against her and have Peter to thank for what happens next. I'd heard all about the terrible things he did. Apparently, one night, when he had run out of money gambling, he stole all of Katherine's jewelry to pawn for fast cash. He was already deep in the hole for a few thousand to some shady people around town and thought he could claw his way out. Not only did he lose that cash, but he then asked Katherine if she could dig into her savings account for a few hundred dollars he claimed he needed for a cousin in Portland.

Even when Katherine found out the sad but predictable truth, she still didn't end her worthless relationship with her ex. If she hadn't have fallen pregnant with Ava, she'd still be with Peter, losing every cent she had to his gambling addiction.

It makes me wonder how far I must take things before she finally cracks.

23

KATHERINE

I know what I saw. There's no denying it. Corey's hiding money from me. All I can ask myself is why? Before we got married, we had already opened a joint account together and told each other our financial history. He knows about all the troubles I had with Peter and how bad he ruined my credit rating. Keeping cash hidden is the last thing anyone should do around me. Yet here I am, scared and confused.

Corey and I went through a dozen boxes, unpacking and sorting their contents as best we could for several hours. The entire time, my eyes were fixated on the box where Corey had concealed the wad of cash. He eventually placed the box up on a shelf at the back of the garage. He'd even tried to tuck it away behind some motor oil bottles to make it seem like the carton had been there all along.

"Is everything okay?" he asked several times as we worked. I gave him whatever lines I could think of to avoid blurting out what I knew. I didn't want to accuse him of anything, but in the same breath I should have demanded to learn what he was up to.

Corey might have a legitimate reason for hiding money away

from me. I know though that I'm only trying to dodge an inevitable confrontation by not asking him. We have an agreement. If either of us needs to purchase something, we have to discuss it first.

We stick to a strict budget to keep the household going strong. Our goal is to save up as much as possible to buy a house here in Battery Beach. There is only so long we can go on renting homes in the area.

Housing in the town isn't as affordable as it could be. And the closer to the water a property is, the steeper the asking price. We're not after some mansion by the ocean, but we don't want to buy anything too far out of the main area just so we can secure a cheap house. After all, this region is where I want Ava to grow up. We need a solid base to work from if we ever hope to settle down.

The rest of our day went by as usual. I struggled to be as normal as possible under the circumstances, but it was clear something was bothering me. Corey tried several times to get me talking, but I kept telling him I wasn't feeling the best.

"Maybe you should go to bed soon? Grab a good night's sleep," he said.

I took up his suggestion to avoid having to broach the subject of the hidden money and went to bed early after putting Ava down. On a normal Sunday night, I often stayed up late trying to fend off the week ahead.

With a bag of rocks in my stomach weighing me down, I lay in bed, staring aimlessly at my phone to distract myself with Facebook. Normally, this rabbit hole of randomness kills the time and pulls my concentration away from my problems. All I can see though is the money being shoved into that box in a hurry. What is it for?

∾

My school day passed by in a blur. For a Monday, it's not the worst time I've ever spent teaching. The kids were often at their craziest on a Monday morning or a Friday afternoon. Maybe I wasn't paying attention to them the way I should have been, but I couldn't help letting my frustrating thoughts seep in.

Corey drove Ava and I home as he always did. We went about our routine like clockwork until it was time for Corey to go to the Monday night poker game at his friend Dan's house.

They arrange the game on a Facebook group I was not a member of, so I didn't have to hear a word about it. He knew my history with Peter. Corey talks about the night in such a way to spare my feelings.

"I'll be back from Dan's around eleven. Don't wait up for me the way you always do."

"Why not?" I ask.

"Because you need your sleep. I can tell something is still off with you. We've hardly spoken today. In fact, maybe I shouldn't go."

"No, don't cancel your plans because of me. I'm just tired and worn down. I'll be fine, okay?"

Corey chuckles. "Got it. You know me, though. I won't be able to help myself. Don't be surprised if I send you multiple texts throughout the evening."

I wrap my arms around him and lean my head against his chest. "That's because you're a good husband." I feel like I'm trying to beam the thought into his brain so he does the right thing and tells me about the money.

"I try," he says as he kisses me on the forehead.

"You better get going," I mumble.

"Yeah, they'll be starting up soon and it's my turn to bring the snacks."

I flash a quick smile at Corey and try not to let him see the concern wrinkling my brow. I don't want to ruin his poker night because I caught him hiding some cash away. Maybe he put it there to buy me a present for my birthday? It's possible he didn't want me to know how much he'd spent or where it was from.

"Have a nice rest," he says as he heads for the door.

"Have a good time."

"Thanks, honey. Oh, I just remembered: don't look at our bank statement online until after your birthday. There might be a little something bought for a certain someone's special day." He smiles at me as he scoops up his car keys.

"Okay, I won't," I reply.

"You better not," he says with a chuckle. "I've got a few fun things coming in the mail, so don't open anything this week unless you want the surprise ruined."

I don't respond and return his happy expression as best I can.

"I'll see you later," he says as the door swings closed. The second the lock catches, I let out my breath. A tightness wraps itself around my chest and squeezes. A sting of pain stabs at my forehead moments before a bead of sweat pokes through my pores.

"Calm down," I tell myself. "Everything will be fine."

I distract the damn anxiety that is minutes away from burrowing deep into my brain by looking at Corey's car through the curtains. He backs out of the drive and rolls into the darkness. He's gone.

I almost drop my cell as I draw it from my handbag. With shaking fingers, I unlock the screen and get to work logging into our bank account online. I screw up the password three times and have to wait a few minutes before being able to attempt another login.

"Stop it," I mutter. "Pull yourself together." I shake my head, embarrassed by how insane I must sound to anyone else. I just need to confirm the money Corey is hiding came from our bank account, then I can regain some focus.

After taking a moment to collect myself, I enter the password correctly. I soon rush through to the right account faster than I should be and wait for the page to load up a list of our recent transactions.

"Come on, come on," I say to myself. Our Internet connection has been an issue from the day we moved in. It only adds another layer of hell to my problem.

"Finally," I say as the site finishes loading. My eyes scan the statement and see the usual purchases listed. Groceries, utility bills. Several transactions from Vegas stick out, but I'm looking for a cash withdrawal from our joint account that can explain the wad Corey so elegantly hid away. I find nothing. Did he win the money on our honeymoon and didn't want me to learn about it? In hindsight, Vegas was a terrible location for a honeymoon but the deal the hotel offered was too good to pass up. I know that can't be it. We were together the whole time.

"This isn't right," I mutter. "Where is it?" I scroll up and down again and again. We rarely get cash out more than once per month, so there's no way I could miss anything. I soon find a transaction that confirms what Corey was telling me about my gift. A purchase from Amazon stares back at me on the screen. It's dated for yesterday. I haven't ordered a single thing from the site in a few weeks. This has to be from Corey buying me a birthday present.

So where did he get the money from?

24

KATHERINE

I try to relax and have a nice evening, but my crazy mind won't let me. That would be too simple. The Amazon transaction flashes through my brain on repeat, mocking me. All I want to do is log into our account and see what the charge is for, but I recognize that would be a huge mistake. If I get caught, Corey will feel cheated that I went snooping around for my gift. But the truth is, I don't care what he's bought me. I just have to know what that damn money he's hiding is for.

There's only one other thing left for me to do before I ruin Corey's present while simultaneously driving myself off the deep end: I need to check the box in the garage. Not only to prove to myself that the money exists, but to count it and attempt to work out what it might be for. It's the only way I'll be able to allow myself to calm the hell down and not assume the worst about my husband.

Moving down the corridor with a purpose, I quickly turn toward Ava's room to check on her. I find the little sweetheart sound asleep in an awkward twisted position. I tuck her in as a grin overtakes the frowning muscles in my forehead. No one else in this world brings me back from the brink of a meltdown faster than my daughter.

Once I finish pulling her blankets up to her chest, I brush her hair out of her face. She doesn't stir and continues to breathe at a steady calming pace. Some days I wish I could trade places with her. To be that young and carefree would be such a blessing. I only want to be able to clear my head at the end of a long day of irrational thoughts.

Satisfied Ava is okay, I walk out the front door and gently close it behind me in case she wakes up and thinks I've left. I can't have her running into the street because I'm too stupid to let go of my obsessive thoughts.

The cold air hangs on my warm breath as I approach the garage wearing a coat over my thin layers. I fumble with my keys as I try to open the side door and get inside the freezing detached room. When Corey and I buy our own place, the house has to have a connected garage. That's assuming our relationship survives whatever has been going on lately.

I grab the handle of the garage door and hold up my keys. They slip from my nervous fingers and fall to the concrete footpath, clattering about in a frustrating mess.

"Dammit," I whisper while squeezing my fists. I scoop up my keys and try to get a solid grip on them. With two hands, I jiggle the key into the tumbler and unlock the door. What am I doing?

I can't help but feel like a hypocrite for being this upset over Corey hiding money. I did the same thing with Peter, stashing small amounts of my wage around the house so I'd have enough funds to put gas in my car or buy toilet paper. The two situations don't compare, but the voice in the back of my head won't let me think otherwise.

Flicking on the dull light to the garage, I wait for the dusty energy-efficient bulb to warm up and provide me with some visibility in the dark space. During these few seconds, I see demons dancing in the shadows, filling my heart with enough anxiety to sink a ship.

I do what little I can to pull myself together and focus. The money needs to be found if I want any hope of sleeping a wink tonight despite the overwhelming sense I'm betraying Corey's trust.

I creep across the cracked and stained concrete to a carton up on a shelf in the corner I know Corey placed there yesterday.

The container is behind some old bottles of motor oil we'll never use. It's not in the most accessible place within the garage. I'm forced to pass around a pile of unorganized gardening equipment so I can bring the box down. Not being as tall as Corey makes the task all that bit harder.

My fingertips brush against the outer flap of the carton as I extend my reach as much as it will go. "Come on, dammit." I grab the cardboard's edge between my index and middle fingers, establishing the world's weakest grip on the container. But it's enough to slide the light object toward me. "A little further," I say to encourage myself. My eyes close so I can dig deep and stretch out as far as possible until the box slips over the side of the shelf and tumbles down, hitting my head.

"Dammit," I yell, bringing my hands to my face. I feel around for blood and find nothing, swearing the edge of the cardboard felt like a knife. I'm such an idiot. Dusting off what's left of my pride, I bend down to retrieve the box so I can search for the money inside.

"What are you doing?" Corey asks.

I almost fall over as my feet buckle while my body spins around. Corey stands in the doorway staring at me, his hand gripping the handle tight.

"Uh, I'm looking for something I need for school."

He steps into the garage and crosses his arms over his chest.

"Is that right? Tell me. What are you searching for? Because I thought we got out everything we both needed for work."

"Um," I say. I don't do most things well under pressure, so lying to my husband's face won't help. There's little choice but to hit him with the truth. "Why are you hiding money from me?" I ask with closed eyes and slowly open them to see his response. He hasn't moved an inch. Instead, he remains in the same position looking more and more angry as each agonizing second passes us by.

Corey stays silent as he ambles toward me. I feel every vein in my body freeze as the blood drains from my soul. What is he doing?

"I can't believe you're forcing me to do this," he says.

"Forcing you to do what?" I rear up a step as he continues on a straight path in my direction. He won't hurt me, will he? This is Corey. I've never seen him so much as squash a bug.

"You've ruined everything, you know that? I can't understand how it's come to this."

"Come to what?" I ask as I feel the shelf ram into my spine. Corey is less than a foot from my face, still staring at me like I just kicked his childhood pet in front of him.

He exhales out of his flared nostrils and bends down to the box, picking it up with one hand. Without breaking eye contact, he digs around inside the carton and pulls out the wad of cash. I don't know whether to feel relieved to know it exists or if I'm supposed to let guilt take hold for being caught looking for it. I go with my only option. "Why do you have this?"

"Why do you think?" he asks, jutting the notes into the limited space between us.

I respond with a slow shrug as I do what I can to stop his eyes from dominating me into submission.

"You're really going to make me say it, aren't you? God, why can't you ever leave things alone? You always have to know everything."

"What are you talking about? What's this money for?"

"It's for your birthday, okay. Annette gave it to me so we could buy you something decent as a joint present. That thing on Amazon was to throw you off the scent. This is her half of the money I was going to put into our account after I purchased your gift this week. I couldn't do that without you knowing about it, so I had no choice but to stash it away for a few days."

My body slumps.

"Happy?"

"No," I reply. "Of course not. I'm so sorry, baby. I didn't mean to ruin things."

"It's too late now, isn't it?" He shoves the cash into my chest. "You might as well give that back to Annette. You can explain to her why you felt the need to screw up your own birthday."

I almost drop the money, not wanting it. "I will. I'll ring her now."

Corey storms off as I try to secure the slipping notes. "Baby, wait. I didn't mean to—"

The door to the garage slams shut before I get in another word. I'm left standing in the cold, holding money that was never meant for anything dishonest. Corey and I have only been married for a short time and I've broken the trust between us.

What have I done?

25

I'm stunned. I never expected Katherine to sabotage herself with such efficiency. I got lucky when she saw the cash being stuffed into that box. I imagined all kinds of scenarios I'd have to work up to force her to discover the hidden funds, but it turns out I didn't have to go down that route.

The money stuck in her mind like a rusty knife. She had to know why it was in the garage and what it was for. She couldn't stop herself from snooping. Today will be interesting to say the least.

The drive to school flashes by as I can't help the expanding grin that's desperate to spread across my face. I can only picture the intense guilt Katherine must feel as she sits next to me in silence. Ava sings in the back seat, oblivious to it all like the ignorant child she is.

Katherine tried countless times to apologize at the start of our drive over the money. I played my part to perfection, showing her how hurt I was while giving out a partial understanding. "Peter really worked you over, didn't he?" I related, milking the pain for what it was worth.

Now there's a brutal quiet between us that only Ava's horrible singing can interrupt.

We reach the school's parking lot fast. I'm too excited for what lays ahead to contemplate time. I find a spot and leave the engine running for the heat in case Katherine has anything else she wants to say. I've got several replies loaded up to make her feel like crap for what she did. At this point, I'm desperate for her to open her mouth and give me more ammunition to work with.

"I guess I should get Ava to before-school care," Katherine says.

"Sure." I've kept my responses short and sharp this morning, hoping they sting. There's nothing worse than talking to someone you've wronged only to receive one- or two-word answers. Sometimes the words a person doesn't utter hurt more than all others.

"Can I ask you something?" I say.

"Yes, please. Anything." Katherine's eyes gaze at me as if they've been dipped in a vat of guilt.

I could make her do whatever I want in this moment, but I have to focus on the plan. "What made you think the money was for gambling?"

Katherine sighs while Ava stirs in the back of the car keen to have her day start. "The poker nights. I thought they could have sparked something. I saw it with Peter. He wasn't always a hopeless addict. But he lost his job and filled the void with gambling. It started off small and expanded from there. I guess I freaked out and feared the worst when I spotted that money. God, I'm such an idiot. I'm so sorry."

She sobs and leans toward me for support. I wrap my arms around her to stifle her pathetic display. "It's fine," I say as I pat her back and wonder how she can do this in front of her daughter. Ava must surrender more and more respect for her mother with every passing day.

"Please forgive me. I can't lose you. I'm so sorry."

I pretend to think about it, casting my eyes off to the side. "It's okay. I'll always be here for you until the end. You know that."

Katherine pulls back from me with a smile as she wipes away her tears. "Thank you. You're too good to me. I don't deserve you in my life."

"Hey, that's not true. Let's not allow this hiccup to destroy what we have," I say, doing my best not to crack as another lie spills from my lips. If Katherine gets any more pitiful than this, I'll puke.

"Oh, I'm such a mess. Not the greatest start to the week."

"No but think about it like this: you'll never forget this birthday."

"No, never. For as long as I live."

I smile at Katherine, pondering her potential end over in my head. I haven't reached that point yet with her and wonder what will happen if she pushes me too far. Until then, I won't be happy until she's rolling around on the ground out of her mind with crippling doubt controlling her every waking thought. All in good time.

"I'd better get Ava moving," Katherine says.

"Tell you what. Why don't I take her for you so you can have a coffee and warm up for the day ahead?"

"Oh my god, thank you, Annette. That would be incredible. I appreciate it so much. You're such an amazing friend."

I think about what I've done to Katherine since she returned from her honeymoon. I messed with the love notes. I spied on her and Corey at the restaurant while I paid off their waiter to screw up Katherine's order. I sent Corey a fake text from a burner phone, knowing Katherine would see the message. I tricked

Corey into hiding money from his suspicious wife and watched from a distance as he hid it away in his garage. I pretended it hurt me when Katherine had ruined the birthday surprise I'd planned. Would she still call me a good friend after hearing these things and everything else I'd done to clutter her mind with doubt?

"I'm serious. You're an amazing person, Annette."

The smile on my face continues. "Yes, I am, aren't I?"

26

KATHERINE

I'm so lucky to have Annette in my life. She came through for me this morning as she always does, helping to drive Ava and I to school even after I screwed up her birthday idea with Corey. I told her everything last night the second Corey gave me the silent treatment. I didn't want to, but I needed to get the guilt off my chest. It would come out by the time my birthday rolled by, so I had no other option but to confess.

Annette was honest with me when I returned her money this morning and told her I wouldn't be celebrating. She relayed her disappointment having been excited to buy me something nice with Corey. She wasn't angry like him, though. He seemed to lose his usual laid-back attitude when faced with such a problem.

I think Annette had the advantage of experiencing my past instead of being told about it. Corey came around long after Peter had left me, but Annette was there before, during, and after that train wreck of a relationship. Countless times she had wasted her breath convincing me to break things off with Peter only to watch me forgive the jerk and give him one more shot.

The man could have committed murder in front of my eyes and gotten away with it.

I sip my cooling coffee in the faculty lounge with some time to spare before my day begins. Because Annette offered to pick Ava and me up this morning, I had to be at school about forty minutes earlier than normal.

"Good morning, Katherine," Susan says as she walks in with a purpose to her step.

"Morning."

"What brings you into the school so early on such a fine day?"

"Oh, you know. My car's in the shop." It's the first lie that pops into my head.

"That's good. I was starting to think my watch had broken." Susan places her belongings down and prepares herself a strong dark coffee while regarding my words.

I doubt she believes me, and I don't care.

"Did you get the email I sent you over the weekend?"

I saw it come up on my cell, but ignored it. "Oh, sorry. I didn't see it. I'll be sure to have a read of it this—"

"Never mind. I've dealt with the issue, but I would appreciate it if you endeavored to monitor your emails over the weekend. Important things happen even when you're off the school grounds."

"I'm sorry," I say as I bury my head between my fingers and squeeze. It's the only way I can stop myself from screaming. I look up after a moment and realize Susan is still blabbing away with her back to me. What's her problem today? It's like she knows I'm having troubles at home and can't wait to rub salt into my open wounds.

"And that's why we need to stay vigilant when it comes to communication around here."

"Got it," I say, standing up in a hurry. My chair grinds backward over the scuffed laminate flooring. I grab my bag and walk away while Susan continues to ramble as if I'm still there. I swear she has it in for me.

As I cross the schoolyard and rush to my classroom, an ocean breeze cuts through me. Corey's disappointed face flashes into my mind. I can't seem to get that moment out of my head when the trust between us broke. He had to understand why I needed to learn what the cash was for. Surely he realized it wasn't a good idea to hide money from me, given my history. I can only hope Annette would have warned him to be careful. If only I hadn't caught him hiding the cash. We wouldn't have had such a cold night together followed by a silent morning.

When Annette offered to pick Ava and me up, it relieved me. Corey and I need some space apart. This way he gets to calm down and forget about my stupid actions while I try to work on my problems. I don't want to throw a bandage over something that will fester below the surface and make our relationship toxic. I can't go through a similar time like that in my life, especially now that I'm married.

Plonking down into my chair, I place my head flat on my arms on the desk, letting my bag fall wherever it chooses to in the mess. The clutter is yet another problem I've allowed to grow out of control. It would take me hours to sort out the piles of printouts and resources strewn about my workstation.

My cell buzzes in my handbag beside my head. Needing the distraction, I fish it out and unlock the screen. Right now would be a fantastic time to look at some shoes online or scroll through Instagram and stare in envy at all the beautiful women my age who seem to have their lives together.

A text notification sits on my home screen, picking me up a little. It's probably Annette sending me some encouragement to get through the day. I set my notifications to be hidden on my lock screen, so I have to unlock my cell and open the text app to see who sent me the message. It's Corey.

My eyes go wide, delivering a jolt of panic down my spine. Unsure why I'm reacting in such a way, my cell drops to the desk. I don't want to read what he has to say, yet I'm also dying to know.

I take a breath and pick up my phone. "It's okay. At least he's talking to me again." I try to ignore the fact that I'm speaking out loud to myself when no one else is around, and I focus on my cell. I read Corey's text and immediately go back and absorb it again as if I'm missing something. Four words is all he has sent me.

We need to talk.

27

ANNETTE

E verything is falling into place. I have Corey and Katherine right where I want them. Katherine is so easy to manipulate. I only wish I'd done something sooner. Why did I wait so long? Deep down I knew what was coming. I guess I never wanted to believe it.

Taking Katherine and her kid to work today was a smart idea. I convinced her that she and Corey needed some time apart, allowing me to get in between them and expand the growing rift I've created. I wonder if either of them will realize what is happening to their relationship. Have they worked out that each problem they've experienced came from my careful planning?

"Morning," Barry says as he paces by me at the front of the office, late as always.

I flash him a smile and reply with, "Morning. How was your weekend?"

"Oh, the usual," he says while continuing through. "And you?"

"Perfect," I say. "I got a lot achieved."

"Glad to hear it." He pushes open the side door after swiping his keycard and rushes for his room.

"Me too," I mutter.

Things are going well. Not only is Katherine beginning to suffer, but I believe I have Corey questioning his decision to marry her. Soon I will break her while showing Corey what a terrible person his wife is. Divorce is the next step.

I've known Katherine for too long now. We both grew up in this town and went to school together. Katherine left for a time to study and 'better herself' with college and travel while I stayed behind. I could never leave Battery Beach or my friends and family the way she so carelessly did. But that's Katherine. She only thinks about herself.

When she returned, at first I was grateful to see her again and have her back in my life. I missed her. Little did I realize I was bending down to her the way I always did like in high school. Katherine was number one back then. All the boys wanted to date her. They'd get me to ask her out on their behalf like I was her secretary. In those days, I let myself be second to her. I even felt thankful for the opportunity. How pathetic.

It's my fault she decided not to leave when she returned to Battery Beach. She was only meant to visit for a few weeks, but I let our old dynamic take hold and convinced her to move back to her hometown. I ended up helping her get a job at BBES by putting in a good word for her with Barry, giving her the means to stay. It was all a lowly administrative assistant like me could offer. Before I knew it, Katherine was offered a teacher position at the school, and I became her loyal sidekick again.

My support got put to the test when Peter came onto the scene. Katherine thought he was so amazing despite his obvious faults. She never once listened to me when I tried to help her understand what kind of guy he was. If he'd never run away when Katherine fell pregnant, she'd still be with him.

Years later, Corey Grayson arrived, looking for a job. His eyes met mine when he walked into the office. I'd never felt that spark with a man before when we exchanged a smile. He made a joke about the parking lot and got me giggling like a schoolgirl. We had an instant connection. I did all I could to convince Barry to hire him.

Barry caved to my suggestion. He was a lazy principal. I even asked if I could give Corey the good news. At the end of Corey's first week, I encouraged the staff to go out for drinks to welcome him to the family. That night, it all happened. Everything fell into place.

I got Corey alone and made sure he knew what I wanted. We kissed outside of the bar by the ocean. The waves crashed hard against the cliff stacks, emitting powerful blasts of energy. It was incredible. For once, I felt like things would work out for me. I had met the perfect man. The future was mine for the taking. But I failed to grab hold quick enough.

Corey took me home that night. We made out on the porch of my house, letting one thing lead to another. But I didn't want to rush into it and ruin what should have been the greatest relationship of my life. Instead of inviting him in, I sent Corey on his way. I felt like an animal fighting its instincts, but it was the right thing to do. At least I thought so.

I told Katherine all about Corey the next morning over coffee. She was both amazed and excited for me all at once.

"So, when are you going to see him again?"

"I don't know. We swapped numbers, but I'm too nervous to call him. I'll mess it up."

"As if. Besides, he's probably desperate to call you but is trying to be cool and wait a few days."

She sounded genuine that day. I thought she was happy for me. The conversation didn't shift toward her or her ex the way it usually did. For once, it was all about me.

But things aren't always as they appear. Behind Katherine's eyes was a cunning plan I never saw coming. She could see that I had found a good guy, so she decided to take him from me. I know that now.

Corey never called. He didn't come to visit me at the office either. A week went by. I tried to talk to him so many times when I spotted him walking by me in a rush to reach the faculty lounge. What had gone wrong? Back then I thought it was something I'd said or done during our time together. Should I have slept with him? Should I have given him what he wanted that night?

I figured it out. It wasn't anything I did or didn't do. It was Katherine. She had swooped in and stolen him. She probably filled his head full of lies about me to force him to shift directions. It's the only explanation that makes sense. Why else would she have gone on a date with him only two weeks later behind my back? It wasn't the first time such a thing had happened.

In high school, Katherine would always go after the boys I told her I liked, fully aware that I didn't possess the same confidence she had to talk to them. Months before she left town for college, she even made out with a guy she knew I'd had a crush on for several years, claiming it just happened one night at a party, that it didn't really mean anything. We both understood that it did. This time was no different.

I'll never forget the day in the faculty lounge at work when Katherine first told me about Corey. It all started so innocently. She made me believe her story. "I've got something weird to tell you. And I hate to be the one to say it, but Corey asked me out."

My heart died in that moment. Time slowed to a crawl as all the possibilities for a happy future I had pictured many times in my head came crashing down. "Are you serious?"

"Yeah, sorry. I said no to him because you two kissed. Plus, I know how much you're into him."

"Wait. How did this happen? I don't understand."

"We've been chatting here and there in the faculty lounge. I guess I was trying to get him to talk about you. I didn't realize he was flirting with me. I certainly wasn't flirting with him, but he asked me out for a drink."

I closed my eyes and tried to remember to breathe. I couldn't think straight. "Are you sure he asked you out?"

She nodded at me with a slight frown. "I'm sorry. I knew I shouldn't have said anything."

"No, you were right to. There's no point in me wasting his time."

"Hey, don't talk like that. Corey's an idiot if he thinks this is okay. He's the one who will miss out. Not you."

I gave Katherine the best smile I could manage. It faded in a heartbeat. How did she think I was believing her? We both knew there was more to the truth than she was letting on.

"Thank you, Kat, but it's hard for me to be mad at him. I should have told him how I feel. I shouldn't have let him go." I thought about that night on the porch in front of my house.

"I'll talk to him and tell him he needs to take you out again."

"No, don't bother. It's no use."

"No, missy. You're not giving up this easily. I'll go have a chat with him at lunchtime."

"Please don't," I begged. But Katherine was so determined. She had that look in her eye.

"You'll see. I'll set him straight."

"Okay, fine," I said, caving. She always knew how to pressure me. All I could do then was pray she actually had pure intentions for once.

I almost thought there was something to hope for in that moment. How pathetic it was to think so.

28

KATHERINE

There's some time before school starts, so I ask Corey to meet with me in his classroom. There's no way he can send me a four-word message and think it won't drive me insane all day long. He agrees to my question with a quick reply, giving me about a ten-minute window to speak with him alone in his room.

My legs pump hard as I rush across the grounds to Corey's end of the school. We are almost on opposite sides of the facility, making the trip that much more painful.

I'm dying to know what he wants to discuss, given we won't have enough time to break out into a full-blown argument. Whatever the reason, I can't help the sinking feeling gurgling inside me. He'll probably come out and confess his regrets over marrying me. Then I'll be on my way back to class to mull the thought over. I know it.

I spot Corey through his window, pacing the classroom. He doesn't wave or offer me a smile as I approach the entrance to his room. What's this all about? I don't know what to think as I feel his burning gaze.

Corey opens the door and lets me in as if he never caught me sneaking around the garage. What's going on?

"Take a seat," he says, patting one of the children's tables for me to use as a chair.

I quickly park myself down with eager eyes and blurt the first thing that pops into my head. "This isn't about my birthday, is it? Because I'm not going to bother celebrating this year after what happened."

Corey takes a quick breath. "It's not about that. I have some news I wanted you to hear from me before anyone else."

"News?" The word seems to confuse me further. I don't know what I was expecting him to say.

"Yes. I finally heard from the school board. They're going to promote me. Starting next week, I'll be a lead teacher."

My brows pop up. Corey has been working to become a lead teacher for some time now. He had everything in place. He had his master's degree, experience, his national certification. All that was holding him back was a nod from the school's board in the district to give him the new title and the additional pay that came with the promotion. I knew so much about the process because I had been trying to achieve the same thing.

"Are you okay?" he asks.

"Ah, yeah. A bit shocked is all."

"Shocked?"

"No, not shocked. I guess I wasn't expecting this."

"So you aren't happy for me. Is that what you're saying?" He crosses his arms. I can feel the tension mounting in his shoulders from where I'm sitting.

"No, you don't understand. I'm over the moon for you. This is amazing. And you've earned it."

Corey nods and turns away. "It's okay, Katherine. I didn't expect this news to thrill you. We've both been chasing the same opportunity in a district that doesn't have the budget to pay teachers what they deserve."

"I'm delighted for you; I swear it. My reaction is coming from a place of confusion. I thought you were calling me in here about last night."

"Right. I guess you could have been expecting another fight, given the path our conversation took."

"Yes," I say, locking eyes with him. Has he brushed aside what happened all because he got the promotion? Is this his way of punishing me by gloating about his new position?

"It's in the past," Corey says. "You had your reasons to assume the worst. I know now not to hide money from you."

My mouth opens to defend my actions, but I stop myself short. Corey has moved on from what happened in his own manner. Sure, it's only because a promotion has inflated his ego, but I might as well take advantage of his improved mood.

"Anyway, I just wanted you to know about all of this before hearing it from Annette or someone else. I don't want there to be an awkward feeling between us whenever I have to talk about my new role."

"There won't be," I say. "I'm your wife and I'm proud of you. They made the right call making you a lead teacher. My time will come when it comes."

Corey's shoulders drop as if the stress of the conversation has rolled off his back. "Thank you for understanding." He opens his arms wide, inviting me in for a hug.

I accept and fall into his embrace. The anxiety I had during my swift walk to Corey's room evaporates. I won't be able to shake the thought of our argument from my head, so I'll focus on Corey's excellent news instead. He deserves this result. He works hard. Plus, it's a good reminder that I need to step up my game and not become bogged down with silly arguments.

"I'd better get going to class," I blurt as we break off our hug.

"Yep. The little devils will pile in soon."

I smile in response to his comment. I hate when teachers of older grades assume the young ones are all terrible pains. You can tell Corey has never taught a kid below the fifth grade.

"I'll see you after school," I say. "That is if Ava and I are still welcome to come home with you."

"Of course," he says. "But that reminds me. With the new job, I will need to arrive at work at least an hour earlier each day and possibly stay late. That's going to be a lot on Ava, not to mention a pain for you. It might be best if we take our own cars to school from now on."

"I thought the promotion didn't kick in until next week?"

"It doesn't, but I've got a bunch to do in preparation. That means longer hours and some extra work at home until I get used to my new responsibilities."

"Okay," I say, knowing that it wouldn't matter if Ava and I were willing to come in early and stay late with him. It's clear he wants the time to himself. I guess he doesn't want the unpredictable problems that can arise from waiting for Ava and me to get ready in the mornings. We've become a burden.

"I'll see you later," he says, showing me out the door with a kiss on the cheek.

I feel the press of his lips against my skin but something is missing. The ferocious love we had for one another in Las Vegas has disappeared.

What's happening to our marriage?

29

KATHERINE

The next two days pass by in a hectic blur. Corey gets up and drives to work while I'm still asleep, leaving me to do everything for Ava to prepare her for the day. Normally, he helps make her breakfast and keeps her in line when she doesn't want to get dressed. He even knows how to do her hair. Now it's all fallen to me again.

Ava and I arrive late to school as expected. I almost had to contact the office and warn Annette I'd miss the first bell. It's not a situation you prefer to be in without a good enough excuse other than to be running late due to incompetence.

I get Ava off to kindergarten. Before-school care has already ended. When I reach my room in a huff, there are several parents waiting out front with their children ready to tear me a new one for arriving two minutes before the first bell.

"Sorry I'm late," I say, praying none of them complain to the office or the principal.

"Do you know what time it is?" asks one of the more argumentative parents.

I do my best to beg for the collective forgiveness of each person I've disappointed and unlock the door. The rude parent grills me further, chasing me up the steps of my classroom. Again I apologize and give out a weak excuse while assuring the group it will never happen again. What's wrong with these people? They act as if they've never been late to work.

I settle into the first few hours of the day and let the rush of the morning fall away, hoping it doesn't become part of the routine. This promotion better be worth the extra hassle is all I can say. When the kids head out for recess, I remember that I have a seminar after school and need Corey to take Ava home.

"Crap," I mutter as the last child leaves the room. I'd never hear the end of it if one of them heard me cuss. I try calling Corey on his cell, knowing he will be available to chat. He doesn't answer, though.

"Great," I say, tapping away to send him a message instead. I guess he's too busy to talk to me. I draft a quick text, explaining the situation while apologizing multiple times. He is trying to get ready for his new role and I'm making his life harder.

A moment later, I see that my message is marked as delivered and read. Corey now knows he needs to pick up Ava. What kind of reply am I going to receive? I watch the three dots come up on my screen to indicate that he is writing back a response. The little animation fades in and out for at least twenty seconds. Is he sending me a big lecture for not reminding him sooner about Ava? This is not what I need, especially with my ruined birthday only a day off.

In a way, I'm glad I told Annette and Corey not to bother celebrating it anymore. It wouldn't feel right, given how badly I ruined things.

The dots stop their dance and disappear. Is he not even going to bother with any kind of reply? A simple 'okay' or a 'fine' is all I require. Either he's too annoyed at me for the whole thing or he got interrupted by a colleague.

With a sigh, I figure the problem is out of my mind. I allow the rest of my day to get underway as best it can, though my brain won't stop thinking about the promotion. I've tried my hardest to be happy for Corey, but after some reflecting, I realize I'm lying to myself. Will my thoughts impact on our marriage?

I'm not jealous of Corey becoming a lead teacher exactly, but I don't understand why I got overlooked for the job. We both applied for the role, helping each other with our applications and the dozen of pages of rambling that came with the process. I never said so, but I thought for sure I would shine through, especially over Corey. I had more experience than him, and the school doesn't need another lead teacher in the higher grades.

Maybe I'm being petty. He got the job, and I didn't. It's as simple as that.

The end of the day comes up faster than I expect, leaving me in a frazzle to arrive on time for my seminar. I make it to the class held in the school with the rest of the first-grade teachers. The presentation is all about exciting and creative ways to encourage better writing skills from the students. I get a lot from the two-hour lecture and exit the school feeling positive for a change, eager to implement what I'd learned.

On my way home, I drop into the grocery store to pick up something to make for dinner. As I approach the automatic double doors, my cell buzzes in my handbag with a call. I fish it out to see the kindergarten's number come up on my caller ID.

"Hello?"

"Hi, Katherine. It's Sheryl here. I've been trying to reach you for the last hour."

"You have? What's wrong? Did Ava leave something behind today?"

"Um, no. She hasn't left anything behind because she's still here."

"What?" I blurt out. Corey didn't pick her up. He can't still be at school. "I'm so sorry. There must have been a mix-up with Corey and me. I'll be there in five minutes."

"We'll be at the front of the parking lot. Goodbye." She hangs up with an annoyed tone in her voice. I can't believe this.

I go to call Corey, but I stop when I realize how angry I am. Instead of unloading my frustration, I decide to wait until Ava and I get home to ask why the hell he didn't pick her up.

When I reach the school, I see Sheryl standing with Ava looking rather agitated. I wonder how many times per week this happens to Sheryl.

"I'm so sorry," I say. "I thought Corey was picking her up, and I suppose he figured the same about me."

"It's fine," Sheryl says with closed eyes, dismissing my poor excuse. "You're here now. That's all that matters."

"Thank you for taking care of Ava. I really appreciate it."

Sheryl speeds along my thanks and apology so she can pass Ava off into my hands and leave. "Please make sure you have a word with your husband. I don't get paid for staying back like this."

"I will. I'm so sorry. This won't happen ever again. I promise."

Sheryl climbs into her car and takes off in a hurry. I wonder how the kindergarten teachers, who were also the daycare workers when the school's day transitioned into after-school care, decided who had to stay whenever this happened. It probably never did, though. No one else would be as stupid as me to think a read text message was enough of a confirmation to assume their husband was picking up their child.

"Where were you, Mommy?" Ava asks as we walk to my car.

"Mommy was at a seminar. Corey was supposed to pick you up today, honey."

"Why didn't he come get me?"

I sigh as I help buckle her into her seat. "I guess he didn't see Mommy's message." I look around and see no other cars in the parking lot. He must be home by now.

Had he forgotten, or was this something else? Was he trying to punish me?

W hen Ava and I come through the front door at home, Corey is on his cell, calling me. My phone stops buzzing in my bag a second after he hangs up. My hands were too full to answer.

"Where have you guys been?" he asks, confusion lining his forehead.

"Where do you think?" I say a little harsher than expected.

He shakes his head with the same look on his face.

"I had my seminar today after school. You were supposed to pick up Ava."

"Oh, right. But you never reminded me. I'm sorry I didn't come collect her, but you know I need to be told on the day."

"I did tell you. I sent you a text."

"A text? Why didn't you try calling me?"

"I tried. You wouldn't answer, so I shot you a message. And don't say you never got it, because I saw that it was delivered and read. You even went to reply but changed your mind halfway through."

"What are you talking about? I never received a text from you let alone started to respond."

I take Ava into the kitchen and place everything down I bought from the grocery store to make dinner. I told Corey I'd sort out our meals from now on seeing as he had to work longer hours than me.

"Don't worry about it," I say. "You were too busy to collect Ava. Next time, tell me so I can ask Annette or someone else to pick her up."

Corey stomps into the kitchen after me. "I didn't ignore a text from you. I never saw one. Here. Look." He passes me his cell and brings up the messaging app. I see a thread between the two of us ending just before the last text I sent asking him to pick up Ava.

"You must have deleted it," I say, handing it back to him.

"Why would I do that? Do you really think I would?"

I try to bite my tongue. It's clear I shouldn't continue to argue like this in front of Ava when I notice her concerned face, but I can't help it. "I don't know. I guess it sounds to me that you didn't want something to interrupt your day, so you pretended not to see my text by deleting it."

Corey's jaw drops open. He continues to shake his head with narrowed brows. "Do you realize how insane you sound right now? I would never do that. But you know what? I'm not going to stand here and take this crap. Catch you later." He heads for the front door.

"Fine by me."

I watch as Corey goes through the motions of his threat, snatching his car keys and wallet. When he's less than a few feet from grasping the chrome handle to leave the house, a knock comes at the door.

"What now?" he mutters, reaching out to answer. He opens the entrance to reveal Annette standing in the dark with a bottle of wine in hand.

"Annette?" I say over Corey's shoulder.

"Hi, guys. Am I interrupting anything?"

"No, of course not," Corey says. "Come on in out of the cold. What brings you here?"

Annette walks inside with some caution in her step. Did she hear us arguing? She must have. "I thought I'd drop in for a minute to congratulate Corey on his promotion. I heard all about it in the office a few days ago."

"Oh, thank you," Corey says. "That's kind of you. Is that what the wine's for?"

Annette looks down at the bottle and up to me. Can she see the look on my face, the one that shows how horribly embarrassed I am for not getting anything for Corey to celebrate his promotion?

"Oh this. Katherine asked me to pick up a bottle of your favorite wine to celebrate, isn't that right?" She stares straight at me with a smile.

I want to mouth a thank you but Corey is waiting to see my response. "Yes. Thank you for doing that, Annette. It's much appreciated."

"It was no bother. You told me what to get. All I did was pick it up."

"Right. Well, you still went above and beyond. How about you stay for dinner?"

"Only if it's no problem for you all."

"Fine by me," Corey says.

"Okay," I say, not waiting for Annette to express otherwise. I need her here to stop Corey and me from arguing. I don't want Ava to see it and I can't trust myself after the day I've had. "Why don't you come into the kitchen while Corey relaxes in the living room." I sound like a fifties housewife.

Annette and I move away from Corey as Ava takes a seat at her tiny table and draws as if she wasn't witnessing two adults yelling at one another.

"Thank you," I whisper to Annette as we reach the kitchen. "You saved my butt back there."

"Don't mention it. Happy to help. By the way, what's going on? I feel like I walked through the middle of a crime scene."

I shake my head as I grab some ingredients I need to make dinner. "Long story."

"I got time," Annette says as she closes the door.

I tell Annette to take a seat. After taking a deep breath, I supply her with the evening's drama, feeling nothing but shame with every word.

"Oh, wow. I'm so sorry for interrupting. I've probably made things worse."

"No, don't be sorry. You're helping to make a nice buffer between us. We can't argue if there's a guest in the house."

"That bad?" Annette asks, leaning forward in her seat with the bottle of wine in her hands.

"Yep. Seems to be this way all the time at the moment. We keep fighting over every little thing."

"The money was not something little, but I've heard that marriage can be like this at first. I guess it's such a huge change in your life. My advice is to push through. Don't let it all get to you. You'll both come out the other side a stronger couple."

"You think so?"

"I know so. You two are perfect together. Everyone sees that."

I stop prepping the meal for a moment and stare at her with a smile. "Thank you, Annette. You're too good to me."

"Yep. I'm cool, aren't I? How are you doing, by the way?"

"With what?"

"You know. The promotion. That's the real reason I dropped in. I knew it wouldn't be easy with one of you getting the position over the other. Especially if the job went to Corey."

I hold back from yelling out how confused I am that he got given the lead teacher job over me and feel a sense of relief that

I'm not the only person who thinks this. "It's been a tough few days. I know I should be happy for him, but I can't help feeling cheated by the whole experience."

"Yeah, it's a bit odd if you ask me. Maybe I can dig around in the office and see what happened."

"No, it's okay. I don't want you getting into any kind of trouble because of me. You being here is enough."

"Okay, I won't interfere. I do, however, insist that you drink a glass of this wine as soon as possible to help ease your mind."

"That's the best thing I've heard all day," I say with a heavy sigh. "Any chance you bought a second bottle? One won't cut it."

Annette gives me a cheeky grin. "I've got another in the car."

31

ANNETTE

Last night was amazing. Katherine and Corey were deep into an argument when I arrived. So much so Katherine didn't hear me pull into the drive thirty seconds after she got home. As usual, I wasn't far away—just around the corner in fact—but no one noticed my car in the dark. Not when there was a battle to fight.

In general, Katherine lets Corey tell her what's right and wrong. But lately, with a little help from me, her true self has emerged. I am showing him her defiant side so he can see what she's really like. By the time I'm finished pulling the wool from his eyes, Corey will thank me for removing Katherine from his life.

Listening in from outside the front of the newlywed's rental, I got to hear exactly how far along Katherine had come. She was charging at Corey full blast with what she believed to be the truth. How could she be wrong when she'd sent him a text that was both delivered and read? Simple really. Well, sort of.

It wasn't easy, but I installed some malware on to his phone that gives me remote access to his messages as if I were holding his cell in my hands. The software is amazing, it even allows me to intercept a message as it's sent to him.

I spent most of my day yesterday waiting for an alert on my cell to tell me when Katherine had sent Corey a text. As soon as I saw the request for someone to collect Ava after school come through, I realized I'd stumbled upon a perfect opportunity to mess with Katherine. What better way to make her think her new husband was gaslighting her than to delete a message he'd supposedly seen? Pretending to respond was the ultimate kicker. It fell in perfectly with what I had planned.

I knew the promotion would already be a sore point. Having them also squabble over who should have picked up Ava only added more fuel to their raging fire.

I couldn't control the smile on my face as Corey and Katherine argued away in front of Ava. Listening in from the front door as quietly as possible, I had to fight the laughter that was dying to burst from my lips. Then it was a matter of waiting for the right moment to interrupt them with a bottle of Corey's favorite wine. Katherine thought I was there to support her. Little did she realize I was only trying to drive a bigger wedge between their bond by preventing that time apart they each needed.

The wine was the best way to make Katherine think I came over to help while also showing Corey that I know him. He has no idea, if I'm being honest, just how well I understand who he is. Katherine, though, barely has a grasp on who her husband is as a person.

I had to watch Corey and Katherine get together. They thought no one realized at the time, so they tried to keep it a secret. Neither wanted anyone to find out that two weeks after Corey kissed me, Katherine had stepped in to 'convince' him to see me again. In reality, she was only there to steal him away. I'm so glad I kept an eye on her when she offered to 'straighten him out' for me.

Did they think they were sparing my feelings by sneaking around behind my back? I mean, they both knew I would find out, eventually. They seemed to figure a month was long enough a time for me to have moved on and forgotten about the most magical night of my life. Little did they know that I could never move on from Corey.

Katherine fed me lies to throw me off her and Corey's scent until they came clean. It took a lot from me not to explode when she first told me how she approached Corey on my behalf.

"I'm so sorry, Annette. I tried to convince him to ask you out again, but he wasn't interested."

I didn't know what was worse: her cruel wording or the fact that I'd seen the way she tried to 'convince' him to give me another shot. I watched from outside Corey's classroom when Katherine first kissed him. How could she do that to me? After years of loyalty, she figured it was okay to destroy any chance I had at true happiness. Just because her ex had run a number on her life didn't mean I needed to fall down to her level.

I shouldn't have been surprised, really. It wasn't the first time Katherine had done something like this. Way back when in high school, she'd not only take an interest in one of the boys I liked, but she made sure he knew that I was not an option after she dumped him only two weeks later.

The secret meetups continued between Katherine and Corey. I followed them wherever they went, even when they drove all the way to Portland for a fancy date out of town. A month after Corey and I shared a perfect kiss, the world found out the truth. Katherine announced to the school that her and Corey were an item. I'll bet Corey wanted to wait longer, but she wouldn't allow it. She probably preferred to tell everyone on day one.

When Katherine first told me about her and Corey, I had to pretend I didn't know. It wasn't hard for me to show her how hurt and betrayed I felt. My pain was real. What she never expected was for me to forgive her so quickly. I had to. I couldn't have her finding out that I was still in love with Corey. There was no way in hell I could give her the satisfaction.

At first I was hopeful. I had one important thing on my side of it all keeping me going; Katherine's relationships were terrible and didn't last. Her ex came and went so many times I'd lost count. There were other guys here and there. None of them survived. I figured Corey would have been no different. I was wrong.

Katherine made things work with Corey. It was as if a bug had burrowed itself into her brain and stopped her from being her usual stupid self. Corey didn't run for the hills the way the others did when they discovered Ava. He was a real man.

Months went by. I played my part even when Corey and Katherine moved in together. I acted like it wasn't a blade to my heart every time I saw them kiss. Each second his hands touched her only caused me more misery. Still, I hung in there, ever hopeful their relationship would run its course and fall apart. It had to.

When Katherine told me about her and Corey deciding to get married, something in my mind snapped. All the restraint I had shown them, all the goodwill I could fake, ceased to exist. I could no longer sit there and pretend everything was okay. I had to act.

As I signed their wedding certificate as a witness, I had to steady my hand to fight the rage from spilling out from my soul. Sure, I could have attacked Katherine there and then, but I had a better idea brewing, despite wanting more than anything to implement that indignation.

I knew without a doubt what I had to do. And now everything is falling into place.

The next day at school, I go about my usual routine with one exception: a quick trip to Corey's room during recess. I'm not supposed to leave my post in case a parent or a student comes in needing something, but I have to follow up my visit to the Grayson household last night. It's time to strike.

I spot Corey in his classroom working away on his laptop. He's such a dedicated educator who deserves to rise through the ranks. Sure, I may have given him a little help without him knowing about it, but I know he would have gotten the promotion on his own.

It wasn't hard to ruin Katherine's application and make Corey's credentials appear amazing by comparison. They each had to submit their forms to me first before I sent the paperwork on to Barry and so on. I spent one night on my computer recreating Katherine's application while making a few modifications. Anything that gave her the advantage over Corey got removed or altered to look irrelevant. It was too easy. Plus, Katherine will never know. The school board never gives feedback to their applicants.

I knock at Corey's door gently, not wanting to disturb him

more than I have to. He lifts his head to the interruption and smiles. I love that beautiful grin almost as much as the way his eyes stare into my being. Every time he looks at me, even if for a split second, I'm back to the night we kissed. I could live in moments like this forever.

"Come in," he calls out to me through the glass of the door.

I return Corey's warm smile and quietly let myself into his room. He keeps his space immaculate unlike Katherine. I don't understand how they live together being such opposites. If I were a teacher, I'd never allow my classroom to fall to pieces the way Katherine's does.

"How are you?" he asks me, thoughtfully beyond a mere formality.

"Oh, you know me. I'm fine."

"That's good. So what can I do for you?"

I walk in further, smiling at him, trying my best to focus on the plan. I sometimes find it hard to place my attention where it needs to go whenever I talk to Corey. All I want to do is fall into his strong arms and feel his warmth against my skin.

"Uh, well, I wanted to ask how you were doing. More specifically check how you and Kat are coping."

One side of Corey's lips pop up into a sardonic grin. "Yeah, not good. Is it that obvious? Or has she filled you in on our latest argument?"

"A bit of both, sorry."

He lets out a sigh and shuts the lid on his computer. "I don't know what's going on between us lately. We were lucky you came over when you did last night to help diffuse things. It was about to get a lot worse."

I stumble on the spot, fighting the temptation to slap myself in the face for helping. I thought interrupting with a helpful bottle of wine was the right call. Whether it was or not doesn't matter. I need to focus on what I came here to achieve.

"Thank you," Corey says.

"Oh, it's okay. I was trying to do what I could to help you guys work through it all. Plus, I kind of knew Katherine wouldn't take the news of the promotion all too well."

Corey chuckles. "Yes, I guess it was the first thing that went through my mind when I found out. I honestly didn't know how to tell her."

"I can imagine. But, she knows now, so don't stress about it. Besides, Kat should be happy to watch your hard work pay off."

"You'd think so. I mean she tells me she's proud of me and excited blah, blah, blah, but ultimately I can see behind her eyes how much she feels wronged by it all."

"Why would she feel 'wronged'?" I ask, pretending I don't know the answer.

"I shouldn't be telling you this," he says, rubbing his neck, "but let's just say that she believes she deserves the promotion more than I do."

"Wow, really? You're both hard-working teachers. Why would she think she deserves it more than you?"

Corey shrugs. "I'm not sure. I mean she admitted some of her jealousy to me this morning, but there's more there. She, uh..." He trails off, shaking his head. It's obvious he's holding back on what he truly wants to express. I could give him another nudge, but I need his venting to feel as organic as possible.

"Anyway, thank you again for the wine. It was a big help. How did you know it was my favorite?"

Because I know you better than you know yourself, is what I want to say, but I stick to the script in my head as best I can. "Katherine told me."

"Come on, Annette. We both know Kat had nothing to do with you bringing over that bottle of wine last night."

"Was it that noticeable? I guess I thought I could make you

both happy. I knew the promotion would upset Kat, but I also didn't think you deserved to have your big moment spoiled."

"It's okay. I'll live."

A silence fills the small space between us. I hold my gaze on him the way I did that night. He doesn't look away. I place my hand on his arm. "If you ever need to talk about anything, you know I'm here for you."

"Thank you. Guess I'd better get back to it," he says, clearing his throat as he turns from me.

"Yeah, me too, I suppose. I'll see you around." I head for the door, frustrated I have to leave. It feels like there is something beginning to spark between us again. All I need is more time alone with Corey to make him forget about his wife.

33

It's my birthday, but it doesn't feel like a day worth thinking about. I came into work early after the disastrous night with Corey. Thank God Annette showed up at our house when she did. She stopped the argument between Corey and me from growing into something far worse. She forced us both to be hospitable.

I felt so ashamed that she knew I'd be upset about Corey receiving the promotion over me. She expected my pathetic anger and tried her best to prevent me from spoiling what should have been a good night. I guess the thing with the texts and Ava not being picked up screwed with my brain a little.

I figure Corey's cell malfunctioned that day. It's the only answer I can think of to explain why my message reported as delivered and read. What's still driving me insane, though, is how the three dots came up. They should only appear when a person is typing a response. I suppose I need to leave the thought alone and write it off as a mystery.

This morning, I tried to be organized, getting Ava ready as fast as I could to put her into before-school care an hour earlier.

I wanted to get to work with plenty of time to spare so I could talk to Corey in private. We needed to chat and clear the air.

After Annette left late last night, Corey went to bed without a word. We can't keep doing this. Our marriage won't survive if we continue fighting this much.

It's lunchtime and I'm sitting alone, eating in my classroom. My mind slips back to the conversation I had with Corey before the chaos of the day began. I dropped Ava off and headed over to his room. He was already hard at it with a steaming cup of coffee at his desk. This promotion was serious business.

"Can I come in?" I asked after opening the door so Corey didn't have to get up.

He stopped writing a note on the pile of papers he was working on and leaned back a little in his chair. "What brings you into work this early?" he asked me in a slightly mocking tone.

"You," I said. "I'm not happy with how things have been lately. I don't mean to interrupt your day, but we need to talk about it."

Corey tapped his pen repeatedly against the edge of his desk, never taking his eyes off mine. "What's happened to us?"

I shook my head as I settled in next to him, dragging out one of the student chairs to sit on. "I don't know. It's all been such a messy blur since we returned from our honeymoon. I wish we could put life on hold and fly back there. Everything was perfect for those five days."

"It was, wasn't it," he said with a coy smile.

"Maybe we can go back there," I said.

"What do you mean?"

"We could pretend we're still on our honeymoon and not let anything come between us the way it has this last week."

Corey sighs. "It's a nice thought, but how are we supposed to imagine being in some perfect moment when we're at each other's throats?"

"That's a fair question, and I will answer you with a simple apology. I'm sorry for being jealous of your promotion. I let my disappointment take control when I should have been happy for you instead. I've been a terrible wife."

"You haven't been. I could have told you the news in a better way. I knew it wouldn't have been what you wanted to hear, considering how much extra work you put into your application."

"It caught me off guard, but I shouldn't have let it go beyond that. When Ava's teacher called me to pick her up after my seminar, I guess I took out the misunderstanding on you. So again, I'm sorry."

"It's okay," he said as he grabbed my hand and gently ran his fingers over my skin. I wished we could have kissed in that moment, but when we first got together, we promised Barry that we'd keep things strictly professional.

"What are you working on?" I asked Corey as I moved in closer to look at the pile of papers on his clean desk. I wish I could work as neat as him.

"A new Math plan. I'm going through some old tests to see if I can make improvements to the way we teach it to the higher grades."

"That's exciting," I said, seeing something I knew I could help him with. Sure, I was a first-grade teacher, but I could teach Math to any year level from preschoolers to seniors in high school. It was my specialty when I was working through my master's. Some days I felt a little underwhelmed, teaching the first grade, but then I'd remember that I love the young ones too much to move on to a greater challenge.

"Yeah, there's a lot here to unpack, but I'm going to present some changes to Barry next week once I figure out this problem the students all seem to have."

"If you need to run anything by me, I'm here for you. I have some useful resources from my master's that would be a big help."

"Thanks," he said, the words spitting out of his lips a little sharp, "but I should be fine."

I backed away. This was something he wanted to do on his own. I guess he was trying to prove himself to everyone so they could see they made the right choice in promoting him.

"I'll leave you to it."

"That would be good, honey. I still have a lot of work to do before the damn kids charge through here like a runaway train."

"Have fun," I said before planting a quick kiss on his cheek. I couldn't help myself.

"What are you doing?" he snapped, pulling away from me.

"There's no one around."

"You don't know that. Anyone could have seen you."

"I'm sorry," I said as I stood from the small chair. I slid it back to where I found it.

"It's fine. Please try to be more careful from now on. I need to show the staff and parents that I'm worthy of this new responsibility."

"Okay. Sorry. I'll see you later then."

"Kat," he said, stopping me.

"Yes?"

"Happy birthday," he said, holding up a small wrapped present.

"You didn't have to do that, remember?" I said as I walked over to him and slowly opened his gift. Inside was a twist link sterling silver bracelet set with small diamonds. It glimmered in the box as the light hit each angle. "Oh Corey. It's beautiful.

Thank you." I went to kiss him on the cheek but remembered I couldn't.

"I figured I'd still get you something even though you said not to."

"You didn't need to but thank you. I really appreciate it."

"Also I didn't mean to bite your head off about the kiss before. People know we're married. I shouldn't be so uptight about it, but I'm under a lot of pressure to make this work. Give me a few weeks to settle into things and I'll take you out for an expensive dinner. Hell, maybe we can go away for a few nights."

I made myself smile to show him I understood. "That would be nice."

"Have a good day, okay? I'll see you at home."

"You too," I said, realizing he no longer wanted me bugging him at school.

The time dragged by until I found myself alone, eating lunch in my classroom, wondering how long I could keep pushing down my feelings.

My head hangs low as I force myself to eat my ham and cheese sandwich. The flavor seems bland and almost nauseating. I hear footsteps approach my room followed by a quick knock. I glance up.

"Need some company?" a voice says to me.

34

ANNETTE

My day picked up its pace after seeing Corey at recess. The seeds I planted in his mind can only grow from here on out. I need to keep nurturing them to flower. It won't take long for him to realize he made a huge mistake marrying that terrible excuse for a human being. If I do my job right, he will welcome a separation and eventual divorce.

As lunchtime arrives, I head for the faculty lounge for a quick coffee. I don't spot Katherine hanging around the way she routinely does or find Corey, for that matter. They both usually sit at the same table having a private conversation while smiling at each other like lovesick puppies. Have I ruined their routine already?

Needing to know, I head toward Katherine's room to see if she's by herself. If I discover her there, miserable and eating alone, my work has been a success.

Thinking about how things have progressed, I only wish I hadn't waited so long to take action. I guess I got swept up in the delusion that Katherine and Corey's relationship would fall apart on its own. If only I had known it would be this easy.

I approach Katherine's room and step up to the doorway,

seeing her alone sitting on her desk like a rebellious teenager. With a single knuckle, I knock on the glass and realize two seconds too late that Corey is already inside. He's relaxing on Katherine's chair. Their held hands snap away from each other.

"Come in, Annette," Katherine calls out with a huge smile on her face. She seems happy. And why wouldn't she be. She was eating lunch with her perfect damn husband. What the hell have I walked in on?

I open the door a crack and poke my head in. "Sorry. I didn't mean to interrupt. I'll leave you both to it."

"No, it's fine," Corey says. "Join us." He ushers me in with a wave.

"Okay," I mutter, like a stunned idiot. I have no choice but to venture inside and be the third wheel to Katherine and Corey as they've somehow become the perfect couple again.

"Have lunch with us," Katherine adds to Corey's invite.

"Oh no, I can't stay. I just needed to ask Kat a quick question."

"Ask away," Corey says.

Katherine leans toward me. "What's up?"

My mouth falls open, but nothing comes out. "I, um. You know what, on the way over here I forgot what I wanted to ask you. How stupid is that?" I force out a chuckle and feel the room close in around me.

"I hate that," Corey says with an awkward laugh.

"Me too," Katherine adds. "If you think of it, I'll be here."

I smile, feeling the phony expression plastered over my face. It starts to burn me. I have to get out. "I'll leave you two be."

"Okay. Have a good one," Corey says, dismissing me. Did I imagine our intimate conversation earlier? I feel myself float out of the room; my legs disconnected from reality. Did any of what we talked about before mean a thing to him? Was he messing with me?

As I walk back to the office at a shuffle, feeling stupid, I divert to the nearest restroom. I find the disabled toilet and rush inside, locking the door behind me. None of the students are around, so I claw at my skull and feel a pure rage swarm within.

I scream out loud and kick the solid gate as hard as I can. What the hell is happening? Katherine and Corey should hate each other. They should accept the cold truth that they don't work as a couple.

I shake my head and realize I've been going about this all wrong. This slow burn is taking too long. I have to show Corey we belong together. I need to step up my game and make Katherine understand what happens when you steal from me.

Her time is coming.

C orey doesn't seem to enjoy being a lead teacher. By the end of the first week of his new role, he looks stressed out and worried. With the weekend now upon us, I hope he tries to take his mind off school for a few hours and relax by spending some time with his family.

It's Saturday afternoon and Corey has spent the morning working on his Math planner again. From what I can see, he has thrown out everything the higher grades had been using and has started from scratch. It seems like the hard way to go about it to me, but I remind myself it's not my problem. I've already offered to help.

"Dammit!" Corey yells from the small desk we have in the corner of the living room.

"Honey?" I say to him while tilting my head sideways toward Ava, gently reminding him not to cuss in front of her. "Please try to stay calm." I'm sitting on the sofa while Ava lies next to me watching her favorite animated show about talking dogs. Thankfully, she seems oblivious to Corey's outburst.

"Sorry. It's this stupid planner. It's driving me insane. If I'm going to help the students improve their results, it needs to be flawless. I can't get things working the way I want them to."

"It's okay. Don't stress about it. You've only been at this for a short time. Why not take a break for the rest of today?"

"No. I promised Barry I'd have something for him Monday."

"Really? That doesn't sound like him to put pressure on a teacher so soon."

"He didn't. It's more that I said I'd show him some progress by Monday. I can't go to school next week and reveal this mess. He won't think I'm up to the job." Corey throws his hands over his face. "God, why did I have to say anything?"

I shift Ava to her own spot on the sofa and wander over to Corey, placing my hand on his shoulder when I reach him. "It's okay, honey. You'll get it worked out. Maybe you need to move aside from it for an hour or two. That helps me with these kinds of things."

Corey lets out a long sigh and takes his hands from his face. "Yeah, you're right."

"I'm always right," I say with a chuckle.

"How could I forget," he says, playing along.

I bend down and kiss him on the cheek. "Come on. Let's go for a walk and get out of this house. The sun's out. It'll be good for us all."

Corey doesn't argue and helps to remove Ava from her position on the sofa. She protests a little to her show being switched off but is happy the second we head outside.

We're not close to the beach, but we can be there in less than ten minutes if we all walk fast enough. As we stroll toward the ocean with Ava between us holding our hands, I can't help but ask Corey about what he's specifically struggling with. We get into the details of his proposed changes to the Math curriculum for the fifth graders. His overall concept sounds ambitious and problematic, but I don't tell him. Instead, I try to point out smaller issues.

"How do you think that will all work with the correlation between place value and operations?" I ask.

"I'm not sure yet. I'm still trying to simplify a system so the kids can better understand place value. It seems to be a severe problem from what I've found in the hundreds of tests I've gone through."

We continue to talk shop while Ava sings to herself, ignorant to our boring conversation. I sometimes wish I could disappear into her carefree mind for a day.

We reach the beach and zip up our coats as a blast of ocean wind rolls in from the waterfront. It's a beautiful sight before us of crashing waves and cliff stacks, but the cold temperature is a letdown given there's some nice sun out. Spring is fading.

"I'm happy to help you," I say to Corey.

"No, it's okay. I have to push through and get it done. Everyone needs to know I'm up for this."

"No one is saying you're not, baby. I'm just offering to support you with a particular problem I'm good at solving. If I were you, I'd take help wherever I could. I sure do whenever I need it. Plus, the school likes results more than anything else. They don't care where they come from. And it's not like I'll run around telling people I helped you."

Corey stares out into the water for a moment, no doubt in thought. "Okay. You're right. I'll accept the help."

"You'll need to ask me better than that."

He turns to me with his crooked smile. "Pretty please, my love, will you help me with my pathetic problem?"

I pretend to consider his request for a second. "I suppose so. But it's going to cost you three milkshakes."

"Done."

Once Ava finishes exploring the beach, we head over to the nearest café and enjoy some milkshakes as a family.

After an hour of fun, we walk home and prepare some dinner. Once Ava heads off to bed, I help Corey with his problem. We have a strong breakthrough within the first few hours, giving Corey something concrete to show Barry on Monday.

"Thank you so much, honey," Corey says. "This is a huge step in the right direction. I can apply this to everything instead of trying to reinvent the wheel. I might even email some of this to Barry so he sees it before Monday."

"That's a good idea. Also, you're welcome. And please remember, I'm happy to help with anything I can."

"Got it," he says, holding my hand.

I pull Corey toward me and drag him to our bedroom. "Come on. Let's go have some fun before this weekend is over."

An interesting email comes by me early Sunday morning. Corey has sent Barry some work he's been plowing through over the weekend like the dedicated man that he is. With back door access to Corey's emails via a virus I put on to his laptop before he left on Friday, I've been able to see everything he sends and receives through his school account. As I go through the attachment he sent to the principal, something becomes clear: Katherine has been helping him.

I saw the mess Corey emailed himself as a backup on Friday. There's no way he has pulled all of this together in such a short time without Katherine shoving her nose into his business. I'm no teacher, but I recognize the language she uses. I know the words she loves to put into action. If she hasn't taken over his project, I'd be almost shocked.

I hate to see Corey struggle this way and have to rely upon some glory hog like Katherine for help. She's always looking for another way to make herself feel important. I'll never forget the time when one of her students came to the office for help, informing me that her father was hitting her mother. I was the one who spent hours comforting the child throughout that day. I was the one to call social services to properly investigate. Yet when the time came for Barry to step in and do his part, Katherine decided to take over without asking me and said it was something a teacher should handle.

Corey shouldn't have allowed Katherine to soil his hard work with her inflated ego. Yet I'm glad he did. There's a beautiful opportunity here that I cannot let pass me by.

I'll deviate from the next phase of my plan for now to implement something that I know will reveal the ever-present fault lines in Corey and Katherine's relationship. It's almost too perfect a situation to ignore.

Come Monday, I will drive an entirely new wedge between the newlyweds. There won't be forgiveness like there was last week when Corey gave in to Katherine's BS. I love this man more than anything in the world, but he needs to show some backbone and realize he has married a manipulative loser who only cares for herself.

If I pull this off, Corey will finally see what has been holding him back all along. And I'll be there to pick up the shattered pieces, ready to glue them together the way they should have been from the start.

37

KATHERINE

Everything is right again. Corey and I feel like we are functioning the way we always have. So much so, he offers to take Ava and me to school, and not too early either. With the effort we achieved on the weekend, he didn't need to rush in first thing to bash his head against the wall trying to pull together something for Barry. By now, the principal will have seen the impressive work Corey sent him.

"Thanks for taking us in to school," I say, making sure Corey understands how much I value him doing so.

"Don't mention it. It's the least I can do considering what you've helped to save me from."

"Hey, it was all you," I say, trying to play down what I did. "I only nudged you in the right direction."

"That 'nudge' was the nicest thing you could have done for me. I'm sorry I was being so stubborn."

"It's okay, honey. The important thing is that you let me in. I only ever want what's best for you."

We smile at each other while Ava groans in the car's back seat. "Can I go now?"

"Of course, sweetie," Corey says. "Why don't we all walk to before-school care."

"Yah!" Ava calls out, overly keen to get going.

Corey and I escort Ava to her room. I only wish we could hold hands to make this moment more special, but I take what I can.

After we sort out Ava, Corey and I head into the faculty lounge to have a coffee together before class starts. Barry sees us coming by his office and calls out.

"Corey. Got a minute? I'd love to chat about what you emailed me yesterday. It's quite interesting."

"Go on," I whisper to Corey with a smile. "I'll meet you at lunch." I send him on his way into Barry's room.

While Corey is busy, I grab a coffee and head to my classroom. My day will be a breeze. I feel energized, so much so that I clean up the mess on my desk and think about how to better organize my class. Sure I didn't get that promotion, but I can make some positive steps for a change with no need for validation.

I wait in my room for Corey at lunchtime. It's become our new spot to have a break together. After five minutes, I realize he is running late to spend any time with me. Figuring a student or parent is holding him up, I start on my lunch. You never know when a problem might come bursting through your door to ruin your limited break, so it's best to eat when you can. I've had parents rush into class without signing in at the office all up in arms about something that could have been addressed in an email. I swear some of these people treat us like robots built to serve them and their children.

Footsteps stomp up and into my room mere seconds after I finish thinking about annoying parents. I spot Corey in the window with a furrow in his brow. He snaps open my door and charges in.

"You lied to me."

"Excuse me? What are you talking about?"

He slaps a piece of paper down on my desk. "Read this and explain it to me."

"Calm down," I say as I pick up the document.

"I'll calm down when you tell me exactly what you were thinking about when you did this."

"Did what?"

"Read it."

I see what appears to be a print-off of an email sent by me to two people in the school: Barbara Cook and Jessica McDaniel. "What's this?"

"Read it," Corey repeats.

"Okay." I continue to read the email and see an urgent subject line. Confused, I discover a message delivered that expresses how much I helped Corey with the work he gave Barry this morning. And the body of the email doesn't say I aided him; it says that I practically wrote the whole thing.

"What the hell? I didn't write this."

"It's from your email account."

"I can see that, but why would I send something like this to Barbara and Jessica? They're the most..." I trail off when I realize what I was about to say.

"Go on, say it."

"No, it doesn't matter."

"It does. You were going to say that Barbara and Jessica are the two biggest gossips in the school."

"Yes," I mutter.

"They didn't disappoint. I had this message passed on to me by several people. Do you have any idea what you've done?"

"I didn't do this. I swear it."

"Don't lie to me. We both saw how jealous you were. Now I don't know if this was a drafted email you never meant to send, but this is pathetic, Katherine. Do you have any clue what this will do for my credibility?"

"I—"

"No!" Corey yells. "I don't want to hear what line of crap you've got for me. I hope you're happy." He charges toward the door and kicks over one of the tiny chairs, knocking over a display stand loaded with the children's artwork. He doesn't stop to pick it up and continues stomping away.

What just happened? Who sent this email?

38

ANNETTE

B y now Corey will have read the email. He'll have seen the viral spreading of the rumor about himself multiple times. It hurts me deep down knowing he is going through this. It truly does. I only want what's best for him, but sometimes that means I have to put Corey through a little pain to show him the truth.

Katherine will deny ever sending the message. What other option does she have? It's kind of ironic, given that she once spread a rumor about me back in high school when we had a fight. She took it upon herself to tell everyone that my parents were related, all because we got into an argument about who would get asked out to prom first.

Katherine knows she didn't send that email, so I have to stop her from demanding to work out who did. There's only one way I can throw her off my scent and it will shatter Katherine into a million pieces at the same time. It's almost too exquisite to appreciate what I've come up with.

I only wish I could be there when Corey confronts his spouse and accuses her of trying to sabotage him. She'll get the talking down to she deserves for all the crap she puts him through. Katherine thinks she's this amazing and supportive wife when in reality she's a selfish, egotistical maniac who only wanted Corey because I had him first.

Part of my plan from the start has been to make Katherine think she is losing her mind, that her husband is purposely screwing with her to break her spirit. The only way to convince her that email is one section of a wider scheme perpetrated by Corey to beat her into submission is to have her believe that he sent out the email to Barbara and Jessica.

Now why would he do that? Why would he intentionally sabotage his own promotion just to bring harm to his wife? One word: control. Katherine has been in this position before. Her ex held her in his grasp for such a long time. It wasn't until she fell pregnant with Ava that his spell broke. The abusive relationship would have gone on forever if it weren't for Ava. I would have had Corey all to myself while Katherine continued to have the man she deserves.

I think about what should have been all the time. So much so I barely sleep some nights. I can't stop myself from imagining what my world should have been like if I had only called Corey after we kissed and pushed to see him again. We'd be married by now. We'd be the ones living together, building the foundations for a lifetime of happiness.

All this business with Katherine is merely a delay. She's a speed bump in our story that needs to be removed. And I intend to do the dirty work required to repair the damage she has caused.

39

I can't believe what I'm staring at as I reread the email Corey printed off and left in my classroom. The crumpled piece of paper got crushed by his anger. I can feel his rage in each crease I attempt to iron out on my desk. As I get the sheet flat enough, several drops of tears splash the ink on the page.

I go over the message I supposedly sent to Barbara and Jessica. Apparently, I spilled to them how I solved Corey's big problem and not him. Someone else in the school did this to screw with me. But no one knew about any of it. I didn't tell a soul I'd helped Corey. Not even Annette. It's not that I don't trust her, but all it would have taken was for her to mention it to another person to start a chain reaction.

So who did this to me?

Barry? No. Why would the principal do something as stupid as that? He has enough drama on his plate on a normal day. He doesn't need more problems from the staff. Unless he wants to fire me and figured this was a good way to shake things up and get me angry. No, it can't be true.

I sound like a crazy person with these thoughts buzzing in my brain, screwing with me. Whoever sent this message from my account has no idea how much damage they've caused between Corey and me.

I struggle through the last few hours of the day, messing up my words as I deliver them to the class. The email rattles around in my head, taking control of my every thought. The kids seem to be able to sense something is wrong and misbehave. I not only lose my authority over them but my ability to focus.

A sigh of relief escapes me when the last child leaves my room for the day with their parent by their side. But any calm I have soon rushes out the door as I remember what has happened today. It feels like a bad dream I can't wake from, so much so the walls of the room close in on me.

My heart races as a layer of sweat builds up on my forehead. My breath comes in uncontrolled rasps. I can feel it coming on, crippling me, dragging me down to the depths to surround me with every fear I hold all at once: a panic attack.

Rushing to my desk, I trip over a chair leg and fall to the floor like a clumsy idiot. On my hands and knees, I crawl to my seat and drag myself up to the drawer in my table I remember has a brown paper bag sitting inside, ready for me to use when hyperventilating.

I pull out the already-crumpled packet and wrap it around my mouth in a hurry and throw my rapid breathing in and out of the pouch. Within a few seconds, my short breaths transition into longer ones as I breathe normally again. The tension in my body fades as I let myself fall to the floor in a heap.

I lie on the ground, eyes closed, praying no one walks in on me in this state. If a parent came back now, forgetting their kid's sweater for example, I'd struggle to explain it. The truth would come out that I was having a panic attack at school. Would I lose my job as a result?

I force myself up and shove the toppled-over chair into place before brushing the dirt off my clothing. It always amazes me how filthy the thin carpet in my room gets every day from a bunch of first-graders running around.

Deciding I need to leave before another attack comes on, I grab a stack of paperwork from my desk and bring it with me. It will be a miracle if I sit down tonight and do this work, but at least I'm attempting to take the task home.

Knowing Ava needs collecting, I realize I must get my head straight before I pick her up. I can't have my daughter seeing that there's yet another problem between Corey and me. At least not until I can no longer hide it.

On autopilot, I hurry to the office, desperate to see Annette. I need her now more than ever to help me somehow solve my impossible problems. If she can't think of a solution, she'll have to listen to me vent my frustrations. I'll take whatever she offers.

I find Annette busy wrapping up a conversation with a parent from behind the Perspex glass in the office. There are two more people in line behind the first, each needing something. Frustrated, I grab a seat in the waiting area.

The clock on the wall ticks louder than it has ever before. I didn't even know the damn thing existed until now. Only the sound of my fingernails tapping against the metal frame of the chair I'm perched on drowns out the rhythm of the ticking. I close my eyes and remember to breathe.

"Kat?" Annette calls out a few feet from me.

I open my eyes to find my friend standing over me, out from the safety of her office.

"What's going on? Are you okay? You look like you're about to pass out."

"Do you have a minute to talk? I need to see you, please."

Annette bites her lower lip and scratches the back of her neck. "I've got a lot of work to—"

"Please," I say, standing. "I need to talk to you. Something messed up has happened today."

"Okay, okay," Annette says as she grabs me around my shoulders and guides me into her office like I'm an escaped dementia patient and sits me down in a spare chair. "What's going on?"

I take in a deep breath and tell her about Corey and the email. It all explodes out of me in a hurry. If anyone can hear our conversation, they'd have to assume I've lost my mind.

Annette had the email forwarded to her but didn't have time to read it until now. "This makes no sense. Why would someone do this to you?"

"I don't know. It's insane, right? It's not like I go around the school making enemies, so why would anyone try to screw up things between Corey and I?"

Annette doesn't answer and shakes her head. "I can't imagine any of the teachers doing this. Not even that old crow Susan. She wouldn't even know how to—"

Annette stops speaking mid-sentence and stares off into the distance.

"What is it?" I ask, gripping her wrist.

She faces me with a smile. "I just thought of something."

40

KATHERINE

T hank God I have Annette as a friend. She's so smart and calm in a crisis. While I hyperventilate and overreact, she thinks up a solution to my problem within a few minutes of hearing it.

After I told Annette about the terrible email sent out to the two gossiping teachers from my account, she had an epiphany.

"You can trace who sent the email."

"What do you mean? It says it came from me."

"No, I mean you might be able to trace which computer the email came from. There are these things in emails called headers in every message you send. I had to learn about our internal system a while back as part of my job. If they sent the email through your school account, we should be able to work out which computer it was from provided it's one in the school's network."

I lean in close to Annette's screen as she goes through a file from the message with a bunch of text I don't understand. She finds something she tells me is called an IP address and looks it up using another program. We both stare at the screen when the name of the computer comes up.

"That can't be right," Annette says. "It has to be some kind of mistake."

I remain silent as I read the computer's identity again and again. The word GRAYSON-COREY-LAPTOP-BBES sits on Annette's screen mocking me.

Annette speaks first. "Someone must have taken his—"

"No. It can't have been stolen. He had it all weekend at home and brought it in to school this morning. It hasn't left his side."

"Someone might have broken into his classroom and—"

"No. They'd need keys, and he'd have told me if the lock or a window was smashed."

"What are you saying then?"

I turn to Annette. The angst that was crippling my face turns into anger. "Corey sent the email."

"Come on. You can't be serious. He would never do that to you."

"Wouldn't he? You and I both know in terms of experience and skill that I deserved the promotion over him. Yet he got it."

"Yeah, but I'm sure things like this happen. They promote the wrong people every day."

"Maybe, but Corey was the one to hand in both our applications."

Annette's eyes shift rapidly left and right as I see her put together everything I'm telling her. "You don't think he—"

"Yes. Corey sabotaged my application for the position. And now he's hell bent on making me seem jealous and pathetic enough to spread rumors around about his job performance."

Annette's mouth drops open as she turns away from me. "This is crazy. Why would he do this to you?"

I feel the tears pouring from my eyes run down my cheeks as my anger dissolves into fear. "Because he's just like Peter. Somehow, that's the only type of man I seem to attract. And now his true self is coming out." I slide my hands over my face and fight the urge to cry. I fail.

"Hey, hey," Annette says, pulling me in tight. "We don't know that for sure. Maybe this is all a strange coincidence. Or maybe it's..."

Annette trails off. I can hear it in her voice that she has no explanation to why Corey is trying to control me the way my ex did.

"It's happening again," I say, "but this time I've married the man."

41

Oh my god. Things couldn't have gone better if I tried. Some days, everything falls into place so well I have to pinch myself to make sure I'm not dreaming.

Katherine ate up every word yesterday. She believed the worst possibilities about her husband with little prompting. I gave her enough information for her to draw her own conclusions.

Things are progressing much faster than I planned. I can barely keep up with the rate at which Katherine and Corey's marriage is falling apart. They're both sinking into place and playing their roles exactly as I want them to without knowing they are being manipulated. I hate doing such a thing to Corey, but Katherine's spell needs breaking.

It's early in the morning. None of the teachers have arrived at school yet except for Corey. He's so devoted to his new position. So much so that I think it's time he got to hear about it from a supportive friend.

I knock on Corey's door and let myself into his room.

"Hey," he says, his voice half deflated. It pains me to identify how badly he's hurting, but I'm here to make him forget his troubles.

"How's everything going?" I ask.

"Oh, you know," he replies from his desk. I can see him grading some papers for his students. All the extra work he's doing as a lead teacher is setting him back a little in his regular classwork.

"That bad, huh?"

"Yeah, it is. I'm sure you've read the email Kat sent."

"I have." I walk up to his workstation, arms wrapped around my body as I do my best to convey my concern to him.

He lets out a heavy sigh and scratches the stubble on his face. "I don't know what to think anymore. How could she have done that to me? I thought she loved me."

I shake my head, forcing myself not to show any frustration. I'm here to support him and not be petty.

"Hey, I'm sure she loves you."

"Really? Then why would she try to sabotage my career? Just to get even because she didn't receive the promotion over me. It's insane, but I'm seeing that nothing is too far-fetched lately."

I move in further and choose to sit on his desk. My right hand extends out and lands softly on his shoulder. "I don't think she meant to sabotage your career. From what I understand, she felt jealous and overreacted. She let her emotions take over. It happens."

He scoffs, crossing his arms over his chest while turning away. "It happens? I don't think so. Only a bad person reacts in such a way. I mean you would never do that for one simple reason: you're not pathetic."

I do my best to contain any excitement that is dying to explode out of me. Corey thinks Katherine is the worst woman on the planet.

"I'm sorry," he says. "You two are good friends, so I shouldn't be putting you in such a position."

"It's fine. You're only trying to vent. We all need to do so from time to time. Otherwise it may come out in ways you won't like."

He shakes his head and wraps a hand over his face. "It's crazier than that. Kat confessed it all to me late last night so I would speak to her again. I thought hearing her admit to what she did would encourage me to get over her betrayal, but honestly, it's made things worse."

He can't be serious. I have to fight hard not to show how shocked I am. Katherine has tried to take the blame for every-thing after she found out that Corey apparently sent the email. Have I broken her already? I understood her past would help speed it all along, but not like this. Corey stares at me waiting for a response.

"Wow. So she admitted it."

"Yep. Every cruel detail. Wait. Did she admit to emailing Barbara and Jessica when you spoke to her?"

"No. I could tell she was jealous, but she maintained her innocence all throughout. I honestly didn't know if she sent the email or not. Hell, I even thought someone did it to mess with her, but I can't think of a single person who despises her."

Corey's gaze fixates on me. I focus in and watch the muscles in his cheeks twitch. He would never say he hates his wife out loud to me, but he might as well be screaming it.

"Anyway, what can I do for you?" Corey asks.

"Oh, nothing. I came here to see how you are. I know you probably wouldn't expect this to concern me being Kat's friend, but I'm worried you may think someone could take away your new position from you."

"What have you heard?" he asks, sitting upright. His eyes remind me of a concerned puppy that's just had its food bowl taken away from it midway through eating.

"Nothing so far. I doubt Barry wants to get mixed up in this. You know he doesn't handle confrontation well."

Corey's shoulders slump. "What a relief. I don't think I could continue teaching here if Barry took this new role from me. Not that I could afford to walk away."

"That won't happen. I'll keep an eye out for anything."

"Thank you," he says, placing a hand on my arm. The touch of his skin sends a rush throughout my body words cannot describe. All I sense are the ends of my hairs on my arms rising.

"Any time. I'm here for you, Corey. And I always will be." I stare into his eyes and try to beam my feelings into his brain. Soon he will be mine again. We can forget about Katherine and finally start our lives together.

Corey's cell beeps out loud, cutting through the mood of the room. I almost grab the damn thing and whip it across the space for daring to interrupt.

Corey looks at his phone. "Oh, crap," he mutters.

"Everything okay?" I ask, needing to clear my throat at the same time from all the excitement.

"Yeah, it's just Kat and Ava are having car troubles. They need me to come pick them up so they can get to school on time."

"I'll do that for you," I offer like the perfect person would.

"That would be amazing. Are you sure you have time?"

I don't. "Plenty. You keep going with your work here while I sort out Kat and Ava."

He lets a sigh of relief flow out of his parted lips. "Thank you so much. You're a good friend, Annette."

Friend. The word hurts me more than he could ever appreciate, but soon I won't just be a friend. I'll be so much more. I'll be his everything.

"I'll get going then," I say as I leave. But a thought occurs to me. One I can't ignore. "Actually, Corey, I have a better idea."

"What's that?"

42

KATHERINE

I don't know what to think when Corey texts me that Annette is coming to pick Ava and me up. On one hand, I'm happy that I have such a dedicated friend willing to help in such a rough time, but on the other, I wish that Corey would be the one to rescue us. Then at least I'd know that he still cares.

I shouldn't want him to be there for me after finding out what he did. Self-sabotaging his career to make me feel bad is definitely something I never expected from him. A good marriage shouldn't have to take the brunt of such an act, but I'm giving him another chance so we can move forward. It's why I admitted to emailing Barbara and Jessica late last night despite knowing it was him.

Corey can be petty. He always needs to be right no matter how much argument it causes. I figure he sent the message to help deflect any guilt he had from getting the promotion. I deserved it over him. He must have known that. Why else would he stoop so low?

I table the thought and listen for Annette's car to pull up and take Ava and me to school. We won't be late if we can get going in the next ten minutes. Corey will need to drive us home after work if he isn't too mad at me still.

Sitting in the living room by the front door, I bite my nails one after the other waiting for Annette. I hear a vehicle approaching and realize it can't be Annette's. Curiosity drives me to look out the window. "What?" I blurt when I see Corey has pulled up in his car. I'm so confused.

"Ava," I say to my daughter. "Turn that off. It's time to go."

"One more episode, Mommy."

"No, baby. Come on."

"Okay," Ava says, dragging her voice along with her body.

We rush outside and head to Corey's sedan after I lock up. I load Ava in and secure her harness before climbing into my seat at the front of the car like I knew Corey was coming. I don't want to say anything. I'm happy he came instead of sending Annette. Maybe he's no longer angry at me, not that he has a right to be.

"Confused?" he asks.

"A little," I admit. "I thought Annette was picking us up."

"She's too busy. Plus, I figured it would be best if I came so you can see I'm not mad at you."

"And? Are you?"

He reverses out of our drive and into the street. "I guess I'm no longer upset, but I won't forget what happened just yet. Besides. You needed me, so here I am."

I smile. I recognize I shouldn't be happy with his reasoning. He caused this latest piece of drama and is now making out that he is the bigger person. Still, having him come to my rescue feels amazing. I don't know what I'd do without him. After Peter left, life wasn't so easy. Raising Ava on my own has been a challenging task. With Corey here, my time is better.

I keep quiet for the rest of the drive into work, not wanting to upset things. I need to let time heal whatever has gone on between us. Maybe one day we can talk about all of this and realize we were both behaving like idiots.

43

KATHERINE

I push through the day, feeling somewhat more positive than when I woke up. Corey had lunch with me, but there was a tension in the air I couldn't quite explain. It was awkward, as if we were on our first date again.

Corey told me he needed to stay back for an hour to get some of his grading finished. Without my car, I couldn't take off home, so I agreed to wait around for him. I'm not going to drive to our house only to return to pick him up either, so thirty minutes after the kids have left, I decide to walk over to see Annette before she leaves for the day.

I find her finishing up in the office, closing her computer down.

"Hey, Kat. I was about to head over to you."

"You were? How come?"

Annette tidies a few items on her desk before answering me. "I've got a proposition for you."

I feel my face tighten with confusion. "A proposition?"

"Yeah. I think it's time you and I went out for a few drinks."

"Like this weekend?"

"No. Tonight."

"Tonight?" I watch Annette as she leaves the office and comes out to the other side of the window I'm used to seeing her behind.

"It's been too long, and there's this bar a few towns over I've heard great things about that we must hit up. They have cheap drinks during the week, and I think you and Corey need some time apart."

I exhale audibly through flared nostrils. "You're not wrong. We finally talked to each other again when he came and picked me up this morning, but there's still some unresolved anger there. It was a little confusing, to be honest. I thought he was sending you to collect Ava and me."

"He had asked me, but I guess he changed his mind."

"It was amazing that he did so, but I can't shake the feeling that we aren't one hundred percent right yet."

"I figured that might be the case," Annette says, guiding me to the front door. "So we need to get you two out of each other's hair."

"You're only saying that so you and I can get drunk."

She gives me a coy smile. "Maybe."

"On a weeknight? Are you crazy?"

"Come on. It'll make us feel like we're not in our thirties if we do something fun during the week for a change."

I run it over in my head. Drinks with Annette would be incredible. "I'll need to ask Corey to take care of Ava. After yesterday I don't know how well that will go down."

"How about this: I'll twist his arm for you. He can't say no to me. Let's tell him now what's happening."

"Oh, you are good," I say, impressed by her commitment to the idea.

"I am, aren't I?"

We walk over to Corey's room. I don't understand why, but I feel nervous about asking him to watch Ava tonight so Annette can take me out for a drink. A wife should feel like she can ask her husband anything, but given recent times, a piece of the faith I had in Corey has vanished.

"Is everything okay?" Annette asks as she loops her arm around my elbow. "You're shaking a little."

"Am I?"

"Yeah, quite a lot," she says as we come to a stop a few hundred feet before Corey's classroom.

Annette casts her eye up and down my face as if she is trying to diagnose me. "Why don't you take a breath in through your nose and slowly let it out of your mouth."

"No, I'm fine. I need to get out of my head for a minute. I'm being pathetic, I know, but I can't seem to shake this bad feeling something awful will happen."

"Like what? We're only telling Corey to watch Ava tonight so you can both take some time to be apart. Don't they say absence makes the heart grow fonder, or some stupid crap like that?"

"Yes, that's the expression."

"So let's go get this over with. I guarantee Corey will be happy to hear my idea."

"Really? You think he doesn't want to be around me that badly."

"No, it's not like that, Kat. You two have just gotten married. It's a huge change in your lives. That takes a toll on any relationship."

I take in what Annette has to say, wondering how she is such an expert. Everything coming out of her mouth makes perfect sense. I only wish I could appreciate it more.

"We're here," Annette says, releasing me from her light grip.

"Time to tell him what's happening, right?"

My hand shakes a little, so I make a fist and squeeze hard to stop the overwhelming dread that's looming from taking over. "Okay."

"You can do this," Annette whispers.

I feel so pathetic, struggling this much to ask my husband for a basic favor that barely requires any effort on his behalf. I'll still be putting Ava to bed. All he must do is help her if she wakes up for any reason.

I raise my clenched fist to Corey's door and knock. I can see him inside with his head down and buried in paperwork. Has he really gotten this far behind in such a short time? Part of being a successful lead teacher is still being able to manage your class while taking on the extra responsibilities. Is Corey struggling?

He glances up and sees us standing outside his room through the glass panel in the door. His brow scrunches in for a moment before he flashes a smile for us to enter.

"There he is," Annette calls out to Corey as we enter.

"Hi, honey," I add.

"Hello," Corey says with some hesitation in his voice. "What's this all about?"

"What? Can't we say hello to our favorite teacher?" Annette says.

Corey gives out a half smile from the side of his mouth and crosses his arms over his chest. He leans back in his chair. "Okay. What is it? Out with it."

Annette glances at me for a second. "I'm taking your wife out for some drinks tonight."

"Tonight? You realize it's the middle of the week, right?"

"We do. You can get cheap drinks if you know where to look. And besides, with the crap this place throws at us all, you're lucky this isn't a nightly occurrence."

Corey chuckles. "Yeah, I hear you."

"So you'll watch Ava then?" Annette asks. I might as well have been in another room given the way this conversation is going.

Corey nods while rolling his eyes off to the side. "Yes.

Someone has to while you two drunks are out trashing the town."

"Ha ha," Annette says in a mocking tone.

"Are you sure?" I ask him.

"Yes. Go have some fun."

"Thank you, honey," I say.

"Don't mention it. Happy to help. You both look like you need a night off."

"I'll make it up to you."

"No need. Put Ava to bed and I'll listen out for her."

"Great. Then it's settled," Annette says. "I'll come pick up Kat at eight tonight and drop her off before school starts."

Corey shakes his head with a broad smile. "Sounds like a terrible plan. We'll see you then."

Annette subtly gives my arm a squeeze as if to tell me how easy this was. "See you soon," I say as she goes to leave.

"Bye now. Be ready for me at eight. Thank you, Corey," she says over her shoulder as she walks away.

Within a moment, Corey and I are alone, facing each other with an awkward silence filling the air. Why does this still feel so strange?

Corey continues to smile at me as if I'm a customer in a store and he is one of the friendly staff waiting to assist me. "I'll be ready to leave soon. Why don't you go collect Ava while I finish up?"

"Sounds like a plan. I'll go sign her out now." I head for the door.

"By the way, Kat."

"Yes?" I turn back to him.

"You could have asked me yourself. You didn't need to bring Annette in."

I want to give him my reasoning, but my mouth won't open to speak. I desperately need to tell him that I feel like we have a serious problem growing over and around our marriage, but I know any such talk may ironically turn into another argument.

"I'm sorry," I say. "Next time I will. I promise."

"Good. Because I want you to feel comfortable enough to ask me anything, okay?"

We both recognize that isn't true given the email debacle. Still, I smile at my husband and pretend everything is fine. A moment later, I leave.

As my feet carry me away from Corey's room, I can't help but realize how difficult the path ahead will be. How are we going to make it through the next few months, let alone the rest of our lives?

I wrap my arms around my body tight and rush to Ava. I need to see her innocent face now more than ever.

44

ANNETTE

Everything is in place for the next phase of this whole ordeal. I can see seeds of doubt sewn deep within Katherine's mind concerning her marriage to Corey. Now I need to propel things in the right direction as quickly as possible.

Earlier in the day, I put the idea into Corey's head to drive Katherine and Ava to school after they had car troubles. It might have seemed like the perfect opportunity to encourage him not to do so, but I needed to set up for tonight. It will be worth the sacrifice.

I honk my horn twice out the front of Katherine and Corey's home, arriving five minutes early. This will appear as a mistake because Katherine is never on time to go anywhere. I guarantee she is still standing by the mirror, slapping makeup on herself. Honking is my way of reminding Corey how frustrating this can be.

Corey opens the entrance and shakes his head at me the way he has many times in the past. It's a simple piece of communication to tell me to come inside and wait for Katherine to get ready.

"Am I too early?" I ask him once I'm out of the car and by the front door.

Corey glances at his watch. "Nope. You're on time. Kat's doing her usual trick where she changes her outfit fifteen times."

I force a chuckle. "Some things never change. Fortunately, I don't suffer from this problem. I pick out an outfit and commit to it, never second-guessing my decision. There's no point."

Corey purses his lips. "Fair enough. I just throw on whatever jumps out at me."

We laugh. I giggle more than is necessary so I can place a hand on his wrist. He doesn't flinch away or seem to mind, so I let my fingers linger for a few seconds longer than is acceptable. We lock eyes for a moment. Goosebumps flood over my skin.

"Can I get you anything to drink?" he asks.

"Some water will be fine."

He nods and smiles at me, warming my insides.

I watch Corey as he leaves the room. Should I follow him into the kitchen and make a move? No. I can't rush things. I know there's something there between us, but I shouldn't do anything yet and spoil our future.

I stay where I'm standing, crippled with indecision. This controlling fear is the reason we are in this mess to begin with. If only I had found the courage to tell Corey how I felt when we kissed instead of waiting for him to make a move. There'd be no need for all this scheming. I would have been Corey's wife.

"Here you go," he says, breaking my thoughts. "Take a seat. I'll check on Kat for you."

"That's okay," I say, sitting. "You don't have to do that. I'm happy to wait here. We've got all night."

Corey shakes his head and laughs. "All night, huh? Planning on a big one?"

"No. Just a few drinks. We'll probably be back before

midnight, knowing Kat. I guess I figured you two might benefit from some time apart."

Corey remains standing at the edge of the room with his arm on the door frame. "It's a good idea, really. Things have been chaotic between us as you know. Hell, right now I could use a week to myself to clear it all up. Does that make me a bad person?"

"Of course not. Like anyone, you should decompress every so often. And tonight will help you both to take some time to think about it all."

Corey's eyes focus on the ground. I can see he's deep in thought, letting my words sink into his brain. With each revelation he has about his wife, I get one step closer to my goal. All I need to do is keep moving.

Katherine finally emerges from her room, having selfishly wasted thirty minutes of my life. Luckily, I spent that time chatting to Corey, ever so carefully filling his head with what he needs to hear.

"Sorry about that," Katherine says. "I didn't mean to take so long; I couldn't decide what to wear."

"That's okay," I say through a feigned grin. Katherine uses this excuse every time we go out as if her inability to organize herself is a one-off event. One year, she even screwed up a birthday dinner surprise she was supposed to organize for me by showing up to the restaurant late. By the time we got to the place, our table had been given away. I had to pretend it didn't bother me.

"Have a good night," Corey says as we head to the front door.

"We will," I reply. "Don't wait up."

"Bye, honey," Katherine says to Corey. He gives his wife a wave and nothing more. She deserves less.

I drive us a few towns over and find a sleazy bar with cheap midweek drinks. The place is half full of loud-mouthed men all trying to talk over one another while some light rock music plays in the background. It's not the best bar to go to if you feel like dancing the night away. Instead, there are plenty of opportunities for young guys to approach us with only one thing on their minds.

I buy Katherine a glass of wine and find us a booth to sit in. I keep her energy levels high with some school gossip, making sure she finishes her drink as quickly as possible. It will be only a matter of time before we get hit on. Then the night can truly begin.

45

I slap the off button on Corey's alarm clock, half confused where I am. The world swirls into existence as I realize I'm at home in bed. With a struggle, I force my eyes to stay open as I try to remember what day it is. Crap, it's Wednesday.

My head is pounding. The bar Annette and I went to last night is nothing but a hazy mess in my mind. In fact, I don't even recall how I got here. How many glasses of wine did I drink?

I reach for my cell on the bedside table and pat around, only to discover it's not on its wireless charging pad. "Come on," I say to myself, not needing the painful task of trying to locate my phone after a drunken night out. I haven't had to do that in a long time.

Giving up after a short while, I look at Corey's alarm clock that he insists on using despite having a smartphone and see that I've slept in for forty minutes. There's no chance in hell I'll be able to get myself and Ava ready in time for school. Plus, I'm guessing Corey went into work early, judging by his absence.

I almost dive out of bed and stumble my way toward our en suite. After only a few steps into the room, I drop to the floor and huddle myself over the toilet and throw up. Apparently, my body can't handle going out for a drink midweek.

I finish vomiting and clean myself up with a two-minute shower. Normally I'd be waking up Ava first so she can dress herself while I do the same, but I need the water on my face so I can think.

I attempt to recall last night. Bits and pieces come to mind. I see Annette laughing away with a drink in her hand as we try to dance in the middle of the bar while some guys hit on us. The rest is a blur. I shake my head and curse myself for letting this happen.

As I walk toward Ava's room, I wonder how Annette and I got home when she was the one driving. From what I remember, she was as drunk as I was. I can only hope nothing bad happened to her.

"Time to get up, baby," I call out as I open Ava's room. Her bed is empty. I roll my eyes, figuring she's in the living room watching TV before school despite knowing better, but then I see a note stuck on the door. How did I miss it before? Focusing on the letters in front of me as best I can, I read the piece of paper.

I noticed that you came home late, so I took Ava into school this morning to give you a sleep in. - Love, Corey

This explains why there was an alarm set on Corey's side of the bed. He also couldn't find my cell and had to do things the old-fashioned way writing me a note. Him sorting Ava out and taking her to school is so thoughtful, especially after letting me go out. I owe him.

Exhaling a pleasant sigh of relief, I take my time getting ready and head to the kitchen for a coffee on autopilot. I brew some ground beans in our machine but become overwhelmed by the smell. Practically gagging, I rush out of the kitchen and squat down in the living room to settle my nausea. How am I going to make it through the day?

After a good five minutes of trying to will myself up, I stand from the sofa and shuffle to the cordless phone we have at the far end of the room. I pick up the handset and find the number for the school sitting in the phone's address book. It feels odd to do things like this when normally I use my cell for everything. I'm glad Corey insists upon having alarm clocks and landline phones.

As I stand there tapping the address book, I know I have a decision to make. Should I call in sick? I'm supposed to phone Barry to do so, but I could call Annette instead, so she covers for me.

With a shake of my head, I turn a few pages and dial our local taxi company. My car is still out of action for a few more days according to our mechanic as he waits on some parts to arrive. The call connects to a grumpy woman who organizes the cab for me. She tells me a driver will be at the front of my house in approximately fifteen minutes.

"Thank you," I reply with gravel in my throat. But before I can hang up, I feel my stomach punch itself again. I rush to the kitchen sink and throw up.

Today will be awful.

46

KATHERINE

I tell the taxi driver to drop me off outside of BBES so I can sneak into the school. It's a good thing my car isn't working. I doubt I could have driven it without crashing into a tree.

I thank the man and give him a generous tip for driving extra slow as requested, not wanting to hurl in the back seat of his car. He nods and drives off in a hurry to his next pickup. I don't know how these guys can compete with all the rideshare companies out there dominating the industry.

Clearing the distracting thoughts from my head, I focus on the daunting walk I have to the faculty lounge. I'd go nonstop to my classroom, but I need to see Annette and make sure she's okay. I forgot to at home before when I had a phone in my hands. My brain feels too fried to think.

The path into school is trickier than it should be. I can't seem to walk in a straight line. We must have been mixing our drinks last night for me to feel this bad. In fact, I haven't gotten this knockout drunk since I was with Peter in my early twenties.

When I step inside the school's office out from the cold, I bump into a student's dad. Gary Cross stares back at me with the permanent frown he always seems to have on his face.

"Miss Armstrong," he says.

"It's Mrs. Grayson now." I've told him this twice.

"Oh right. You're married. Congratulations," he says in a huff.

"Thank you. What can I do for you?" I already know a complaint is coming.

"It's about Tom's report card from last semester."

"Last semester? What about it?"

"I went over each of his academic performance scores and I feel you gave him a lot of threes where he clearly had earned a four."

It takes everything I have not to roll my eyes. Gary is one of those parents who rarely get involved in their kid's lives. But the second he does, he reaches out too far and analyzes every report or note sent home regarding his son.

"Mr. Cross, if you'd like to discuss this further, we can arrange a meeting after school."

"No, I want to talk about it now."

"I'm sorry but I don't have the time."

He stares at me with his beady eyes and rubs his balding head. "Fine. I'll return after school this afternoon."

"I have a meeting scheduled then. It will have to be tomorrow." The lie flows out of my mouth without thought. There's no way in hell I could stand to discuss this moron's son for any length of time today. It won't help anyone.

He sighs heavily. "So be it," he says as his nostrils flare at me. He storms off out the office before I can say another word. I shake my head and continue.

Annette isn't at her post, sending a blow to my already churning stomach, so I move to the faculty lounge, hoping she's grabbing herself a coffee.

A minute later, I find her doing exactly that while chatting to some teachers. I let out a long breath and move over to her.

"Kat! How are you?" Annette calls out to me louder than I can handle. She seems to be too bubbly for my liking. How is she not bent over the sink, begging for death to grab her with two bony hands?

"Did you get home okay?" I ask.

"Yeah, no sweat. Why?"

"Oh, no reason."

"Are you okay, Kat? You look like you've got the flu."

My forehead is sweating as if I've run a marathon despite the room not being overly warm.

"Kat?"

"Um, sorry. I'm not feeling the best, you know?"

Annette pulls me away from the other teachers. "Because of last night? You barely had two drinks."

"Are you serious?" I ask as I try to recall exactly what went on during our visit to the bar. "I figured you and I must have drunk until they kicked us out, given the way I feel."

Annette stares at me with concern lining her forehead. "Honey, we were only out for a few hours. I dropped you off at ten thirty."

"How is that possible? Corey left me a note saying I didn't get in until late."

Annette snaps her neck back a touch and screws up her nose. "No, that can't be right. I drove you home after a short while because we both figured we'd be too tired if we stayed any longer. Don't you remember?"

I don't. Not at all. Did Corey leave me the note to mess with me? Better yet, why do I feel like I've had so much to drink when I barely had two glasses of wine? What did he do?

"What is it? Are you remembering something?"

I try to push any dark thoughts out of my head. It couldn't be possible. "It's nothing. I guess I mustn't be feeling well and shouldn't have had those drinks. Obviously, I can't handle them anymore."

"Kat. You can't be serious? We have more to drink when we go out for dinner. This is crazy. You shouldn't look like someone has run you over with a truck after only two glasses of wine."

"I know. I know. It's weird. I just need to push through the day and not throw up again."

"You've been vomiting?"

I nod, giving her a forced smile to try to make light of the subject. It doesn't get Annette off my case any less than she already is.

"Maybe you should have a nice strong cup of coffee. Here take mine." Annette grabs her mug from the kitchen bench and holds it under my nose. The smell is overpowering, so I step back and move for the exit to find some fresh air. My stomach twists.

Barry walks in and almost collides with me. "Mrs. Grayson. Please watch where you're—"

He doesn't finish his sentence. Instead, he flinches as I throw up onto his jacket. "What the hell?" Barry yells out.

"I'm so sorry, Barry," I mumble through the disgusting taste in my mouth. "I'm not feeling—"

More vomit comes up, pulling me to the floor.

"My god. This is the last thing I need today," Barry says.

Annette rushes over and helps me up. "I'll take her to the restroom."

"Please. Then I think it's time you head home, Mrs. Grayson," Barry says, bending down to grab my attention.

"Yes, Barry. Thank you. I'm so sorry." I glance around the room to see everyone gawking at me with their mouths open.

"Don't thank me yet. I'll be sending the bill for the steam

clean this carpet will need. Not to mention the dry cleaning for my jacket."

"Okay," I reply. What else can I say?

"Let's go," Annette says, pulling me along. She hands me a few tissues from her pocket. I wipe away the mess and walk with her to the restrooms. "I'll take you home, okay?"

"Thank you," I reply without another word. I feel like death.

"Just trying to help. Something is messing with your system. Maybe you ate spoiled food before we went out."

It's a reasonable theory to have, but it doesn't explain enough for this to be food poisoning. Someone steps on my grave as I shudder. A terrifying thought has entered my mind, and I can't shake it.

What if Corey slipped me something in my sleep?

47

After dropping off Katherine, I can't wipe the joy from my face. Did she really throw up all over the principal in front of the staff? My god, I couldn't have planned things to go this way if I tried.

The GHB I slipped into Katherine's wine last night was still working hard, so I had to help her into her house to her bed.

Spiking her drink was a delicate process to pull off. A full dose would have made her look like a zombie in any of the selfies I'd later encourage her and the sleazy guy to take. I had to put in a small amount of the liquid at a time to give her an over-whelming feeling of euphoria. Then, once she'd taken enough photos, I hit her with the rest of the vial to help wipe her memory.

"I don't know what's wrong with me?" Katherine said over and over when I placed her in her bed. "I never react this way to a few drinks."

"Maybe you've come down with something like a virus?"

"Yeah, maybe. I wish I knew where my cell was."

I could hear the doubt circling around in her head when

Katherine answered me. But it didn't matter. By the time she wakes up later on today from her hangover, I will have cemented the idea within enough people's brains that Katherine spent the evening drinking.

"Anne," Katherine said.

I gritted my teeth, hearing the short form of my name. "Yes?"

"You mentioned dropping me off at ten thirty, but Corey's note told me I didn't get in until late."

"That's weird," I said.

"Corey may have been confused. He was probably asleep and thought it was later than that. He goes to bed early during the week."

"Sounds reasonable to me."

"I guess it doesn't matter, does it? Anyway, thank you for helping me," Katherine said with half-shut eyes.

"Just trying to be a good friend," I replied.

"You're an amazing friend. I don't know what I'd do without you." Katherine started to blink.

"I'm okay."

"No, you're more than okay. You're—"

Katherine coughed three or four times. So much so she had to sit up.

"Are you all right?" I asked with an arm on her shoulder.

She shook her head. "No. My head is killing me. Any chance you could fetch me an aspirin from the en suite and a glass of water?"

"Not a problem," I replied, screaming obscenities on the inside. I had better things to do than to play nurse for Katherine. God knows I'd done it countless times before she left for college. Katherine would drink herself stupid while I stayed relatively sober to make sure her parents never found out what we were up to.

I walked into the en suite. Instantly I could smell Corey in the small space. I spotted one of his work shirts hanging on a clothes hook. It fell into my hands within a few seconds as I wrapped it around my face, breathing in his scent. His powerful aftershave grabbed my full attention, so much so that it pulled me to that amazing night we kissed. I allowed the memory to flood my mind.

"Did you find it?" Katherine asked, ruining the flawless image in my head.

"Still looking. Don't get up." Reality couldn't allow me a few seconds to fall back into the most perfect moment of my life. Instead, it wanted me to play doctor for a moron who had no idea about what I did to her last night.

It was a beautiful few hours. Not only did I slip Katherine the GHB, but I also collected some interesting photos that I don't think Corey will enjoy seeing. I can't wait to see his reaction when he realizes what his wife got up to on a weeknight.

I took another breath in of Corey's shirt, closing my eyes as if I were breathing in a drug. Soon I won't have to sneak around his house to smell that powerful essence he leaves wherever he goes. It will cover my home. Our home.

"Here you go," I said to Katherine when I handed her the aspirin and some water.

"Thank you so much for this and for getting me home. I can't imagine what I'd do without you."

I smiled at Katherine as she took slow blinks, tucking her in a moment later. "Get some rest. You're going to need it."

Katherine's eyes fell shut before she heard my ominous warning. Within a minute, she was lightly snoring while I held a spare pillow in my hand. It tempted me to end her life there and then. But a hazy smothering wasn't enough of a punishment.

I drove away from the Grayson household with one clear

image in my head. Soon, Corey will feel disgusted that he ever married Katherine. I'll show him exactly the person she is. He'll understand the terrible error he made. Divorce will be his only option. Then I'll be there to pick up the pieces.

48

I traveled back to school and resumed working for a few hours. Every so often, I'd hear the whispers of passing teachers talking about Katherine's career-destroying moment in the faculty lounge. She'll never live it down.

After lunch, I walk over to Corey's room, knowing he has some student-free time. While his students are busy running around in the gym with the PE teacher, I will make my next move. I know word has reached him by now regarding Katherine's actions. He's sent her multiple texts asking her what made her vomit all over Barry this morning. Each message reads angrier than the last. I know this because I have his wife's cell.

I have the perfect cover story to return Katherine's phone. Corey has no idea the device is even missing. All he'll be thinking about instead is how badly his spouse's actions have reflected on him. Especially with this promotion.

I knock on Corey's door and find him at the front of the room, standing by the whiteboard with a marker in hand. He turns to me and ushers me inside. The look on his face says it all. I can see anguish and uncertainty lining his forehead.

"Everything okay?" I ask once I enter.

"Not really," Corey replies. He returns the cap to the white-board marker and shoves it on the built-in ledge. His shoulders slump. I hate seeing him like this, but I know it's necessary.

"I can come back if this isn't a good time."

"No, it's fine," he says, facing me. "How can I help you?"

"I found this," I say holding up the stolen cell. It was so easy to take from Katherine last night once the drug had kicked in. "I think it might be Kat's."

"Oh, okay. I didn't know she'd lost it."

"I didn't either until today. I only noticed it on my way back from taking her home this morning."

"Where was it?"

"Sitting on the ground near your driveway. I'd say Kat dropped it last night. I would have given it to her, but I didn't want to wake her up. She's probably still asleep."

Corey's brow tightens as he shakes his head. "That explains why she hasn't responded to my texts."

"That's the other issue. I'm not one hundred percent sure this is hers. I mean, it looks like it from the case, but the lock screen is blank. Usually there's a photo of you and Kat on there, but all I can see is a black background. I'd unlock the thing to find out more, but I don't know her passcode."

"I'll take a look," Corey says as we step toward each other. I hand him the phone and give him my best face filled with concern, throwing in a hint of confusion for good measure.

Corey punches the passcode 26739 in as I had only a few minutes prior. I wonder if he knows that it spells out his name.

I move in close and stand over his shoulder to see the screen unlock to the photo app I made sure was open a moment ago. Sitting there are a series of selfies from last night. I encouraged some drunken asshole to take them with an intoxicated Katherine. The two have their arms wrapped around each other with drinks in hand.

"What the hell?" Corey lets out. His fingers jab at the screen and swipes through the photos, seeing Katherine and this sleazy moron kissing one another on the cheek. Smiles and laughter cover their faces.

"Did you know about this?" Corey spits out, snapping his neck toward me.

"Not at all. I don't understand. This guy was sniffing around while we were there, but I kept telling him to leave us alone."

"Were you in the bathroom for a long time or something?" Corey asks, desperate for an explanation.

"No. I didn't go once. This makes no sense, unless..." I trail off as if lost in thought.

"Unless what?"

I lock eyes with Corey and shake my head. "It can't be right."

"What can't be right? Tell me."

I take a breath in and let it out slowly. "Look at the time they took the photo."

Corey taps a few commands into Kat's cell. "It says two in the morning."

"Oh, no. I dropped her off at your place at ten thirty. She kept threatening me that she wanted to stay out longer, that she would return to the bar once I'd gotten her home. I thought she was joking. She must have ordered an Uber to go back there."

"Are you serious?"

I don't have to be. That's exactly what we did. I used Kat's cell to get us an Uber from her house to the bar after we'd already come home in my car. Later, once enough incriminating photos existed, I got us another Uber to Katherine's home, again using her cell. I shoved Katherine through the front door with her keys and directed her down toward the main bedroom before sneaking away with her stolen cell. From there it was a matter of walking down the street and around the corner to retrieve my car.

It was a lot of messing about in one night, but Katherine's rideshare history on her cell paints an undeniable picture, and Corey is now checking it.

"What in the...?" His voice trails off as he sees where Katherine has been. "She went back there after you dropped her off."

"Oh my god. Are you serious?"

"Look," he says, showing me Katherine's Uber account. "She even gave the driver a huge tip."

I particularly enjoyed that little extra. "That's just... I don't know what to say, Corey. I'm shocked."

Corey's mouth hangs open as he shakes his head. But his surprise is transitioning into anger. The veins on his temple pulsate as he exhales louder than is needed to breathe. "Who is this son of a—?"

"I'm so sorry, Corey," I blurt, not wanting him to think this was the doing of another man. I redirect his rage. "I should have taken her seriously when she said this. I figured it was a joke."

"Don't be sorry. This isn't your fault. Katherine must have a problem she's not dealing with. I'd hoped things might get better for us, but I guess not. Instead, she's out there doing this sort of thing on a work night."

I lay my hand on Corey's elbow and brush his arm up and down. "I'm so sorry I invited her out. I thought some time apart would help you both but look what I've done. I'm so stupid." My arm pulls away. I turn on the waterworks like a tap, covering my face with both hands.

"Hey, hey. It's okay, Annette. Like I said, this isn't your fault. You were trying to be a good friend to us both." His arm wraps around my shoulders and squeezes me tight for a moment. I shudder to his touch and do my best to maintain the supposed sadness I'm attempting to display.

"You're not mad at me?"

"No. Not in the slightest. You're not the one out there betraying my trust, especially after everything that's been happening lately. God, why would Kat act this way? Is it for attention? Is it to punish me?"

I remain silent for a moment, letting Corey fret over each question. "Whatever has gotten into her, you don't deserve it. Kat should appreciate what an amazing man she has and not take you for granted."

Corey smiles at me out of the corner of his mouth, blushing at the same time. "You don't have to say that. I have my faults too."

"Everyone does, but some are much worse than others."

"Yes, they are."

A quiet seeps into the room as I pretend to hang my head down in thought. I take a peek at Corey to see a shattered look on his face as Katherine's cell hangs by his side, loose in one hand. Is he contemplating his relationship with Katherine over in his mind? Has he finally realized she's not the one?

"Thanks for returning this, Annette," Corey says, avoiding my eyes.

"Any time. Is there anything I can do to help? I could drive Ava home for you today."

"No, it's okay. I'll pick her up. I need to take some time to think about everything."

"Okay. That's probably for the best. If you need anything, I'm here for you." I grab his hand and brush my thumb over the back of his fingers. "I hope your day improves."

"Me too," he says, looking me in the eyes.

I give Corey one last smile with a hint of what I really want him to feel before I exit his classroom.

"Annette."

I stop short of the doorknob with my arm extended out to

twist it open. The huge grin on my face is almost uncontrollable. I contain it as best I can and turn to Corey.

"Thank you for being here for me despite our history. It means more to me than you'll ever know."

My heart slams against my chest. Finally, he's acknowledged our past. I'm so close to getting him. I just need to keep my focus.

"I'll always be here for you, Corey. No matter what."

49

KATHERINE

The sound of Corey and Ava coming through the front door with a bang wakes me. I was only half asleep, so I don't freak out when I wake during the day. My head pounds even worse than before, feeling like an egg that's got a crack in it. Whatever's hit me has done so with fury.

I've stopped throwing up finally. For hours after Annette dropped me home, I couldn't keep so much as a glass of water down. My body was trying to remove the evil that had entered my system in whatever manner it could, leaving me dehydrated.

After a slow stumble to the en suite, I realize every muscle in my soul hurts. I swear I'm recovering from being run over by multiple buses the way I'm shuffling about like my legs need to go through a swift round of rehabilitation.

My eyes avoid the mirror at all costs. I can't stand the thought of seeing myself at the moment. I'll deal with that problem later if I ever feel a lick of energy return to my body.

"Mommy?" Ava asks, knocking on my bedroom door.

"Come in, sweetheart. I'm in the bathroom," I reply as I run the tap to splash some water on my face.

The door gently opens with a squeak, so I quickly pat myself dry with a towel. Ava's footsteps move toward me one small patter at a time until I see her eyes.

"Are you okay, Mommy?" she asks, a single wrinkle over her forehead.

"I'm okay, honey. Come here." I open my arms and drop to my knees to invite her in for a hug. She rushes over and dives into my chest the way she used to when she was three.

"Corey said you weren't feeling well and that you'd made a mess."

"Yeah, I did, sweetheart. Mommy was silly last night. Now she's paying the price."

Ava stares back at me, confused by the situation. I don't have the energy to go into detail more than I have, so I change the subject. "And how was your day? Did you have fun?"

"It was amazing!"

Ava fills me in on almost every activity she did over the day. It's nice to listen to her talk passionately about cutting something out with scissors 'without going outside of the line' as she so proudly tells me.

"Wow. That sounds like a cool time to me. Are you hungry?" I ask.

"Yes!" she shouts.

"Okay. Why don't you go watch some TV while Mommy fixes you a snack before dinner?"

Ava nods with a big grin, one that warms my heart every time I see it. I'll never forget how that smile got me through the darkest of days when I had to single-handedly take care of Ava as a baby. She could give me hell for an entire day and then bring me back from the brink with her beautiful giggle.

Ava rushes off before I can get to my feet. It seems like a long way up as I groan out loud. Never have I felt so drained of energy. This is the last time I go out on a school night.

A slow walk takes me to the kitchen. I find Corey starting on dinner. "You don't have to do that. I'm happy to cook."

"It's fine. You're not in any kind of state to be doing this, so please sit down."

His words come out sharp around the edges. He's upset with me. No doubt for the whole incident in the faculty lounge. I guess me making a fool out of myself reflects even worse on him now we're married. Still, I can't help what happened to me. All I had was two glasses of wine. I swear it.

"I can make dinner," I say. "You've had a long day of work. It's only fair."

"It's only fair, is it? Well then, go for it. Make us some dinner. If you can handle it, that is." He walks off before I think of a single thing to answer back. What the hell was that all about?

Corey leaves me alone in the kitchen when I need his support more than ever. I'm so run down I don't know how I'll prepare this meal without feeling worse. It's not like I plan on eating any of it. Corey got out the ingredients necessary to make a basic meatloaf. The thawed ground beef is already getting to me, causing me to gag.

I fight through the churn in my stomach and follow the recipe as best I can while a thick layer of sweat coats my forehead. Slapping together a simple meal shouldn't take this much out of me but it does, so I quickly shove it in the oven. Before I leave the kitchen, I grab out a small packet of potato chips and give them to Ava on my way through to the bedroom. I need to lie down for a moment.

When my head hits one of our thick memory foam pillows, my eyes close. I want a minute to rest and recuperate to get through making dinner. But before I know it, I'm slipping away into a dream.

A hazy image of the bar from last night slides in front of me. I see flashes of Annette's face laughing as we enjoy a few glasses of wine. Then things transition into a strange mess. Some guys come over and hit on us, but I don't tell them I'm married. In fact, each time they make a move on me, I don't seem to mind. I laugh at first, but soon I become drained of all energy and realize my breathing has slowed down. I no longer have a sensation of elation consuming me, but the impression that I've disconnected from my body. That's when one guy kisses me.

I snap awake and try to stand in a hurry. My feet ache underneath my weakened knees. Sweat soaks my head even worse than before as I struggle to remember where I am. My bedroom slowly rolls into focus, reminding me I'm at home making dinner for Corey and Ava.

"Oh, crap," I yell, realizing I've fallen asleep with a meatloaf in the oven.

When I reach the kitchen, I find Corey pulling out the burning dish as smoke fills the room. He throws the ruined meal into the sink and runs the tap over it, spoiling any chance I had to cut off the charred outer layer to save the rest.

The smoke alarm down the hall blazes away as Corey turns around and faces me with yet another horrified look of disappointment. He brushes by me, heading for the alarm without saying a word.

Can this day get any worse?

50

KATHERINE

"I'm sorry," I say to Corey as he paces around the kitchen, making a sandwich for Ava's dinner. There isn't enough time left in the day to make her anything else. He doesn't respond.

"I needed to rest my eyes for a moment but forgot to set an alarm. I'd normally use my cell to do so, but I don't know where the damn thing is."

Corey stops what he's doing and pulls something out the front pocket of his jeans. He places my phone on the small dining table and turns away.

"Oh my god. Where did you find that? I thought I lost it last night."

"Nope. You dropped it near the front of the house when you finally came home."

I walk to the table and scoop up my phone, not realizing how badly I missed the device. It took today to make me understand the dependence we have on these damn things. I go to unlock my cell to check the million notifications that will demand attention when something Corey said hits me.

"Wait, what time do you think I came home last night?"

"Around two."

I cross my arms. "But Annette said she dropped me here at ten thirty."

Corey breathes out loudly. "She did." He faces me with Ava's sandwich ready to go. "But you decided to charge back out to the bar on your own." He walks off out of the kitchen through to the living room before I reply. I follow and watch him deliver the meal to Ava.

"Here, sweetie," he says to Ava's excited eyes.

"Thank you," she replies, using the good manners I'd taught her.

Corey brushes by me, ignoring the look on my face. He can't have missed my mouth hanging half open as I try to put two words together.

"Wait," I say as we both head into the kitchen. Corey doesn't stop and makes another sandwich. I can only assume it's for himself. "What do you mean I went back out? I came home with Annette. She dropped me off. You must have thought it was later than ten thirty."

With only a glimpse over his shoulder, Corey nods toward my cell. "Check your Uber history."

"My Uber history? Why?"

"Do it," he says firmly.

"Okay. Not sure what that's got to do with anything but—"

I see on my phone multiple trips made last night. The first one started after ten thirty from our house, with the destination being the bar Annette and I visited. I find a return trip below the record with me arriving back home after two. "What the hell?"

"That's not all, Kat."

I pull my attention away from my rideshare history and glance up to Corey. "What do you mean?"

"Look at the photos you took last night."

"Photos? What photos?"

He scoffs at me. "Wow. You're unbelievable."

"What?"

Corey's brow tightens as he storms over and snatches my cell. He taps at the screen harder than is necessary and hands it back. "This."

I take my phone and see a series of selfies from the bar last night with me and some guy getting more than a little friendly with one another. My heart beats so hard in my chest it hurts.

"I don't remember—"

"How convenient. You were too drunk to remember that you were practically cheating on me."

"I wasn't. I wouldn't."

"Really? I think these photos tell a different story, don't you?"

I can't deny it. Each image is more damning than the last. There I am, sitting on some guy's lap with my arms around him, laughing, with a drink in hand. In the next image, he's nuzzling his mouth into my neck. Then I'm kissing him on the cheek. In every photo I look happy. And to make matters worse, Annette isn't in a single picture. She really dropped me home, but I took it upon myself to go back out.

"Corey. I don't remember this. I swear to you. Someone must have slipped something into my drink. Maybe this guy did."

"You don't appear to be out of your mind on some drug in any of these photos. You look like you were out to have a good night."

"That's not it. I don't even recall this guy's name or speaking to him beyond a few short words."

"Of course you don't. You were both too busy grabbing one another to waste time chatting. Answer me this simple question, Katherine: if this happened when you were taking selfies, what did you do when your cell wasn't being used?"

My jaw falls open. I remember someone kissed me last night but hoped it was a bad dream. Did I cheat on my husband? I can't be sure, but it's looking more and more possible with every passing second.

"Well?" Corey presses.

"I don't know. But whatever happened was not what I wanted. I went out to have a drink with a friend and nothing more."

"Oh, then that's fine. No problem at all," Corey says, exaggerating each word with sarcasm.

I feel my hands shake as I stumble my way into a seat at our small dining table. The surface trembles beneath me as I grip it. "This can't be happening," I whisper.

"It is, though, Kat. You don't get a free pass on this just because you drank too much to remember."

"That's not what I—"

"I don't want to hear it. You told me what you're like when you drink too much. I rarely worry about you going out because you always have Annette by your side keeping you from being you. But it wasn't enough for you last night. You waited until she dropped you home and ran back to that place so you could do whatever you wanted."

I wrap my hands around my face and feel my body convulse as I sob uncontrollably. He's right. When I was with Peter, I'd drink to forget. So much so that I would either pass out or make a fool out of myself. It's the reason I only ever have a couple of glasses of wine with Annette and call it a night.

"I thought we had something special," Corey says.

I glance up to him as I cry and see him staring at a framed picture he's holding in his hands. The photo is of Corey, Ava, and me all cuddled up together.

"I thought you were the one the way we hit it off. I never expected things to fall apart the second we got married." His eyes drop from the frame and focus on mine. "Is that what this is all about? You never wanted to marry me?"

"I love you," I blurt through the tears. "And I love being your wife. I can't understand why we're having so many problems, but I don't regret marrying you." I rise from the chair and do my best to stop crying. "We can still make this work, Corey. This is a rough patch and nothing more. We can push through it. We can—"

"Enough!" Corey shouts, throwing his hands out wide. The photo frame flies through the air and smashes hard against the kitchen floor. Pieces of glass spray out across the tiles, but he doesn't remove his eyes from mine. He takes a step toward me with a sneer on his lips.

"Mommy?" Ava calls from the doorway.

"It's okay, sweetie," I say as I rush to her side. "Corey and I are just having a little—"

I don't get to finish my sentence as Corey brushes past us. He storms through the lounge and grabs his keys on the way through.

"Where are you going?" I call after him.

Without looking back, he says, "Out."

51

I can't help but to be proud of my work. Today, I pulled off what I thought was the impossible. I made Corey feel nothing but loathing for his wife. That look of betrayal on his face was so intense, I could see the rage boiling his insides. He hated Katherine in that moment, but I didn't enjoy putting him through any pain.

Soon I will take Corey's intensity and turn it into a passionate relationship with me. He won't ever have to experience a complete lack of loyalty again. I'll show him how better off this world can be without Katherine. She only holds him back.

By now, Corey will have confronted her. There is no way around such a discovery. I gave him enough evidence to prove once and for all that she's not devoted to him. He cannot deny that he chose wrong and married a woman ill fitted to be his wife.

So what happens now? The tracking virus I installed on Corey's cell tells me he's at a bar in town. Perhaps he might run into me there and find a sympathetic shoulder to cry on, so to speak. I'll listen to him unload his frustrations and help guide him on the right path. By the end of the night, we will have kissed, and he'll realize that he's wasted the last six months of his life with the wrong person.

I get ready as fast as I can, while giving myself enough time to look perfect for Corey. I'm styling my hair and dressing the same as I had on that night we kissed, hoping the sight of me will trigger a wave of emotions within him.

Never will I forget our short but amazing moment together. And I know Corey hasn't tried to push it to the back of his mind for Katherine. I'm still in there. She didn't deserve to have someone as thoughtful and caring as Corey taking care of her and her daughter. Instead, the universe threw her a bone while it screwed me out of eternal happiness.

A wave of giddy nerves washes over me as I think about seeing Corey. The second our lips meet, I'll again be complete. This constant pain that is my existence will be erased by Corey's flawless soul. My life can resume and return to the path it strayed from.

As I finish my makeup and hair, my cell buzzes on the surface of the vanity unit I'm staring at. I scoop up my phone to see Katherine calling. "No," I blurt. But I have to answer it so she sees me as the caring friend who will always be there for her. I can't have her thinking I had anything to do with her being drugged.

"Hey," I say.

Sniffles and sobbing greet me on the other end of the line. "Anne."

"What is it? What's wrong?"

"It's Corey. He thinks I..."

It's clear the two lovebirds have had their argument. "He thinks you what?"

"I can't explain. It's too much for the phone. I need to see you, now."

Dammit. What was I thinking answering my cell?

"Please. Are you free? Can you come over?"

"But isn't he—?"

"He's gone out. I think to a bar, maybe. I don't know, but he's not here and I need you. Please, help me."

"I..." My voice trails off as I try to think of a way out of this. I have to get to that bar while Corey is vulnerable. This opportunity can't be wasted. But a caring friend wouldn't say no to someone this desperate. And if I tell Katherine I'm too busy to help her, she will grow suspicious of my actions. She might work out what I've been up to and ruin the whole thing.

With a sigh, I recognize what I must do to keep the wheels turning on my plan. As painful as it is to throw away such a golden opportunity with Corey, I have to remind myself to be patient. I've waited this long. What's another few days?

"I'll be there in ten," I say, fighting off the scream dying to escape my lips.

"Thank you, Annette. You're amazing. I don't know what I'd do without you."

If only she knew the truth.

52

KATHERINE

Putting Ava to bed was a challenge. She could see that something was wrong no matter how hard I tried to hide it. My daughter has this impeccable ability to penetrate any lies I feed her when I'm nervous.

I pace up and down the short length of the living room as I wait for Annette to come over and save me. It's pathetic that I'm about to unleash all of my crap upon her, but I can't help it. I need to get out my frustrations and fears into the world even if she's only listening to me blab away. Everything that has happened is drilling a hole through my brain. So much so, I swear it will kill me.

Annette's car pulls up. I know the sound of her engine from all the times she's driven me places. I rush to the front door and open it before she knocks. My arms fly out wide, ready for her to console me and hear the hell I'm about to spring upon her. We hug for a moment.

"Thank you so much for coming. I don't even know where to begin," I say, tears welling in my eyes.

"It's okay. Start at the beginning, I guess. What's happened?"

I practically pull Annette inside to the sofa and sit down

beside her. "It's about last night. Apparently, I went back to the bar after you brought me home."

"What? Really?"

"Yes. I took an Uber there, got drunk, and ordered another ride home a few hours later. I have to ask you, what was I like when you dropped me off here? Did I seem out of it to you?"

"No, not at all. You'd had two glasses of red. That's it. You wanted to call it a night and get to bed."

I feel my eyes turn away as my face tightens up. "Then why did I go back to the bar?" I whisper, unsure if I'm asking Annette or just wishing there was an explanation.

"Maybe I was boring company."

"No, you could never bore me. I'm the dull one who can't handle a few drinks."

"Whatever happened, it's over now."

I give Annette a shaky sigh. "It's not over. Corey hates me."

"Hates you? Why? Because of what you did in the faculty lounge?"

"No. It's far worse than that." I unlock my cell and bring up the photos from the bar. I slowly hold my phone up to Annette and watch her jaw drop as she sees the shots of me and the unknown sleaze hitting it off.

"These are from last night?"

"Yeah. You can see the time and date I took each photo. Do you remember seeing this guy?"

"Vaguely. I think he hit on you not long after we got there."

"So that happened. I can recall that part of the night in my head, but not this."

Annette hands me my cell. "So I'm guessing Corey has seen these."

"Yeah," I mutter, fighting off more tears. "I don't know how to explain something I have no memory of. There's no way in hell

I'd ever cheat on him but looking at these photos makes me think I may have. And he thinks so too."

"Oh God," Annette blurts, covering her mouth with her hand a moment later.

"Exactly," I reply. "It's appalling. And Corey is furious. I don't know what'll happen next. This could be it for our marriage." I feel my hands shake again. The tremble works its way down into my fingers until I drop my cell to the floor. It bounces on the carpet.

"Hey, hey. It's okay," Annette says, wrapping her arms around me. "Everything's going to work out. I promise."

I lift my head and study her eyes. "You think so?"

"I know so. Things might seem terrible now, but I guarantee this will all come to an end."

Annette smiles at me, trying to raise my gaze further. "I hope you're right."

"Hey, I'm always right," Annette says with a chuckle.

"Yeah, you are."

"Which makes what I have to say next so hard."

I stop breathing for a second. "What do you mean?"

Annette lets out a sigh and glances away from me, closing her eyes. She opens them and refocuses on me. "What I'm about to say to you I say as a dear friend. One who cares deeply."

"Okay," I whisper.

"I think it's time you asked yourself one of the hardest questions you'll ever have to face."

My eyelids push my brow up into my forehead. "What?"

"Do you think marrying Corey was a good idea?"

"You mean a mistake?"

"Hear me out. You guys are a wonderful couple. You always have been, but the second you two rushed into marriage, things have gone from one disaster to the next."

"We've had a few difficulties," I say, suddenly feeling offended, "but we can push through it."

"Can you, though? Last night aside, you've been at each other's throats almost every day from what you tell me. Is that the sign of a happy marriage?"

My head spins as I pull my focus away from Annette and stare at the floor. I feel like a powerful migraine is about to knock me flat. "We need to go see a marriage counselor. I know we'll get through this. We have to."

Annette lifts my chin up with her finger so I have to face her eyes. "What about Ava? Is all of this arguing good for her?"

I shake my head. "You don't understand. I don't want to fight in front of her, but it happens."

"And it keeps happening and is damaging her in ways you'll never realize until it's too late."

"No, she's a strong girl."

"I know she is, Kat, but is it really fair for her to have to deal with this situation?"

I snap my head away from Annette's. "You don't know what you're talking about. You don't have kids. How could you possibly understand what it's like to sacrifice for them day in, day out, and get no thanks for your efforts?"

We fall silent. I keep my eyes from Annette's knowing I've said something hurtful, but I don't care. I'm too angry to apologize.

"You're right. I don't have kids, but I know what you've been through with Ava. Who do you think has been there whenever you've needed help from the day she was born?"

She's right. Annette may not have a child of her own, but she knows how hard it's been for me. She's witnessed the good and the bad. I need to apologize.

"Don't. It's fine. It's clear you're upset over what I said about you and Corey. Maybe I'm wrong about you guys and everything will somehow be okay but think about what's best for Ava and yourself. I'd hate to watch you fall into another downward spiral the way you did with Peter."

I stand from the sofa in a hurry, not wanting to accept what Annette has to say. It can't be true. Corey and I belong together. We're a good couple.

"That won't happen," I say. "Corey and I are married. Peter would never have committed to something so serious. Hell, the second he found out I was pregnant he raced away."

Annette stands and steps toward me. "Peter ran away, but it was no surprise, was it? He was a terrible boyfriend from the start, and you allowed him to treat you that way."

"But Corey isn't."

"No but ask yourself a question you've been avoiding since the moment Corey proposed to you."

I shake my head, feeling my body shift from side to side. I realize what she is getting at and I don't want to face it. Not now.

"Come on, Kat. Don't make me be the one to say it."

"You don't understand."

"You know I do."

We stare at each other, each holding our gaze. I blink first and lower my eyes. "I can't do this."

"Fine. I'll ask then."

"No. Please."

"Did you want to get married?"

The question flows out of Annette's mouth and hits my ears without stopping. She's known this all along and has held her tongue. Until now.

"Well, did you? Did you want to marry Corey when he asked you?"

A sigh escapes me. "No."

53

I hit Katherine with everything I had last night and sent her a devastating blow at the perfect time. It was obvious from the word go that Katherine didn't want to get married when Corey surprised her with an unplanned proposal. I remember the lack of excitement in her eyes when she told me the news. It even left me believing she might back out of the relationship. But instead of being honest with Corey, she doubled down.

I don't know which hurt me more at the time: knowing that Katherine never wanted to marry Corey or finding out that he had asked her. But it didn't matter. My feelings were thrown out like worthless trash. They forced me to be their witness at the courthouse when they got married. I had to sign their marriage license. I had to give my approval to the world no matter how much pain it caused me. That day sent me over the edge.

Until that point, I had handled seeing Corey and Katherine together as best I could. It was a waiting game. I knew I just had to push through until Katherine screwed things up the way she always did. But then Corey popped the question.

It was clear he hadn't thought it through, and that Katherine wanted to run until her feet bled. But they got married. Part of me knows I should have said something, anything to stop the wedding from going through. I was there. I could have made them each understand the mistake, but I remained silent.

I don't know if it was anger holding me back or the fear that I had finally lost Corey to my supposed best friend. Either way, I failed. And now, I alone must right what's wrong unless Katherine sees the light.

I'll consider this Katherine's last chance to do what she should have done the second Corey asked her to marry him. She never deserved to receive that amazing question from such a perfect man. If she can see past her ego and come to her senses, then I won't have to escalate this situation any further.

But I'm not one to take chances. Especially on someone as stupid as Katherine. While she's contemplating her life and the terrible choices made, I'll continue with the plan and follow each step. I'll do whatever it takes to claim what is mine.

Soon, I won't be responsible for my actions.

54

KATHERINE

Corey didn't come home last night, so I barely slept. I alternated between sitting at the end of my bed, listening out for the sound of his car, and pacing up and down the corridor. I did what I could to not disturb Ava, but on multiple occasions she woke up to the tone of me muttering to myself.

"Go back to sleep, sweetie," I said as I gently ran my hand over her forehead the way I did when she was only two years old.

"Mommy, I heard a scary noise."

"That was probably the wind, honey. Nothing to worry about."

"Okay. Can you read me a story?"

"Sure, baby. Which one do you want to hear?" It was only fair.

Morning trickles into existence as I finally fall asleep on the sofa in the living room, hoping to catch Corey sneaking in through the front door. The sound of chirping birds only adds to the throbbing pain in my head.

I shuffle toward the kitchen with both eyes half shut, feeling my way to the coffeemaker. I could just about make myself a strong espresso blindfolded, given how well I knew the machine.

Within a few minutes, I'm sitting at the dining table close to the kitchen, slurping down the hot beverage as fast as possible. I need the caffeine to kick in if I'm going to survive the kids.

After my absence yesterday I needed a good night's sleep so I could charge into work and prove myself to Barry and the rest of the staff. But if any of them were to see me now, I'd be lucky to still have a job by the end of the day.

Why didn't Corey come home? I know I'd also be furious if I found selfies of him and some unknown woman almost kissing on his cell. But would I have left like this? I honestly can't answer the question.

What if nothing got slipped into my drink? Maybe I made the conscious decision to return to the bar on my own. I guess deep down I was still harboring anger toward Corey for the whole promotion drama. Maybe that's why I felt the need to run back there and get drunk.

But there's more to it than that. There was a painful truth to what Annette said last night. As upset as she's made me, I can't be mad at her for trying to be honest with me about Corey. I didn't want to marry him. At least not this early. But he stared into my eyes that morning, begging me to take the next giant leap forward. I wasn't only scared to commit; I was worried, and still am, for my daughter.

Corey has always been amazing with Ava from the first day he met her. I trust him with her welfare. And that's not what has me concerned. All this chaos that has enveloped mine and Corey's relationship has the potential to do so much damage to Ava. I'm afraid more than anything else that if Corey and I don't make it through this rough patch, Ava could lose the only man in her life who is a positive father figure. That will have a lasting impact on the way she views men.

I reach the end of my cup without realizing it until I try to take another sip. My neck snaps toward the doorway to the kitchen as I hear footsteps coming through the living room. "Corey?"

The footfalls continue until I see Ava poke her head in. "Hi, Mommy."

"Hi, baby. Why are you awake so early?"

"I couldn't sleep," she says as she rubs her eyes with her knuckles.

"I'm sorry, honey. Are you feeling okay?" A wave of guilt hits me in the chest. This is my fault. I kept waking her up last night, breaking her cycle. What a terrible mother I've become.

"Guess so," she says a second before a huge yawn breaks through.

Pushing up from the dining table, I step toward my daughter. "Come here, sweetie," I say as I bend down and scoop her up into a big hug. Ava does what she can to stop me from smothering her with kisses as she giggles at me. I'll never grow sick of hearing her innocent laugh.

"Mommy," she says with a full smile.

"What is it?"

"Where's Corey?"

The sun is rising. Even Ava knows he would still be here on one of his long days to school.

"Did he come home yet?"

I was hoping she didn't notice. "Um, yeah. He did. He had to go into school super early this morning because he has a lot of work to do with his new promotion."

"Okay," she replies, somewhat skeptical.

I hate lying to my kid. She always seems to see through

anything I tell her. Even a white lie like this. I almost want to spew out the truth to prepare her for what may come next. How would I go about informing Ava that Corey won't be around anymore if he decides this marriage isn't worth the hassle?

"Are you hungry?" I ask, changing the subject. "We can have a nice big breakfast to help us wake up a little before we leave." I haven't even worked out how we're getting to school yet. With my car still in the shop, Corey would have taken us. But he's not here.

Ava's eyes drop away from mine. "Can I stay home today?"

I place a hand on her small shoulder. "Why do you want to stay home?"

"Because I'm tired."

"I know it would be nice to take it easy, honey, but we both have to go to school even though it would be more fun to lie around all day on the sofa watching TV."

"But, Mommy."

"But nothing. Come along. Let's have some breakfast together." I take Ava's hand and guide her into the kitchen. She reluctantly accepts.

It would be nice to pretend to be sick today, but after yesterday I have no choice but to go into school and face the music.

55

I risked a lot saying what I said to Katherine. Most of it came out without me thinking. It almost felt strange being so honest, given the number of lies I've been spinning lately. But I know once she has settled down and had a chance to think, Katherine will realize there is a harsh truth behind every word spoken.

I came into work early today, hoping to catch Corey alone. Last night would have been the better time to speak with him while he was so vulnerable after finding those photos on Kat's phone. Still, I persevere.

The parking lot is almost empty apart from Corey's sedan parked in its usual spot. He's such an enthusiastic worker. He makes ninety percent of the teachers in this school look lazy. I park my car as far away from his as possible so no one suspects I'm here to see him. I can't let my hard work come unstuck by a simple mistake.

The cold morning fills my lungs and wakes me. I don't know how Corey does this five days a week, but it doesn't surprise me. He's never shied from a challenge. Every time I watch him interact with Kat's annoying kid, I wonder to myself how he does it. How can he stand taking care of her, knowing full well she's not his child?

I rush into the office and dump my stuff off in a hurry, then head into the faculty lounge to prepare two cups of coffee. One for myself and the other for Corey. It's a long way to carry a pair of hot mugs, but Corey will see exactly how much I appreciate him when he sees me walking in with these.

To make the walk easier, I brought two travel cups from home to avoid burning myself.

When I find Corey pacing up and down his classroom, I instantly feel the tension that has manifested between him and Katherine. I resist smiling, knowing that I am the mastermind behind their relationship's descent. It was all too easy. There were gaping holes in their relationship to exploit, making the task all that much simpler to concentrate on. Now all I need to do is finish the job.

I knock on the door with the back of my knuckles. Corey snaps around in my direction almost alarmed to see anyone else so early. I hate interrupting and keeping him from his important work, but after last night, I have to focus and take what is mine before Katherine ruins everything again.

"Annette?" Corey walks over to me and yanks the door open. "What are you doing here?"

"I spent a few hours with Katherine last night. After hearing about the argument, I figured that you also may need someone to talk to."

Corey smiles at me out of the corner of his mouth. "And is that coffee for me?"

"Of course. It might be early, but even I can't handle two cups in the morning."

"You're a lifesaver. So, how did I come across according to Katherine?"

"I'm not here to take sides. I'm only here to help you. You guys are both my friends, and both have feelings."

"Whoa. Please don't go all emotional with me. Because I've had enough of it over the last few days. I just want to move on with things, you know?"

"Yeah, I understand. But I suppose now isn't the time to close people out. As hard as it is, you need to get everything off your chest and talk to someone who cares." If only I wasn't holding these damn coffee cups, I'd be touching him to accentuate how much I care.

Corey grabs one mug and asks, "Is this mine?" He ignores what I've said without missing a beat. I understand his frustration and not wanting to deal with things, but I can see that he didn't sleep last night.

Corey walks into the room away from me and takes a swig of the cup. It's not the right one. This latest argument with Katherine must have him rattled. I'm so close to witnessing him crack. Soon he'll break his spirit free from his wife's spell. I just have to push through any resistance.

"Oh God," Corey says. "This is your coffee, isn't it? I'm so sorry. I don't know what I'm doing anymore."

"It's okay, Corey. That's why I'm here. Anyone can see you need to talk about all of this."

He places the drink down and shakes his head. "I can't understand how everything's gone downhill so fast. It's like there's a curse on my and Kat's marriage."

"I don't know about a curse, but there have been a few tricky situations for you guys to get through. More so than what the average couple usually faces in the first few weeks after getting married."

"That's an understatement." Corey's eyes stay glued to the floor. I see him mulling it all over in his head. Am I going to like the conclusion he eventually comes to? Or can I push him in the best direction?

"Here," I say as I approach him with the correct mug. "Drink this. It'll make you feel better."

Corey smiles at me the way I've only ever seen him grin moments before we kissed. I don't waste another second and take a step into his personal space. He lifts my coffee to me, and we swap them hand-in-hand as close to each other as two friends can. I gaze up into his pupils and lean toward his lips. I feel my body tremble as we both shut our eyes a split second before it finally happens.

The honk of a horn out in the parking lot stops us both. Corey's eyes snap open and he draws his head back from mine. "Wait? This isn't right. What am I doing? I'm so sorry." He turns and takes three hurried steps away.

I go to speak, but what words can I use without confessing my true feelings to him? If I do, he'll know all along that I've been up to something to get in the way of him and Katherine. "It's okay," I say. "We were both caught up in the moment. Don't worry about it."

"No. I am worried about this. I was about to cheat on my wife with her best friend. What kind of husband am I? I have to speak to Kat and talk things out."

I step toward him, my arm extended, but he shudders further back from me like I'm on fire. I want to say to him that he's the best husband anyone could hope for, more than Katherine deserves, but I freeze in place, powerless to move.

"You need to go, Annette. I'm sorry for trying to kiss you."

"No, please, don't push me away. We didn't even kiss. It meant nothing." The words come out of my mouth through a shaky voice filled with pain. Why can't I tell him the truth? Why can't I make him see who he should have been with all this time?

"Please, Annette. I need to fix things with Katherine. It's my fault she did what she did at that bar. I drove her away when I should have realized we needed help."

I'm too late. He is already falling back to her. Whatever she holds over him I can't stop. At least not while she's still alive. It's clear now what must happen. Part of me hoped it would never come to this, but here we are.

My plan has failed, so it's time to push forward and do what it takes to see this through. Soon Katherine won't be around to get in my way.

56

As I reach the BBES parking lot, I receive a text from Corey. His message is longer than normal and says that we need to have a chat before school. He must wish to have a serious discussion as he doesn't want to meet in his classroom. I'm guessing he wants to avoid the possibility of us having a heated argument out in the open for the other teachers to see. It's fair enough, considering the way we have been speaking to one another lately.

I walk Ava to her before-school care room feeling nervous the entire time. It hits me hard that I don't know what Corey will say. Is he going to break this marriage apart and end things before we even reach the one-month mark?

How did we get to this point? It seems like only yesterday that we were enjoying ourselves in Nevada, taking in the millions of lights The Strip in Las Vegas offered. Now we are here, on the verge of ending it all, both of us unsure of the other. I thought I knew Corey. Sure, we've only been together for six-plus months, but I feel in that time that we'd discovered everything about each other.

"How are you today, Ava?" asks one of the before-school

teachers. Her name escapes me, but she is a young graduate eager to prove herself. I feel I may be losing my drive for this line of work, especially after missing out on the promotion because of Corey's jealousy. I still can't believe he'd do such a thing to get ahead, considering I'm his wife. Then again, most of what's happened since we got back from our honeymoon has been unbelievable.

Ava and the young teacher chat away like they're old friends. I've zoned out their conversation with some self-absorbed thoughts I need to stop having. How will I ever cope at work if things don't go right at home? I barely made it through the years I had to deal with Peter. Fortunately, back then I didn't have a child to look after. Just a grown man who knew better.

After dropping Ava off, I head out to meet Corey. He said he'd be having a coffee behind the old sports shed on the far side of the school. No one goes there anymore, so we can be alone and speak as loudly as we want.

As I make the lengthy trip across the grounds, I feel the chill in the air grabbing hold of my body. I grasp at my middle and wrap both arms around my chest, but it does little to stop the cool ocean winds from cutting through my jacket. I accidentally grabbed the wrong one this morning like an idiot. It's not surprising, though, as I can't seem to focus on anything anymore.

The cold reminds me of a better time when Corey and I first got together and were dating in secret, fearful that Annette might find out. We were taking a stroll along the beach, looking out at the mighty waves as they bashed in and around the degrading cliff stacks of Battery Beach. The walk was an impromptu idea we seemed to have at the same time.

"Wow. It's colder out here than I realized," Corey said to me. He hadn't been in town that long and was still getting used to the difference in temperature here.

"Yeah, it takes a while to adjust to the coast. Growing up here gives you an extra layer of skin."

Corey looked away from me and out to the water. "What do you think Annette will be like when she finds out about us?"

The mention of Annette's name had me on edge. "I expect at first she might be mad, but she'll understand that we never intended for this to happen. It just did."

"I hope you're right. I'd hate to come between you two. You guys have been friends forever and I wouldn't want to ruin that."

I grabbed Corey by the chin and turned him toward me. "I know Annette. She's not like that. And I also believe once she gets over this, she will accept you as a friend."

Corey looked down the beach before us and nodded. "I only wish I had gotten to know you first. Then Annette and I would have never kissed that night. It must feel strange knowing that I made out with your best friend."

"It's all in the past. Come on. We better get you back to the warmth of the café before you freeze to death."

I don't understand why I'm thinking about Corey and Annette. Maybe it's my guilt resurfacing. She has been nothing but amazing since Corey and I got together. I only ever saw the hurt in her eyes for a short moment before she realized there was never anything between her and Corey to begin with. I felt rotten for weeks, but I eventually accepted things as they were.

Corey's proposal made me feel guilty all over again. When I told Annette, I didn't know what to expect from her. But she didn't show me even the tiniest hint of a problem. Instead, she welcomed it and wanted to be as big a part of our nuptials as possible. I can't imagine why I thought she'd be any different.

I reach the old sports sheds and see no sign of Corey. I walk right around the back and sides of the shed and still don't find him anywhere. After checking the text from him twice, confusion sets in, so I make a call to him instead of trying to tap out a garbled message.

"Where are you?" I say to myself. Looking at the time on my cell, I realize I need to be in the classroom in fifteen minutes or else I'll be late.

Impatience takes control fast as his phone rings out. "What the hell?" Either he is running behind, or he told me the wrong location to meet. I try calling him again but, on this occasion, it goes straight to voicemail. "Yeah, I'm here at the meeting spot. Where are you? I have to get back soon if you don't show up."

I hit the end call button and let my cell drop by my side in my hand. A long-winded sigh escapes me as I shake my head and mutter obscenities. "Where in hell is–?"

A bright flash fills my eyes with pain, replacing my world with a high-pitched deafening tone.

The light fades, gradually restoring my sight and sound.

I take a moment to realize, but the unkempt grass surrounding the old sports shed is pressing against my face. I try to move but no muscles in my body seem to function.

A darkness seeps in at the edges of my retinas, engulfing my vision. I feel the life fade from me as my eyelids scream to fall shut. A figure looms into my blurry view that can only belong to one person.

Corey is standing over me.

My eyelids crack open, each feeling like they weigh a ton. I slowly blink until my vision focuses. My hearing soon follows and allows in the rhythmic pattern of what must be a heart rate monitor.

I try to move, but my body feels like it's made of concrete. All I seem to be able to do is swivel my head. My brain throbs as if it's doubled in size.

"She's waking up," says a familiar voice. The sound comes from a person I know so well, but I'm having a hard time remembering who they are. Then everything clicks. It's Corey.

I push myself up and away from him as best I can, but his thick hands grab me by the shoulders.

"Hey, it's okay. Try not to move. You're in the hospital."

I don't speak. What are you supposed to say to a man who has attacked you? I stare at Corey and realize he has been by my side, waiting for me to wake up.

"Honey? Do you understand what's happening?"

Before I'm forced to answer him, a nurse comes into the room and takes over. She directs Corey to move back and take a seat in a chair that sits beside my bed while she checks over me.

"Hello there. My name is Judy. Do you know where you are?"

"In a hospital," I say with a croaky voice. I try to clear my throat but feel instant pain.

"That's right. You're in the Providence Bayside Hospital. You've taken a blow to the back of the head. Can you tell me what day it is?"

I think about the question for a moment and answer, "It's Thursday the fifth."

The nurse looks down at me with pursed lips. "It's actually Friday, sorry. You've been unconscious for almost twenty-four hours.

I try to sit up. "You can't be serious. I've been out of it for an entire day?"

"Yes. Your husband brought you in here after he found you unconscious and bleeding on the ground at the school. Can you tell me what you remember?"

The nurse inspects me while I shift my eyes from her to Corey, unsure what to answer. She checks my blood pressure and asks me again what I recall.

What the hell am I supposed to say in front of Corey when I'm certain he was the one who hit me over the head?

"I'm not sure what happened," I say, sounding less than convincing.

The nurse must recognize the concern and reservation I have, talking about what's happened to me. Does she see me pleading with her to get Corey out of the room?

"Mr. Grayson," the nurse says, turning to Corey. "Why don't you wait outside for a minute. I need to chat with your wife, if that's okay?"

"I'm not going anywhere," Corey says. "Someone's attacked her. Why else would she have taken a blow so hard to the back of the head that it's left her unconscious for a day?"

"Please, Mr. Grayson. I must speak with Katherine alone for a moment to sort this out."

"Why alone? Anything you have to talk about you can say in front of me."

The nurse presses a button on the wall. "I'm sure that's true, but when a patient comes in under these circumstances, we are required to hear what they have to say in private. It is standard protocol."

"I don't give a damn what you're supposed to do. I told you, I'm not going anywhere until I know she is safe."

Judy smiles at Corey with a weak mouth as her eyes shift left and right. She doesn't answer him until a few more nurses move into the space. One of them matches Corey's height and build.

"What's this?"

"Please, Mr. Grayson. Step out of the room for a minute."

Corey stands from his chair and leans forward. "Wait, you can't seriously think I did this to her."

"We're not accusing you of anything, Mr. Grayson. Again we're simply trying to obtain the facts from your wife without any outside influence."

Corey flashes me a look. "I didn't do this to you," he says, shaking his head. "Don't let them convince you of anything. I would never do something like this. Do you understand me?"

"Mr. Grayson," one of the other nurses says. "This way, please. Don't make us call security."

Corey's eyes linger on me. After too long a time, they shift to the nurse. "Fine."

The two extra nurses guide Corey out and away, closing the door behind them. I soon realize my bed is the only one in the room. Was I put in here intentionally? Did the staff know at some point that they would have to question me?

Judy refocuses on me. "I'm sorry we had to do that, but you and I need to speak alone."

I nod faster than is normal as I feel a layer of sweat sweep across my forehead. Am I really in a hospital bed? Am I really about to say what I know to be true beyond any doubt?

"Katherine? Are you okay? Try to remember to breathe. And please, take your time answering my questions."

I nod again, knowing Corey can't hear me, but it's hard not to imagine him listening in to this conversation.

"Tell me what you think has happened."

I close my eyes, not wanting to say what my mind is shouting at me.

"It's okay," Judy says as she places a hand over mine on the bed. "Take as long as you need."

"I don't even know where to begin, but I suspect my husband has attacked me."

Judy subtly shakes her head. She has probably heard this a million times before but still has to show the same level of empathy. "What makes you think your husband has attacked you?"

I feel the room closing in on me from all sides as my breathing becomes more and more rapid by the second. "We've been fighting a lot lately. Corey thinks I cheated on him a few days ago, but I swear I didn't. We spent the night apart to cool off after a huge fight. In the morning, at the school where we teach, he sent me a text asking to meet up before our classes started. He wanted to talk to me alone in private behind the school's old sports shed. I figured this was so no one would hear us arguing. The next thing I realized something had struck my skull so hard that I barely remember hitting the ground."

Judy shakes her head again. "Did you see your attacker?"

"No. I mean, I saw Corey stand over me moments before I fell unconscious. It had to have been him. No one else knew I was there."

"I see," she says.

"Please don't let him back in here. I'm so scared he'll find out what I know."

"It's okay, Katherine. One of the other nurses is calling the police to let them take over from here. Your husband won't be allowed into the room."

"Thank you. I'm sorry for causing all of this fuss."

"Don't apologize at all. You have nothing to be apologetic for."

I show my understanding while attempting to comprehend what is happening. I know Corey has done this to me, but what has brought him to this moment? Am I really that horrible a wife that he felt the need to beat me over the head? Was he trying to kill me, or send me a message?

The nurse continues checking over me as I sob.

"Hey, hey. Everything will be okay. The police are on their way. You're safe now, and no one can lay another hand on you."

She must think Corey beats me, that I'm nothing but a downtrodden victim who's been hospitalized by her husband's actions. I never expected I'd be in this situation, ever. It seems impossible to me that I would be with someone who I believed had it in them to do such a thing to me. Not even Peter would stoop this low.

The door to my room opens. I feel every one of my muscles tense as I look up to catch a nurse standing in the doorway.

"It's okay, Katherine," the nurse says. "It's just your friend coming in. She's been waiting for a long time to see you."

Annette walks in with both hands interlaced, her brows twisted in with concern.

"Hi, Kat," Annette says.

58

I leave the hospital, resisting an intense urge to laugh. Katherine believes beyond any doubt that Corey has attacked her. Soon, the police will arrive to take her statement. The responding officers will then ask Corey to come down to the station for questioning. He'll have no choice but to oblige them, but the detectives will struggle to prove he had anything to do with the assault.

Katherine has no proof of her attacker. From our conversation, she is assuming it was Corey. She has no idea he has a solid alibi to save him from arrest, thanks to me.

Corey won't ever find out that I sent the message from his phone using the spyware I installed on the device. The second Katherine read the text from Corey and responded to it, I deleted the message from his cell using the spyware. I did the same on Katherine's phone after I struck her over the head with a metal pole I found lying around.

After leaving Katherine unconscious, I rushed over to the office while calling Corey's cell to ask him to meet me in the faculty lounge. I told Corey some lie about Barry needing to speak to him urgently which got him there in a hurry. I couldn't risk him not coming because of our discussion from earlier that morning.

Over half a dozen staff members saw Corey in the busy break room. I kept him waiting there long enough for people to see us chatting away after. I then apologized for what had happened in his classroom between us and asked if he'd spoken with Katherine yet.

"Are you positive you want to hear this?"

"I am. What you said made sense before. Plus, I need to make sure that everything is okay between you and Katherine."

"I'm not sure. I guess I was hoping to speak with Kat before school started, but there wasn't enough time to go over it all. We'll hash it out tonight."

"That's understandable. You guys have a lot to talk about."

"We do. I hope we can push through this, provided I'm not too late."

"I know Kat. I'm sure she will also want to start fresh and move forward."

"We'll see, I guess... So, Barry wants to see me?"

"Yes. He did, but he had to go, sorry. I'll find out what he wanted and let you know."

"Thanks, Annette."

After smoothing things over with Corey, one of Katherine's students entered the office with his mom. I rushed to my work-station and feigned confusion, pretending I didn't know why Katherine wasn't in her classroom. I called Corey and told him what was going on, suggesting he check his cell for any texts from Kat. He apparently found a voicemail from Kat telling him she was waiting to meet up behind the old sports shed.

By now the police will have taken Corey aside and asked him some impossible questions. I never wanted to put him through this kind of stress, but I couldn't attack Katherine without first showing him how unhinged his spouse had become.

Once the authorities see Corey's cell and realize that everything Katherine has told them doesn't add up, he will be free to go. No doubt he'll tell them the truth about their recent arguments and marital troubles, only adding to the fact that his wife's mental health is questionable at best.

After it all comes out, Corey will recognize that Katherine isn't worth fighting for. And she will think her husband is trying to kill her. If Katherine plays her part well and doesn't interfere with Corey and I being together, then I won't have to take this to the final level. But if she allows her stubbornness to keep their pointless marriage afloat, God help me I will have no choice but to act accordingly.

I climb into my car, satisfied that I'd bounced back after such an intense holdup with Corey this morning. Part of me wanted to give up, but I can't quit on him. Not now or ever.

He will be mine no matter what.

59

KATHERINE

Corey moved out. I didn't give him a choice. Just because he has the police fooled doesn't mean I'm falling for his lies anymore. I still don't know how this all happened. Maybe my memory is a little hazy and messed up after the attack, but I know it was him who did this to me.

I swear to God he sent me a text demanding to meet up behind the sports shed. Surely my mind didn't dream that up post-concussion. If it has, then I don't know what is real and what is not.

I'm at home with Ava, cuddling her on the sofa. We're watching one of her favorite shows, but I'm taking next to little notice of anything that's happening on the screen. All I can think about is Corey. It's been almost a week without a word between us. How can I speak to the man who harmed me? He was meant to protect me, but instead he allowed his anger to come close to ending my life. I am so afraid, yet my heart also feels broken.

How can you both love and fear a man at the same time?

Annette has been amazing throughout this last week, making sure that I feel safe at all times. I swear some days I'm the worst friend in the world. Everything always seems to be about me and my dramas. I never make the effort to ask how things are going in her life. It's so hard to when Corey's chaos envelops my every thought.

Annette isn't here at the moment, meaning I am quietly terrified for both Ava and me. So much so that I had to take out a restraining order against Corey to feel any semblance of security.

"Mommy? Where's Corey?"

Ava has asked me this question so many times that I'm running out of excuses to tell her. "He had to go away, sweetie. Remember?"

"I know that, but where's he gone?"

How am I supposed to answer that? This poor girl hasn't had a father her whole life and now I've had no choice but to send off the one man she trusted. I guess I trusted him too and never thought he would lay so much as a finger on me. I was wrong.

Darkness sweeps in and casts strong shadows outside. Ava doesn't have to go to bed for another hour. We had dinner earlier, not needing to wait around for Corey to come home. Despite Ava's bedtime being a short while off, I will no doubt keep her awake until she begs for sleep. I can't stand to be alone right now.

I know that the restraining order means Corey can't touch me, but I still don't feel safe, especially at night. The slightest noise outside makes me jump off the sofa and into a state of panic. So many times now, I've heard a tiny disturbance in the street that sends me charging to the nearest window only to find nothing but the trees swaying in the wind. I don't know how much more of this I can stand.

It gets to nine thirty when Ava finally asks me to take her to bed. With all the resistance and bribery I can come up with, I give in to her request and slowly carry her down the hallway. I drag out the process as far as possible — something I will pay for in the morning when Ava is too tired to function.

I contemplate going to sleep myself when I see the door to my bedroom, but I know what is waiting for me in that room: fear and loneliness. I loathe sleeping in such a huge bed by myself. And I also hate trying to fall asleep all the while knowing that my husband attacked me and put me in hospital. It's not the best mix.

After a few hours of pointless TV watching, I send Annette a late-night message, instantly feeling like the world's worst friend if I'm waking her. She told me to call or text any time day or night, but I realize that's something people respond with when they are friends with someone as frustrating as me.

Annette messages me back straight away and asks if I want her to come around for a few hours despite both of us having to work in the morning. I accept her offer without a moment's hesitation. I know I should say no and that I'll be okay, but we both recognize that isn't the case and won't be for a long time.

Waiting for Annette to make the short trip over to my place, I wonder what's keeping her up this late? She's normally in bed early compared to me. One of my bad habits has always been staying up too long on a work night. It's half the reason I'm so unorganized to get Ava and myself off to school each day. But this is different. Things have changed in such a crazy way that I don't know what to think anymore about anything.

Why has my life fallen apart?

60

ANNETTE

What a week it's been. Corey and Katherine are no longer living together, and I can't see them ever making things work again. It's almost too good to be true.

No one in their right mind believes Corey attacked his wife. I've listened in to the rumors and whispers that have floated around the school. None of them suspect Corey of any wrongdoing. Instead, they all think Katherine has lost it.

I couldn't have asked for things to have worked out any better than this. If everything continues the way it has, then I won't need to take this endeavor any further than it's already pushed me. I can go through with my original idea where Corey and I run away from this dump of a town forever.

I know that once Corey and I reunite, he will leave Battery Beach if I ask him to. He hasn't lived here long enough to allow the town's hooks to sink into his brain. I've let this place hold me back all along.

It's kind of ironic. All these years, I resented Katherine for abandoning me when she left town to go to college and travel around the world. But now I see the true wisdom in the idea. Part of me wonders what things could have been like if I had gone with her, but I knew back then that I could never have discarded the people I loved to pursue my own selfish desires. Now, there's only one person I love.

It's one in the morning, and I am leaving Katherine's house to travel home and get some sleep before work starts. I hate every minute I'm forced to spend with her. It's bad enough getting her moronic texts at random times of the day. But having no choice but to rush to her place so late at night is driving me to my limit.

"Thank you so much for seeing me," Katherine said when I came through the front door a few hours ago. She made it sound like I was her therapist squeezing her in for an emergency appointment. I might as well have been one, given the amount of crap I've had to listen to over the last week. It's hard to pretend you care about a person's problems when you are causing them.

"Any time. You know I'm here for you." I struggle not to laugh, hearing the lies as they spill out of my mouth.

"I'm so sorry to keep annoying you so much, it's just I can't sleep anymore. And I realize that Corey wouldn't dare violate the restraining order I've had put against him, but it doesn't stop my crazy brain from going around in circles."

Katherine holds on to this whole restraining order thing like it'll last forever. I doubt she realizes that within a few weeks the police will drop it when they determine that Corey has done nothing wrong. They never made him leave his house; he volunteered to.

Who could blame him?

Katherine had become a special kind of intolerable. There was a jittering in her eyes as she constantly looked left and right and over each shoulder. I've got her on edge.

I spent the next three hours listening to Katherine drone on and on about Corey and everything that led up to her having no choice but to kick him out of his own home.

I wanted to scream at her. I wanted to shout how she should have been kicked out to the streets like a dog that'd stolen its master's dinner. But I knew I couldn't. Soon Katherine's rambling wouldn't matter. Soon I'll be leaving this place with the man of my dreams.

"Thank you again for listening to me," Katherine said when she finally let me leave.

"Anytime," I replied. That was when I noticed a look in Katherine's eyes, one that told me she had a question to ask. "What is it?"

"I know I shouldn't be bothering you like this, but I have a huge favor to ask."

My head tilted a little. "Yes?"

Katherine let out a quick sigh. "Is there any chance Ava and I can come stay with you next week?"

"At my house? For the whole week?"

"Yes. I need to get away from this place. All of Corey's stuff is still here and I can't stop thinking about him. I figure being apart from that mess might help me process and deal with what is going on."

I wanted to say that she was lying, that she only needed to use my house to feel safe, but again I resisted saying what I truly felt. "That sounds like a wonderful idea, Kat," I said, all the while dreading the plan.

"Thank you, thank you, thank you. I promise we won't get in your way. I'll give you some money for any food we eat and some more for the utilities."

"Unnecessary," I said, playing my part as the loyal friend.

"You're too good to Ava and me."

"Just trying to help. I know this is a rough time for you both."

Katherine sobbed as she wrapped her arms around me. She gripped me tighter than expected. So much so I had to break her hold.

"Sorry," Katherine said.

"It's okay." I tried to leave by heading to my car, but she wasn't done.

"I don't suppose Ava and I could come around as early as this Saturday?"

Frozen in the driveway, I had my back to Katherine. If she could have seen my face at that moment, she would have known instantly the disdain I felt toward her. It was bad enough having her and her stupid kid at my house during the week. Now I would lose my damn weekend.

I turned to Katherine and smiled. "Sounds like a plan."

She let me go after thanking me again for the hundredth time.

Now that I have finally escaped from Katherine for the night, I feel exhausted. Spending the next week with her will be painful. So much so, that I may have to do everything I can to drive her back to her home. Besides, I won't be hanging around my house. I've got another friend to help. One who is more deserving of my attention.

61

School has been difficult. Every teacher I walk past has this look in their eyes that tells me what they truly think. No one believes Corey attacked me or that he is capable of such an act, so I have to continue on with my life knowing what I know. Everyone around me assumes the worst while I have to swallow my fears and teach my class in the same place I got ambushed.

To say I'm on edge is an understatement. Sure, it would be insane for Corey to attack me again in the school, but he's done it before and gotten away with it. Every corner I walk around feels like it could be my last.

The kids have noticed my weakness and are naturally acting out in response to my waning authority. With each hour that passes, they are seeing me for the washed-up excuse of a teacher that I have become. I don't know what I can do to make myself concentrate and focus on my job.

Barry tried to send me away on leave, but I can't be at home, especially with Ava still needing to go to school each day. I could have used the time off to better recover, but I insisted on coming back after only a few days. So much so that I had to beg a doctor to sign off on the idea.

It's early, and I'm late again. A parent is waiting outside my classroom with their kid. I should have been in my room already with the door unlocked to allow kids to come in but trying to arrive here on time has become an even harder task than before. When I wake up in the morning, I've usually been asleep for less than three hours and feel like death. I struggle to get Ava and myself into my car now that it's been fixed and on our way to school.

"Mrs. Grayson," the parent calls to me as I unlock the door. Hearing my new surname stops me. It sounds like a rusty blade being dragged over a steel pole and makes me shudder. I don't even know how or what I'm supposed to do to have my name changed back to Armstrong.

"How can I help you?" I ask the parent, seeing that look of reservation in her eyes.

"I understand things have been rough for you lately, but Jackson's had no homework all week. Usually by now you've given the class some."

"I'm sorry," I say, bringing my hand over my face as I shake my head. "I guess I've forgotten all about it. I'll send some home today."

"Thank you," Mrs. Wilson says, "but I feel it would be best if you take some time off and let another teacher come in."

"Excuse me? Do you have any idea what you're asking of me?"

"Yes, I do. Clearly you are going through something at the moment and need to think of the kids first."

"I am thinking of the children by coming here. Having their usual teacher disappear doesn't help in any way."

"It does when their regular teacher isn't coping."

I open my mouth to retort, but I realize I'm getting into an argument with a parent. That never bodes well for anyone. Focusing all my ability to show confidence, I clear my throat and respond. "If you have anything you wish to discuss, we can meet with the principal and go over your concerns."

I turn back to the door and open the classroom as more parents and students arrive. I don't have the time or the energy to deal with this kind of hell first thing. These people know someone attacked me and put me in hospital. They're also aware that I think my husband is responsible, yet they still treat me this way.

Before I take three steps into my classroom, Barry calls. "Mrs. Grayson. Do you have a minute?"

"No, sorry," I say as I face him. "I've just opened my room."

"That's okay. I'm sending someone down to watch the class for a moment. We really need to talk."

I want to run and scream, not caring where I go. As long as it's away from here. Barry leaves me with little choice but to comply in front of all the parents that have lined up with their children behind me. "Okay then."

"Thank you, Katherine," he says as one of the regular substitute teachers arrives. They have all the gear with them as if they are planning on coming into my room for the day. Barry doesn't want to talk; he's sending me home.

"What's this?" I blurt at him before we're clear of the parents.

Barry ushers me to follow and sighs. "You know what this is."

"No, I don't. So why don't you tell me what this is all about."

"Not here, Katherine."

"Yes here, Barry. Whatever you have to say get it out already. I've got a class to teach."

"I'm afraid you don't. I'm sending you home for the next few weeks until you feel that you are up to the job."

I cross my arms over my chest. "Why?" Every parent and student watches our exchange despite the substitute teacher's best efforts.

"To be frank, your job performance has taken a massive

tumble. You've only been back for a few days, but I have nothing but complaints spilling into my office."

"What the hell are you talking about?" I know I've been off my game a little, but considering everything that's happened, I highly doubt many people have called up to complain about me.

Barry guides me away from the gawking crowd for a minute until we're alone. "Look, Katherine, I've had multiple emails sent from parents complaining about you and your conduct in the classroom. They all know about the attack. And because of the incident, there's a strong consideration whether you are fit for duty."

"I am, dammit. I might have made a few understandable mistakes here and there, but you're acting like I'm a danger to the children. I'm not and never will be."

"No one is saying that you're a danger to the children, okay? The concern here is your mental state and if you can function at an acceptable level to teach and care for your class. The welfare of the kids must come first."

I stumble backward until I feel something solid bump into my back. "Are you firing me?" I stammer.

Barry shakes his head but says nothing to confirm that he's not thinking about it. I know what he's like. At the first sign of trouble with a teacher he will do anything he can to make them want to resign or move on. He can't seem to handle things when teachers are the ones causing him grief. If I were a parent, he'd bend over backwards to accommodate me.

"Come along, Katherine. We can talk more about this in my office."

My eyebrows narrow in. "No. I'm going home. You've already decided everything. There's nothing left to discuss." I walk away from Barry and head toward the parking lot. He doesn't call out to try to stop me. I don't know if I will ever return to this school.

62

ANNETTE

I watch Katherine leave school from the front of the office through the glass of the door. Apparently, Barry has acted faster than I expected he would in response to the fake complaints I sent him. I marked them all as anonymous to make it difficult to follow up each complaint on an individual level. Combined with three real criticisms from the usual whining parents it must have made the situation impossible to ignore.

A small snicker escapes my lips as I watch Katherine climb into her car and slam the door. Any minute now my cell will ring with her on the other end ready to moan. But I won't answer my phone if it rings. Not today. I'm too busy to help her out and be the one she dumps all of her emotional trash onto. She can wait until I get home.

Barry is so scared of the parents and their ability to have him fired. He acts like they're all his collective boss some days. The emails he received came via the school app that allows parents, teachers, and the admin staff to communicate school-related issues between one another. I sent the complaints at different times using various levels of wording via the anonymous feed-back forms each classroom has associated with it.

With the three real complaints backing up the fake ones, Barry would have freaked out and jumped into action to have Katherine removed from the classroom as quickly as possible. He can't fire her, though. At least not yet. There's a long-winded process behind that, requiring actual proof that Katherine can no longer teach at the school. All the spineless administrator can do at the moment is force her to take leave and pray the situation resolves itself.

My cell buzzes in my pocket. It's Katherine sending me a lengthy text about what's happened. She's still in the parking lot, sitting in her car, from what I can tell. The message is littered with spelling mistakes and words jammed together. Normally she sends me proofread texts as if it matters to the world that her boring communications use the correct spelling and grammar. She's probably crying over her cell letting her tears splash on the screen. I can only hope.

At the end of the message, Katherine has asked me to pick up Ava after school. She's already informed the teachers there that either me or Katherine will come to collect her at four. Reluctant to reply, I have no choice but to say yes. The world needs to see what a great friend I am for the moment. I have to appear happy to offer her help and drive Ava home to my place like a mindless chauffeur.

I mutter away to myself all day, annoyed that I have to collect Ava when Katherine could easily make the trip back to school herself. She thanked me again and again and explained how she was too embarrassed to show her face at school after Barry kicked her out. I pretended to care as Katherine eventually requested the inevitable. By the end of the school day, I've apparently agreed to drive Ava to and from school for the rest of the week while Katherine lays around my house feeling sorry for herself.

I guess I'll have to make the best of the situation and ensure Katherine has a pleasant stay.

63

After three days of being away from the school on leave, I'm already bored out of my mind. I feel bad for asking Annette to drive Ava to kindergarten and back each day, but I can't face the judgmental faces of the parents and teachers. At least not until I've had enough time to get used to the fact that I will now have a permanent stain on my teaching record.

I never once contemplated that my job would be in jeopardy after I survived the hard years spent with Peter. My career became my focus outside of Ava. I rarely worried about dating and only ever went out with Annette occasionally to a bar for the night, avoiding drinking more than a few glasses of wine. Look at me now.

Not only have I lost what I thought was an amazing relationship with Corey, but I'm facing the prospect of losing my career. I could have obliterated all of my hard work in a short amount of time because I married a psycho. How did I let myself fall into the arms of another guy like Peter? One who is worse than my terrible ex? I don't think I will ever find a good person.

Maybe the universe is proving to tell me something. Maybe all this time I shouldn't have been worried about finding some man to save me from the world when I should have been the one to do so. I allowed myself to become dependent on Corey in as little a time as possible. That's why I should never have said yes when he casually sprung a proposal on me. I wasn't ready for such a commitment. And apparently, he regretted the decision as well.

I still find it hard to fathom that Corey attacked me the way he did. Did he plan it out entirely, or was he coming to yell at me and let his anger take over? I'll never know as there's no chance in hell I will ever speak to him again, especially given the impact of his actions.

Annette's home is large. She inherited the two-level house from her aunt a few years ago that is reasonably close to the water in Battery Beach. I would kill to have this place compared to the small rental I live in now. That's not to say that this house is perfect. Someone built it in the fifties meaning it's long overdue for a renovation. It's rather big for one person to exist in. I'm always surprised Annette doesn't rent out a few rooms for extra cash. But then again, she loves her privacy.

Bored, I walk around the house, looking for something to do. I don't know what I'm hoping to find as I amble from room to room absently exploring the layout. I discover the door to the basement, and try the handle. It's locked, giving me some relief that Ava won't accidentally find her way in there and trip down the steps.

There is still too long to go before Ava and Annette get home to help relieve this crippling tedium that is my forced leave. I feel like I should do something constructive to pass the time, but my mind is all over the place at the moment.

One minute, I want to forgive Corey and take him back. The next, I wish someone would send him to prison for what he did and hope that he gets hurts on the inside. I go around in circles throughout the day.

Finally, I settle onto Annette's comfy sofa and watch a movie. I need to escape for a few hours so I put on a comedy that hopefully won't remind me of anything to do with Corey.

About twenty minutes into the film, I hear a heavy bump outside. "What the...?" I mutter. I pause the film and try to pinpoint where I thought the noise came from. It's almost impossible with the ambient ocean waves crashing in the distance, so I return to watching the comedy.

A minute later, the same loud bang interrupts me. This time I locate the source of the disturbance. It sounds like someone had hit the back door of Annette's house with a brick, given how heavy it was. I have no choice but to pause the film again and see what's going on.

"Is anyone there?" I call out as I shuffle toward the back door. The place seems to have fallen quiet during my approach to investigate the sounds ruining my escapism. When I reach the rear entry to the home, I lean out my hand to unlock the deadbolt using the key that lives in the lock. I try turning it left then right but receive a lot of resistance. Annette didn't really give me much of a tour of the place and only showed Ava and me the basics.

Pressing my body into the door, I feel the key turn away from the frame until it unlocks with a loud crack. "Ouch," I let out as a sharp pain throbs in my thumb and index finger. I shake my fingers to ease the discomfort as best I can and grab the doorknob with my other hand.

Standing alone at Annette's back door to her aging home, I draw in a breath through my nose and let it slowly out of my mouth to give myself the courage to focus. It shouldn't take this much effort to open a simple door, but I guess I'm more scared of what I might find than I realize.

I yank the door open, pulling it toward me and shift to the side to see Annette's empty backyard greet me. "Hello?" I call out. "Is anyone there?"

Nothing but a gentle breeze responds.

Shaking my head, I decide to close the door and deadbolt the lock. I return to the living room, chuckling to myself for letting a few noises scare me.

Minutes later, I'm back into the film and have lost my thoughts in the simple plot, enjoying the laughs as they come. At least I know I can still stand to watch such a movie. My depressing life hasn't ruined my sense of humor yet.

After ten minutes, I grab myself a glass of juice from the kitchen and rush to the paused movie. The main character is frozen on screen, pulling an awkward face as I sit down. I take a big gulp of the liquid right as the large TV switches off.

"What did I do?" I ask myself.

I hit buttons on the remote and cuss under my breath. I was enjoying the film and now the damn TV is broken. How am I going to explain this to Annette? Frustrated, I go to leave the room to look for something else to do when I realize the floor lamp I had on beside me is also off.

Creeping up to the dusty brass pole, I hit the switch with my foot a few times. The power to the house must be off. "That's just gr—"

The same loud bang smashes harder than before on the rear door. I stumble back and away from the direction of the thump and realize I'm not alone. I check the time on my cell and know that Ava and Annette won't be home for another hour and a half. Is someone trying to break in?

I look for something I can use to defend myself with and find nothing in the living room worth a damn. Fearing the worst, I charge for the kitchen to grab a sharp knife. The biggest one slides out of its holder into my hands at the same moment as a realization hits my brain.

This is the exact time during the week when Corey has no students in his classroom.

64

I don't know what to do. The heavy pounding on the rear door continues as I remain in the same place on the hardwood flooring of Annette's house. It has to be Corey out there coming to follow up his attack on me while I'm all alone. I try to yell to ward off the threat, but my voice only comes out as a trembling squeak.

My body shuts down. I close my eyes, trying to make him go away. Then the noise stops.

I exhale my shaky breath and stare at the back door from a safe distance. "Hello?" I cry out too softly. No one responds. The large kitchen knife in my hands shudders so much I'm convinced I might drop it. I have to pull myself together and do something, anything to get out of here before it's too late. God knows I won't be able to use the blade in my hand to defend myself.

"Hello?" I call out again. Still, I get nothing in return. All I hear are the birds happily chirping as if there isn't a murderous psychopath lurking around the backyard of Annette's house. If only I could fly away at a moment's notice.

. . .

After more time than I am proud to admit passes by, I will my legs to function. They have to pull me toward my phone so I can call for help. But I can't seem to hold my attention on anything other than the back door. All my mind sees is Corey bursting through any second to charge at me. My head throbs.

Waking from my crippling fear, I rush to my cell in the living room and attempt to scoop it up with sweaty hands. I take far too many attempts to unlock the damn thing with my thumbprint, so I'm forced to punch in the passcode instead before the device locks me out.

Once I get into my cell, I stare at the home screen unsure who I should call. I want to get the police out here more than anything else, but I also don't want them rushing out only to find nobody. The limited number of officers in this region have already marked me down as a liar, given the lack of evidence I had to prove I knew my attacker. They still think I tripped over backward and struck my head on a rock, but there was nothing like that at the scene.

I could call Annette to rush home and do a sweep of the perimeter to scare Corey off but then I'd be putting her in danger. I don't want to be responsible for her falling into harm's way, so I get my answer.

My call to the police is taking longer than it should. The operator asks me too many questions. If Corey finds an entry into the house, I'll be dead before help can arrive. "Please. I need you to send some officers right now. Someone is outside about to break in. If that happens..." My voice trails off. I can't finish the thought out loud without a lump in my throat forming.

"Take it easy, ma'am. Two police officers are on their way to your location as we speak. Stay on the line with me and remember to breathe."

"Okay. I will," I say, feeling some relief slow my increasing heart rate.

"Now, what I need you to do is find somewhere safe to hide. Can you think of anywhere in your friend's home that could be a good option?"

My head spins around with thought. If only I could get into the basement, I could probably hide myself well and barricade the door, turning the space into a makeshift panic room. Why did Annette have to lock it?

"Ma'am?"

"Um, I'm trying to think of something."

"Can I suggest the bathroom? Perhaps one upstairs."

"Okay," I say as I slowly head for the stairs in the next room. The knife leads the way, extended out to make myself look as imposing as my cowering body will allow. I don't know why I'm expecting Corey to jump out, but every wall I can't see behind only serves to frighten the hell out of me.

"When you get into the bathroom, I suggest you lock or block the door as best you can and then lay down and hide inside the bathtub. Can you do that for me?"

"I'll try," I reply as I reach the bottom of the stairwell. My eyes run up the length of the wooden steps and see the darkened landing. Not much light reaches the top floor hallway based on the house's design.

One creaking step at a time, I ascend while checking over my shoulder for anyone silently following me. I know such a thing would be impossible in this old house, given that every square inch of the floor makes a noise when you walk over it. Still, I need to check.

"Are you there yet, ma'am?"

"Almost," I whisper. I still have to travel another dozen or so feet at the top of the stairs before I can make it to the bathroom.

As I reach the second floor, I hear the thump again on the lower level. "He's back," I half shout into my cell while my legs lock in place.

"Calm down, ma'am. Everything will be okay. I need you to find the bathroom like we discussed and quickly and quietly make the room secure."

"I... I can do that. I have to." The cell falls away from my face for a moment as I try to slow down my breathing. I can't let this crippling panic take over my system. Not yet.

"Ma'am?" the operator's voice calls out. "Are you there? Hello?"

"I'm here," I respond as I move toward the bathroom. My grip on the knife tightens so much my knuckles turn white. When I get to the bathroom door, I hear shouting coming from downstairs. "He's yelling out to me," I whisper into my phone.

"Ignore that. Focus on what needs doing."

A louder bang echoes through the lower floor and reaches my ears, reverberating throughout the house. I shut my eyes, squeezing them tight to block out the terror charging for me from below. But I can't concentrate. All I can see is Corey's damning face. Why does he hate me so much? How could he have hurt me the way he has?

"Ma'am?" the operator shouts.

"I'm here."

"That's good. Have you barricaded the bathroom?"

I move into the tiled room and shut the door gently. The large knife in my hand finds its way on top of the vanity. I search for a means to stop Corey from charging in here if he breaks into Annette's house.

"There's nothing I can use to barricade myself in," I say, realizing the consequences of my discovery.

"Does the door have a lock?"

I check three times and only find an old handle and a keyhole. "I'd need the key, and it's not here."

"That's okay," the operator says as if none of this is a problem. The voice shouts out again. I can't understand the words from up here, but I know it's the deep rumblings of an angry man. More thumping follows. "He's getting madder. He's going to find me."

"We won't let that happen, ma'am. Search around and go through the cupboards. There has to be something you can use to block up the door."

"Okay, okay. I'll try again." I place my cell down and open the vanity. Nothing jumps out at me. I look in the bathtub and shower combo. It's empty. There's no magical device that will prevent a furious man from plowing through the bathroom door. "There's nothing here," I yell out to myself as the noise below continues.

"Ma'am?" the operator calls through my cell. I don't have the courage to tell her I've come up empty or that I'm ready to give in. But then I see the answer before me, sitting there all along.

I grab my phone. "It's okay. I found something."

"How was she today?" I ask Ava's teacher as I pick her up. "Fantastic. She had an incredible day."

"That's wonderful," I reply as I stroke Ava's head and give her a smile. "Your mommy will be so pleased to hear. Now what do we say to Mrs. Roberts?"

"Thank you," Ava says as she wraps her arms around her teacher.

"You're most welcome, Ava."

"Come along, honey," I say, offering Ava my hand. "We need to go home and relax."

"Can I play iPad?"

Ava had been using my iPad like it's a drug giving her less and less of a high with each session. Katherine has an older clunky model at her house, so it's no surprise that Ava has thrown herself into mine the way she has. The best part for me is how the device keeps the kid busy. It's less time I have to waste interacting with her.

"We'll see. Depends what Mommy says, okay?"

Half defeated, Ava's shoulders drop along with her smile. "That means no, doesn't it?"

"No, it means we'll see, okay?"

Ava takes her eyes off me as we walk to the parking lot. Katherine tries to limit how much time Ava spends on the iPad, but with everything that's been going on, Katherine's too distracted to care.

The drive home is as boring as always until we reach my house. "What's all this?" I call out.

"Auntie Annette?" Ava asks me in the rearview mirror.

We both stare out at a police car parked in the driveway with its lights on. "I don't know. I think we need to give your mommy a call, though."

Snatching my cell out from my handbag, I dial Katherine and listen as my call goes to voicemail. "Hello, Kat. It's Annette. Is everything okay? I'm outside my house with Ava and there's a police car sitting here. Talk to you soon."

I hang up and watch as Ava's eyes bulge in the mirror. "Is Mommy okay?"

"I'm sure she is, but I think we should see what's going on first."

Ava nods sharply. I watch her eyes jump from one spot to the next as she attempts to understand the situation.

I turn around to Ava and grab her focus. "I need to have a look inside. Can you stay in the car for me?"

"Will you lock the doors?" Ava asks.

"Of course. Now don't stress. I'll be back in a minute."

Ava nods again with her mouth open, not removing her eyes from the flashing lights.

I exit my sedan and lock the doors as promised. Taking things slowly, I approach my front door with caution. "Interest-ing," I mutter when I find the entrance ajar. The last thing I want to do is walk into the middle of a few stressed-out police officers, so I knock on my own door. "Hello?"

Silence.

I poke my head inside and put on a face that registers shock. If Katherine or the police see me, I need them to think I'm unaware of what has happened. To be honest, I didn't expect Katherine to call the cops when I bashed on the back door a few hours ago. She really believes it was Corey who attacked her. I guess timing this piece of psychological drama with his student-free time did the trick.

"Annette?" Katherine calls from upstairs. I can hear terror in her struggling voice. I don't doubt she'll attempt to join the dots and blame Corey for the disturbance. Again, though, he has the perfect alibi. I made sure Barry dropped in to check on him during his student-free time to see how things were going. He loved my idea and had an in-depth conversation with Corey while I was out terrorizing Katherine.

A male and a female police officer walk down the stairs ahead of Katherine. They each have a glazed-over look in their eyes like they've had to listen to her life story. If Katherine called them not long after I started the banging, then they must have been chatting to her for a while.

"Annette!" Katherine calls to me as she rushes through the officers down the stairs. She runs with open arms and wraps herself around me. "I'm so glad you're home. He tried to get to me while I was alone. He tried to break in."

"Break in? Who?"

Through a mess of tears, Katherine replies. "Corey. He knew I was by myself and came here when he had no kids to teach so no one would suspect a thing."

"Are you sure?"

Katherine confirms what she believes while twitching as if she is unable to contain her emotions.

"Did you see him?"

She shakes her head too far left and right like a child trying to avoid getting into trouble with their parents. It's like staring into Ava's eyes for a moment. "No, but I heard him yelling out as he tried to break the back door."

"Ma'am," says one officer to me, stepping forward. Her fists cling to the utility belt at her sides. "As I said to Mrs. Grayson before, that yelling she picked up on was my colleague here calling out."

"I know what I heard," Katherine snaps over her shoulder at the officer. The policewoman throws her hands up in defeat and turns away from us, muttering to her partner.

I contain the smile begging to crack through as I witness Katherine's rapid descent into madness take shape. Wait until she finds out that Corey was in a room with the school's principal during the break-in attempt.

Katherine grabs my arms. "Hang on. Where's Ava? Why isn't she with you?"

"It's okay. She's safe in my car out front. I locked the doors and the child lock is also engaged. She's perfectly fine. We'll go grab her in a moment."

Katherine exhales slowly as she releases me. "Thank you. If anything ever happened to her, I don't know what I'd do."

"Nothing will ever happen to her," I reply.

"Okay. You're right. She's safe. She'll always be safe."

"Ma'am," the male officer says to me, ignoring Katherine's muttering. "Is this your property?"

"Yes. Katherine is staying here for a few weeks because... Well, I'm sure you know why by now."

The officer nods as he chews gum, keeping a stoic look on his face the entire time.

"Why do you ask?" I need to determine if they plan on investigating this at all.

"Primarily to get an understanding of the security setup you have in the home. Do you have any cameras or an alarm system?"

"No. Nothing like that. Just the locks on the doors."

The officer shows no emotional response to my answer. "Can I talk to you privately for a moment?"

I turn to Katherine. "Take my car keys and go see Ava. I'm sure a hug from her will make everything better." I hold up my keys the way I would to an excited puppy.

"Yeah. You're right. Thank you," she says as she takes the mess of keys from my hands.

I wait for Katherine to leave, with the other officer following her close behind. "What did you need to ask me, sir?" I say to her partner.

"This is a little awkward, but your friend here really needs to seek some professional counseling. Maybe a therapist. She seems on edge and frankly paranoid that her husband is out to get her."

"It's okay. I'm aware."

"I'm sure you are, but she doesn't seem to be coping all that well and may be suffering from a form of PTSD."

I resist scoffing at the officer's free diagnosis of Katherine's mental state. "She was attacked, so that makes sense. Can I ask if you are planning on speaking to Corey about any of this?"

"Her husband? Of course. We need to determine his where-abouts during the incident, but I'll bet you a month's pay that he didn't do this."

My heart rate spikes. Is he saying that he thinks someone else was here trying to gain entry to the house? I did my best to sneak out of the school without being seen while Barry distracted Corey.

"No, I won't be surprised if this all turns out to be Mrs.

Grayson's PTSD causing her to hear things that weren't really there."

I breathe a silent sigh of relief at this terrible police officer's assumption and continue to listen to him ramble on and on about his theories that align perfectly with everything I hoped to achieve. Katherine's accusations will fall on deaf ears and only work against her.

"Thank you for your help today. Sorry to bother you," I say to the man as he wraps up and heads for the front door to leave. Katherine carries Ava inside as the officers move toward their patrol car.

"Are you going to arrest Corey now?" Katherine asks.

The female officer sighs as she exchanges a look with her colleague. "He will be questioned, informally."

"Informally? What the hell does that mean? Arrest him, right now. He did this."

"Mrs. Grayson—"

"Don't call me that!" Katherine shouts.

"Try to remain calm. I can assure you we will speak to your husband and inform you if we place him under arrest for any further investigation. Okay?"

"Thank you," I say, interjecting. I wave the two officers off and close the door.

"This is insane," Katherine says as she places Ava down and locks the front door for me. "Corey did this. I know he did."

Katherine continues to mutter and walks away. Apparently, I've broken her in the space of a few hours. Once Corey speaks with the police, he'll forever see Katherine as the crazy person he shouldn't have married. Now all I need to do is to be there for him. It's only a matter of time before we will be together.

I call the local police department for the tenth time, demanding to know when they will arrest Corey. It's been six hours since he tried to break into Annette's house to attack me and they've done nothing.

"Don't you dare put me on hold again," I say to the officer on the other end.

"Ma'am, as I said before, the responding officers spoke to your husband. They accounted his whereabouts for the time that you claimed someone was trying to attack you."

"It wasn't 'someone' trying to attack me. It was Corey. And whatever he's said to your colleagues is a lie. He was here trying to silence me."

"Ma'am, please. We're going around in circles again. I'm sorry this outcome upsets you."

"He had no students in his classroom this afternoon. He left the school, while no one was looking, to assault me again."

"Ma'am, he was with the principal during the same time-frame you claim he was trying to break into your friend's home. Now I'm no detective but that paints a clear picture that your husband is innocent of any—"

I jab my finger at my cell to end the call and throw the damn thing down on Annette's dining table. "He's lying. Corey couldn't have been with Barry." I slam my elbows on the hard surface and wrap my hands around my face.

Annette sits down beside me. "Are you okay?"

I feel tears worm their way through the gaps in my fingers and pull my arms away from my head. "No, I'm not. This is all so crazy. How could Corey have been with Barry?"

Annette flashes me an awkward smile that tells me she knows something I won't be happy to hear.

"Was Corey with Barry?"

"Yes," she says. "They had a long meeting. Just the two of them. Barry wanted to see how everything was going with the promotion and with you."

My mouth falls open. "Barry must be in on it. Maybe they're working together to—"

Annette's hand drops to my wrist. "Come on, Kat. We both know that can't be true."

I shake my head. "It has to be. Otherwise what the hell does this all mean? I didn't imagine the noises."

"No one is saying you did. But maybe the stress you've been experiencing has manifested itself into something strange."

"No, no, no," I say. "That's a load of crap. What I heard today was more than noise. I felt the vibrations through the core of this house. Corey was here to finish what he started. He may have you all fooled, but I won't rest until I see him behind bars or worse."

"Kat, please—"

"No. Forget it. I don't want to hear any more theories or excuses. I know what I know." Feeling a shudder run down my spine, I push myself back and stand, moving away from the dining table and Annette. I shouldn't be getting mad at her, but I can't help the rage flowing through my body.

Frustrated, I walk off before I say something to Annette I'll truly regret, so I drag myself upstairs to the spare room I've been sleeping in these last few days. Ava is already asleep down the hall.

As I am about to give up on this day and go to bed, I hear a car pull up outside the front of Annette's house. A tightness grabs me, compelling me to investigate by looking through the window. Gently, I draw the curtain aside and look down to see a police car.

"What now?" I say out loud, wondering what more the police have to say for themselves. Maybe they didn't enjoy me hanging up before. If only they could appreciate how uptight I'm feeling. Corey attacked me for reasons I can't understand and got away with it. And this afternoon, he came for me again to finish the job.

I let the curtain fall into place and cover the window again. If the police want to talk to me, they can come up here and knock on my door. I refuse to help them after the way they've treated and spoken to me. No one from the department will listen to what I have to say.

Shaking my head, I move over to the queen-sized bed Annette has in this spare room. I fall onto the inviting mattress, forced down by the weight of the world. All I want to do is sleep and not wake until everything in my life is back to the way it should be.

I roll on my side and pull the covers up to my chest. Voices below the flooring of the bedroom mumble away as Annette speaks with the police. She must have invited them inside as if the visit is nothing more than a casual affair. If they didn't want to help me on the phone, then why are they here? I know Corey's already been questioned and deemed to be innocent of any wrongdoing. If they are here to rub that in my face, then I'll make a formal complaint to their bosses.

Multiple footsteps charge their way upstairs toward my bedroom. "Seriously?" I say, throwing my bedding off me. I swing my legs out and sit upright, ready to speak to these people.

A few moments later, the knock comes at my door. With my arms crossed over my chest, I say, "Come in."

The door pushes inward and creaks open to reveal one of the police officers who attended my call from earlier today.

"Katherine? Officer Pauline Jensen here. How are you doing?"

"You know how I'm doing." I can't help the frustration in my voice. "What do you want?"

The officer exhales as her eyes drop to the floor for a few seconds. "I understand you've been through a lot today, but there is someone here who you need to speak with." She glances off to her right side out of view of the room and moves aside.

"Okay," I say, wondering what kind of useless idea they've come up with.

Footsteps clump along the wooden flooring, making the surface creak and groan. Corey steps into the middle of the door frame and looks straight at me. I feel my body lurch back in the bed until I smack hard into the wall.

"What the hell is he doing here?"

W hy is Corey here? He barely said a word to me when he came in with the police officer. I tried to get more than a greeting out of him, but all he would say is that he needed to speak with Katherine urgently.

I stand outside and out of view of my spare bedroom as the police officer and Corey talk to Katherine. My mind runs amok as I try to fathom what this could all be. Do they know it was me who bashed on the back door earlier today to mess with Katherine? They couldn't. And if they knew, why haven't they arrested me?

I just need to remain calm and appear as a supportive friend and nothing more. I'm too close to the finish line to ruin everything I've worked so hard to achieve. Whatever this is, I'm sure it can't be good for Katherine if Corey felt the need to have a police officer accompany him.

"Katherine," Corey says.

"Get him out of here!" Katherine yells. "He's trying to kill me!"

"Katherine. It's okay," Officer Jensen says. "He's not trying to harm you. He's here to help."

I try to move a little closer to the conversation without

drawing attention to myself. My creaking floorboards make the task a difficult one, but I have to know what Corey is doing.

"He has you all fooled!" Katherine yells. "Why don't you believe me when I tell you this man is trying to kill me."

"Katherine, please," Corey says, practically begging. "I would never lay a finger on you. I'm here because I'm worried about you. At first, I was angry with everything you'd done, but now I've realized that you're not acting like yourself. You need help."

"I don't need help. What I need is for you to leave me alone. I'm not falling for any of your charm. No one will believe me until I end up in a body bag."

Corey goes to speak again, but Officer Jensen places an arm on his shoulder and gently pulls him back. She steps forward to take over, out of my range of view. "Katherine. We don't know what happened here today, but we have overwhelming proof that Corey was not behind any of it. The only reason he is here right now is because he is deeply worried about your well-being and mental state."

"There's nothing wrong with my mental state. I know what happened."

Why is Corey concerned about Katherine? I ask myself. Sure, he's a nice guy who cares about people, but how can he care about Katherine after everything that's taken place? What more do I have to do to convince him that they don't belong together?

"Katherine, please listen to me," Corey begs. "You don't sound like the woman I married. You sound like someone who needs help, and I'm here to offer it to you. I'm not going anywhere until you understand that I love you and will do anything to support you through this."

"No," I whisper as I stumble back from the room. This can't be right. This can't be real. Please tell me Corey didn't say that he still loves Katherine. He doesn't mean it. This has to be an act to lock her up in some mental facility.

"I don't understand," Katherine says, her voice cracking. "You attacked me. You came here today to do so again, and now you're claiming you want to help me? This is all a big lie."

"This isn't a lie. When we got married, I made a promise to be there for you no matter what. Now I'm doing just that. I want our life together back on track."

I feel the floor tilt up and force me away from the conversation. My legs weaken as I hold out a shaky hand to grab the balustrade. He still wishes to be with her. He wants everything to return to the way it was. I've failed. It's over. Corey wants his wife back.

What was I thinking? There was a reason he never called me after we kissed. I wasn't good enough for him then, and I'm not now. I've wasted my time chasing after a man who doesn't love me.

"No," I mutter. It can't be true. He loves me. I know it. This is all an act. He's trying to do the right thing because he's the perfect man.

I'm not giving up. I've come too far. Corey needs one final push, and I have no choice but to make that happen.

68

I argued as hard as I could with Corey and Officer Jensen until I had no choice but to instruct them to leave. I could tell they wanted to haul me away and throw me into some psych ward like a crazy patient who'd gone off their meds. But I'm not one of those individuals. I know exactly what Corey is trying to do. He can't get to me without people knowing, so he is doing the next best thing by working to have me committed into some hellhole of a mental hospital.

It's the following evening. Outside the weather is rough. An icy wind hits the house every so often, accompanied by the occasional spot of rain. After Corey and the police officer tried to 'help' me, I didn't speak to Annette. I felt slightly betrayed that she failed to come running to my defense, but then again, I shouldn't have expected her to. I can't blame her for believing Corey over me. He has meticulously planned this all out by making sure he had solid alibis each time he came for me. It would be hard to work against such logic.

I stumble downstairs, hoping to find Annette. Even if she doesn't believe me, I just want to talk to her and hear a friendly voice no matter what she has to say.

Ava is in bed. I put her down as best I could. I couldn't read her a bedtime story or go through our usual routine. My mind is too scattered and frazzled to handle such a task. Plus, I could sense in Ava's eyes that she knew something was wrong. The last thing I need is for my own daughter to think I've lost it.

"Annette? Where are you?" I call out when I get to the living room.

"I'm here," she says from the sofa.

I move forward and see that she is lying down, hidden from view. "Can we talk?"

I hear a groan come from Annette's mouth. "Okay," she says a moment before she sits upright.

My hands reach out to the back of the sofa as I guide myself quickly around to, and down on, an adjacent armchair. I sit on the edge of the seat with wide eyes, trying to gain Annette's full attention. She can't hate me the way the rest of them do. I've lost too much as it is.

Annette glances at me. "What do you want to talk about?" Her voice lacks its usual level of care.

"I want you to understand why I don't believe Corey when he says he didn't attack me."

Annette holds a palm up to me while closing her eyes. "Don't take this the wrong way, but I don't want to hear that right now."

"I get where you're coming from. I truly do. But I need to unload everything in my head before I lose my mind, and I thought I could rely on my best friend to listen to me no matter how crazy she thinks I sound."

Annette focuses on me. "There's no point."

"What do you mean there's no point?"

Annette stares at me. "Don't worry."

I feel my mouth open to ask her what the hell she's on about, but I stop before a single word escapes me. Annette seems frustrated. It's obvious that I've ruined this friendship by accusing Corey of trying to kill me. What did I expect her to think?

"I'm sorry for putting you in the middle of all of this," I say to Annette. "I never hoped for any of this to affect you."

"Don't be sorry."

"But I am. What's happening between Corey and me shouldn't have to impact you the way it has."

Annette chuckles to herself. "I've gone about this all wrong from the start."

What does she mean by that? It feels like we're having two different conversations. "Is everything okay, Annette?"

"Don't worry about me, Kat. This will all work out in the end."

"Are you saying that the truth will come out about Corey?"

"One way or the other," she says, looking away from me.

I don't know what to make of Annette's behavior. She doesn't seem to be herself. It's like she's waking up from a dream and is mumbling nonsense.

She pushes herself up and stands in front of me. "I have to go see my mom in Portland."

"Right now?" I say. "You realize it's eight o'clock, right?"

"I do. I forgot to tell you about it with everything that's been going on."

Before I can respond, a heavy downpour of rain pounces hard outside. It's loud on the old house.

"Sounds like quite the storm is coming," Annette says as she walks off. "Goodnight."

"Goodnight," I whisper, wishing my friend didn't hate me.

69

KATHERINE - NOW

Corey is trying to kill me. As if sending me to the hospital with a severe concussion wasn't adequate, as if tormenting me in front of a police officer didn't give him enough joy, he's come to end my life. All I keep asking myself is why.

But I don't have time to think about the why. Corey is about to stab me with the thick blade of his hunting knife. I do everything it takes to pull my attention away from him and focus on yanking open the window so I can escape death. With my back to a man who is trying to kill me, I open the pane of glass out into the stormy night.

I launch myself through the opening, bashing my shins into the frame of the window as I realize how steep the roof is. My body twists around while my hands claw to grab hold of the bay so I don't fall down from the second floor of the house and break my neck. I stop myself from tumbling down and look up to see the knife swinging out into the night. The blade slices through the rain and comes close to cutting me. With no other choice, I release my failing grip on the window frame and let myself slide down the roof toward the edge of the building.

A voice screams, following me down. I take a few moments to realize it's my own. It only stops when I slow my descent using my bare feet on the slippery metal surface of Annette's old house. My legs slam into the guttering of the roof, but the aging material holds firm enough to prevent me from going clean off the edge.

For a moment, I stare out into the thick rain pounding down and discover how high up I am from the ground. My heart beats so hard it feels like it might break my ribs.

With as much caution as I can exercise, I slowly turn my head and up to the window bay and find that Corey isn't following me along the dangerous path. He has disappeared inside. Is he looking for something to help push me over the edge? My gaze stays fixed on the opening above, waiting for my attacker to return with a solid object to throw at me. But the terrifying moment doesn't come.

I snap out of my trance and work out how the hell I'll survive this. My options are limited. I could try to hang off the side of the house and drop two floors down to the hard ground below or make my way along the guttering to a valley in the roof that belongs to the first floor. Not wanting to break both my legs, I edge myself across the cold metal on my butt, shuffling toward the relative safety of a lower section of the building.

The guttering creaks and moans from my weight as I proceed. Each time I place pressure on the next section, the previous area my foot was pressing on snaps outward. I keep moving, trying to increase my speed as a large piece of the guttering gives way and submits to gravity. Realizing the full length of guttering my feet are pushing on is about to break off the side of the house, I roll myself over and desperately try to cling on to the slippery roof with my fingers. There's nothing to hold on to, so I press my body against the cold surface like I'm on the edge of a mountain.

I can't move.

All I can do is pray my weakening grip holds out long enough for someone to find me.

70

KATHERINE

A rumble in the distance tells me the storm is getting worse as I cling desperately to a steep roof slick with rainfall. Thunder radiates out from lightning that has already passed across the region. Did Corey wait until there was bad weather to end this all? Or had he gotten lucky?

With not much choice, I call out for help, but my voice gets drowned in the rain, too heavy to fight. But I continue to yell, nonetheless.

No one is coming for me. Annette had to leave for the night to go visit her mom. Corey must have known that I would be alone in the house with Ava.

The stabbing pain in my stomach makes me wonder what this monster has done with my daughter. Does his hatred extend out to her? He was always good to Ava. So much so that I believe she genuinely loves him. She doesn't understand why I no longer want Corey in our lives. How do you explain to a five-year-old that you've had to leave your husband because he is trying to murder you?

As my grip on the roof fades, I can't help but wonder what drove Corey to this moment. Am I really that terrible a person that he feels his only option is to take my life? I don't deserve this. I've been nothing but a loyal and supportive partner to Corey, even through all of his torture these past few weeks. If he never hit me over the back of the head, I'd have still forgiven him for the promotion debacle. Our relationship was more important to me than my career. Now I realize how stupid I was to think such a thing.

My fingers let go.

I feel a sudden yank pull me downward as I lose my grasp on the roof. My legs pass over the edge and pull the rest of me down with them, but I cling on to the fresh edge of the crumbling metal. My body is hanging off the side of the second floor.

"Help!" I yell out, desperation coating my voice. "Please, help me!" But it's no use. Annette's neighbors are too far away to hear me. I have to save myself.

Feeling my arms, hands, and fingers burning to let go, I shuffle along the edge, straining to advance toward the lower valley of the first floor. It's all I can do before my body finally gives up and lets me fall.

I move across the roof one small hand grip at a time, slowly progressing to the valley. It's less than ten feet away from me but it's too far to try to swing out and drop onto it. Again, the metal of the ancient house buckles under my weight. I ignore the ominous sound and continue to inch along the edge until I give in to gravity.

I plunge to the lower valley and land on its peak. My hands grab what they can and help me throw my legs up and over more freezing cold metal. A smile cracks across my face once I realize I'm no longer going to smash into the solid ground below. I practically hug the valley, thanking it for being there. That's when I notice a small window above me that I could easily reach. The ground is still too far down to drop to without potentially snapping an ankle, so I scoot myself along back toward the house.

I'll be okay. I'll get away from Corey, I tell myself. By now he must have fled, knowing that I will call the police the second I can. I wonder what alibi he has lined up this time.

Pushing myself up to my feet on the slippery surface of the roof, I reach for the wall of the house with my spare hand. A moment later, I pull my body to the window and grab its frame. Both of my arms ache with a burn I'll feel for days, but I don't care. I'm alive.

The fixed window provides sunlight to the stairwell within, meaning I'll have to determine a means to smash the glass out and crawl my way through. Inside, there's a decent drop to the lower level. I'm not in the clear yet.

As I try to work out how to get back into the warmth of Annette's house without cutting myself on old glass, I hear a thump behind me. I glance over my shoulder and see a ladder propped up at the edge of the valley's peak. My grip on the window frame tightens.

Is it Corey? Would he really go to this much trouble to kill me, risking his own life for the chance to plunge a hunting knife into my chest?

My eyes dance left and right as I hear the ladder squeak and strain under the weight of a person climbing up toward me. In a panic, I pull off my sweater and wrap it around my fist as fast as humanly possible. The window behind me has to go.

The pane shatters with ease but leaves a jiggered mess in its wake. I do what I can to clean it until I slice my palm open on a smashed blade of glass. I yell out and seize my hand, using the destroyed sweater to stem the blood that is now gushing out.

There are still too many sharp edges stuck in the window frame for me to crawl through the opening without slashing my body to shreds. Devoid of options, I give up on getting back into the house and try to think of a better idea.

But I don't have time to brainstorm.

A figure pops up at the end of the valley and climbs up and over the top of the ladder and stands on the same roof as me. A hood covers their head, casting a thick shadow over their face. It's only then that I realize I'm not staring at Corey. He's much taller than whoever is standing in front of me.

"Hello, Katherine," I hear a voice say to me through the heavy rain. The figure is brandishing the same hunting knife I saw earlier. That weapon made me leap through a second-floor window onto a steep roof during a dangerous storm. I can't work out who it is I'm staring at. If only it weren't raining, I'd be able to tell who has climbed a ladder in the middle of the night to reach me.

I get my answer when Annette pulls her hood back and reveals her face. A thousand realizations hit me at once. How could I have been so stupid?

71

KATHERINE

"**W**hat's the matter, Katherine?" Annette asks me.

My jaw drops and pulls my mouth open. "What are you—?"

"Confused?" Annette asks as she twirls the knife in her hand.

"Why are you—?"

"Oh, come on. You can't seriously be this stupid."

"All of this. Everything that's happened. It was you, wasn't it?"

"Guilty," Annette says as she throws her arms out wide while still maintaining a solid grasp on the sharp blade.

"But why?" I ask on autopilot. The betrayal hasn't set in yet and will take some time to become a reality in my mind.

Annette takes another step toward me on the narrow peak of the valley and closes the small gap between us a little further. "You really must be this stupid if you don't understand why."

I know why she has done this. The moment I saw her face, I knew why we were standing on a hazardous roof in the middle of the night getting soaked by the rain. But I can't accept the truth.

"Say it," she says, reading my mind.

"Corey," I mutter.

"That's right. You thought that you could steal him from me and that I'd give up."

"I didn't take him from you. You and Corey never dated."

"But you knew how much I liked him and how badly I wanted to see him again."

"Of course I knew. But it doesn't mean I tried to ruin your chances with him. He came to me. I didn't approach him. We hit it off straight away and never meant for you to get hurt."

"Well I did!" Annette yells. Her voice pierces through the rain and smashes into my eardrums. I witness an intensity in her eyes that is hyper focused. How long has she been planning all of this?

Annette moves closer to me again, one foot over the other, balancing without effort. "You knew exactly what you were doing. You couldn't stand to see me finally meet someone that might take me away from this hellhole of a town and out from your shadow. So what did you do? You sought Corey out and did everything in your power to claim him before I even had the chance to tell him how I truly felt." Annette raises the knife and points it toward my eyes.

"It's not true. Corey and I getting together was bad timing. Nothing more. I'm sorry things didn't work out the way you hoped, but after that night, he only saw you as a good friend."

"You're lying to me. I know what you did. You got in under his skin and turned him against me. I don't doubt that you filled his head with lies about me so he would never want to see me again."

"Annette, I—"

"Enough! I won't stand here for another second and listen to your attempt to confuse me. I will admit this has all gone on far longer than I ever expected. It would seem Corey is too decent a human being to understand when the person he has married is nothing but a piece of garbage. I never wanted things to come to this point, but here we are. You've left me no other option."

Annette walks closer to me, holding the knife firm as I back up to the house. I feel the wall and the broken glass touch my spine. Pain shoots through my skin that I ignore as adrenaline takes over and throws me into survival mode.

"Don't make this harder than it has to be. For once in your life you won't have your way."

"Please, Annette. I've always been there for you and you've always been there for me. Don't do this. I'll get you help."

Annette swings the knife at me before she is within range, throwing her off balance a little. I feel the blade slicing through the air and come close to my eyes. "I don't need help. You do. You can't see what a disgraceful person you are. How can you call yourself a friend after what you did to me?"

I'm dead. There's way too much rage exploding out of Annette's soul for her to see reason. It's clear to me now that something has changed within her mind. She's not the person I once knew, and I can't stop her. And to make the situation worse, I have nowhere to go.

With my only other choice being death, I charge at Annette while she regains her footing. I reach for the knife, but she fights back, flexing and bending her arms away from me until I trip past her. My body drops hard to the roof and rolls, but I clutch tightly on to the metal surface. I claw my way to my knees and realize that Annette has dropped her knife.

We lock eyes.

I stare at Annette. She stares at me and heaves with a combination of rage and breathlessness. I glance over my shoulder and see the ladder within reach.

"Oh, no you don't," Annette mutters.

I ignore her threat and scurry to the ladder. My hands

extend out to grab the top rung, but I feel a force shove me hard in my back.

I fly forward and crash through the ladder. As my body tumbles out into the dark void, I understand Annette has finally finished what she started.

I did it. It's done. I've finally eliminated everything that stands between Corey and me. No longer will Katherine be able to maintain her manipulative hold over the man who I love more than anyone else ever could.

She landed hard. I watched Katherine go face forward and collide with the ground in such a sickly fashion that there's no chance in hell she could be alive. Still, I have to check. I can't leave her body lying there for all to see.

I find a safe way to the driveway below without a ladder, knowing that there is a small garden shed attached to the side of the valley Katherine obviously didn't understand was there. She could have almost escaped me if she'd known that little fact. But I would have caught up with her, eventually. She still thought Corey was the one haunting her dreams, judging by the confusion on her face.

With my feet on solid ground, I walk up to Katherine with a smile that's filled with relief. She drove me to this moment. I did everything I could to have her believe Corey was a bad husband, yet that wasn't enough. I had to make her fear for her own life, but the damage she'd done to Corey's mind would not allow him to let her go.

Katherine's body is limp on the ground. She's face down in the mud where she belongs. I'm tempted to leave her there, but given she left me with no option but to kill her, I now have to dispose of her body and convince Corey and everyone else she fled town. If it weren't for Ava, the task wouldn't be so hard. She is sleeping in her room drugged up on enough cough medicine to see her through till midday tomorrow.

Sometimes I feel sorry for Ava. It's not her fault that her mother is the worst parent in the world. I'm sure Ava's grandmother will do a better job of raising her.

Squatting down, I check Katherine for a pulse. I don't find one and try a second and third time to make sure I'm not doing it wrong. The CPR courses I've completed through the school over the years have finally come in handy.

Katherine's gone. Luckily for me, Katherine fell and landed close to her own car. Her sedan is shielding her body from the neighbors and the street. It's about the only thing she's ever done right.

With the cover of the darkness and heavy rain, I grab Katherine by the ankles and drag her back to my house to take her into the basement and do what is necessary. I'm not looking forward to what comes next but, I did what I could to prepare myself for this moment.

The Internet is a wonderful thing and can provide someone with education on any topic imaginable. Using a teacher's laptop in their classroom while they were at lunch, I researched the proper disposal of a body. There's no chance they'll trace any of it back to me. Plus, no one will think to look there to begin with.

It takes some time, but I pull Katherine's body into my house, across the hardwood floors to the basement door. I unlock the entrance with its only key and switch on the lights, giving myself a few moments to breathe.

At the bottom of the stairs, I have everything laid out. Plastic sheets and rope wait for Katherine's body. I was expecting to have to deal with a lot more blood, but she is only bleeding a little from her arm and forehead.

Dragging Katherine down to the basement could make too much of a mess and spread her DNA around, especially if her head thuds along each step. Instead, I lay down a thick pile of blankets and roll her onto them to help get her body to the basement.

I reach the bottom of the stairs after an exhausting effort and drop her legs to the floor. After a quick breath, I walk out to the setup I've prepared in the dust-covered room.

I took a while to draw up enough courage to go through this, but she forced me to this point. I guess a part of me knew this day was coming from the start. It's not the first time I've had to take matters into my own hands when a supposed friend has betrayed me.

Katherine was away from Battery Beach when my former best friend Lisa took it upon herself to date my ex-boyfriend less than a week after he had dumped me. I didn't kill her like I should have, but I made it clear that if she ever stepped foot in this town again, it would be a deadly mistake.

This time is worse. Corey is my soulmate. There's no doubt in my mind that we will be together forever. No one else knows him the way I do. I learned more about him with a single kiss than any of the shallow women he has been with in the past.

I was right to throw Katherine off the roof. She wouldn't have been easy to threaten out of town. Scaring her off would never work.

I close my eyes and breathe in for a moment to draw in all the focus needed to clean up. When I exhale my held breath, I shift my gaze to the bone saw laid out in the middle of the room. I only take two steps toward the tool when I hear a groan.

Spinning round, my eyes land on Katherine. She's still alive. I mustn't have checked her pulse right.

I instantly run for a hammer I have sitting on an old workstation in the corner. My fist grabs hold of the wooden handle and squeezes tight. I need to finish this now before I lose my nerve.

"Corey," Katherine whispers. Her eyes are closed. "Help..."

"He's not coming," I mutter. "Ever."

I rush to Katherine and drop over her chest, hammer in hand. My hand raises it up high without question, ready to silence her. "You did this to yourself."

73

The hammer drops from my hand to the floor after I step away from Katherine. My breath sucks in and out as I struggle to maintain the overwhelming amount of adrenaline flowing through me like a river.

I wanted to do it more than any other act in my life. It's not that I'm incapable of giving Katherine what I know she deserves, but a better idea came into my head as her eyes opened at the last second and stared straight into mine. She didn't beg for her life or even try to fight back. I assumed most people would rebel in their final moment of existence. Instead, Katherine accepted her fate and waited for me to strike.

That didn't sit well with me. I need to see nothing but utter defeat in her eyes in her last moments.

"Annette, please... What are you doing? This isn't you," Katherine whispers.

"No talking. We're past that."

"Please... You can still—"

"I said don't talk to me!" I charge over to Katherine. Her eyes follow mine as I bend down and scoop up the hammer. Again, I crouch over her chest and raise the weapon in my hand up high, readying it to silence Katherine forever. Maybe killing her will be enough satisfaction. Maybe I don't need to take this thing to the final level.

"You're better than this," Katherine says through a croaky voice. Her eyelids are only half open as if she is gradually losing consciousness.

I let my arm lower calmly as my shoulders ease up. Katherine's eyes fully close. Her begging must have taken all the energy she had left. It pains me to my stomach to place the hammer down on the floor, but I know the payoff will be so much more if I can escalate what has already begun.

Katherine is still breathing. I observe the rise and fall of her chest and stand to take a step back from her body. I know what I must do now as I pace up and down the limited space of the basement.

"You thought I'd end your life this easily," I say to Katherine. But she doesn't respond. She's either unconscious or is the world's greatest actor. After taking that fall and being dragged down the steps, I highly doubt this is an act.

This is perfect. Everything I worked so hard to achieve is coming together. If only I could enjoy this moment forever. But I know it's time.

My idea is so simple and will confirm what I already know to be true in my heart.

I pull my cell out of my back pocket and unlock it. Within moments, I navigate my way to my list of contacts and hover my finger over Corey's name.

I need him now more than ever before. Together, we will end Katherine's life.

74

ANNETTE

I've spent almost an hour getting everything ready for Corey to arrive. I can't wait for him to get here and be part of Katherine's final moments. Together we will repair the past. Then we can leave this place and the pathetic people that dwell within the region. Corey's not from this town, so I know he won't have any problem leaving it behind to start our new life. Then we can wipe the last six months clean from our minds.

Standing almost outside my front door while rain continues to soak the ground, I wait as calmly as possible for Corey to appear.

A set of headlights twist and turn around the corner ahead and charge straight for my house. I see Corey arrive in his sedan. He slams on the brakes as he hits my driveway, causing his tires to screech. In less than a second, he leaps out from the driver's seat and rushes toward me, his door slamming in a hurry.

"Where do you think she's gone?" Corey says, referring to Katherine. I told him over the phone that she had grabbed Ava and run away, only leaving behind a simple note. I had to shift Katherine's car and park it a few streets over from mine to help sell the story.

"I don't know, sorry. I only realized when I got up in the middle of the night to drink some water that she'd left with Ava."

Corey shakes his head. "I've tried calling her cell, but she won't answer. I think it might be switched off as it keeps going to voicemail." He clutches his forehead with both hands and squeezes. "This is insane. Where the—?"

"Hey, it's okay. I promise you, before this night is through, everything will be the way it should be."

Corey's eyes lift from the ground and focus on mine. "How can you be so sure? Her behavior has been so erratic since we got married. What if she has—?"

"Hey, hey," I say to him as I place both hands behind his elbows. "Don't panic. I'm confident they're both fine. Come inside with me, out of the rain."

Corey resists as I gently pull him toward the house. "No, we should search for Katherine and Ava. Grab what you need and meet me in my car. I'm gonna drive us around town so we can find them."

I expected this to be his response. "That's a good idea, but I think you should come inside first. I have to show you something that I know will help."

"We really don't have time to—"

"Follow me, please. You need to see this before we do anything."

Corey glances over his shoulder at his car and then to me. "Okay, but whatever this is, make it quick. They could be anywhere by now, and the longer we take to leave, the further away they get."

"I understand," I say as I grab Corey's hand and lead him inside. Once we're in through my front door, I close it behind us. He walks further into my house and scratches the back of his head. He is too eager to rush out and save Katherine, but I know that's because he's a good man who always wants to do the right thing. Even though no one would hold it against him if he let Katherine go, he continues to be there for her. That will change before the night is through.

"What did you want to show me? And how does it help us find Katherine and Ava?" Corey asks, facing me.

I step up to him and get inside his personal space. "Before I show you, I need you to understand something. Everything that's happened leading up to tonight has been for one simple reason: you and Katherine don't belong together."

"What?"

"Hear me out. You have to admit that your marriage with Katherine has been nothing but a train wreck."

"I'll admit that we've had some hard luck over the last few weeks, but—"

"Is it bad luck, or is the universe trying to tell you that things will never work out for you and Katherine? Come on, think about this."

Corey exhales louder than the rain beating down outside. "I know what you're saying, and I guess there's a lot of truth to it."

I step closer. "You did everything you could. You gave her chance after chance, but it still wasn't enough for her, was it?"

Corey's eyes drop to the floor. "No."

"So why fight for her? Why put yourself through hell to rush around and find her?"

Corey glances to the front door as if he can see through it to his car. I grab his jaw and gently guide him to me. "Let her go."

"Okay," he says. "You're right."

A warm tingle rushes down and over every inch of my skin as I pull his head toward mine. I kiss Corey and feel him kiss me back. My eyes flutter with ecstasy, making me draw him in tighter. Our tongues meet and become one.

Our lips stay together for what feels like an eternity. When they finally part, I gaze into his soul and thank him for seeing the truth. "I love you," I say. The words fall out of my mouth. I stored them away in my heart the second we first met. His eyes narrow in on mine.

A smile breaks through my intense stare as I don't dare to shift my focus from Corey's face. "You have no idea how long I've waited to tell you that."

"Annette, I didn't know—"

"Shh. It's okay. Everything will be as it should soon enough. Follow me." I pull Corey by the hand and guide him toward the basement. I left the door wide open with the light on. "After you," I say, pointing him down the steps. He needs to see this first.

We take the stairs slowly and descend into the depths of the cellar. It's not until we reach the bottom that Corey sees Katherine tied to a chair around the bend at the back wall of the underground room. He doesn't utter a word.

I drift past him and into the space toward Katherine. She's gagged and can't move an inch.

"What's this?" Corey asks.

"Our greatest test."

"What do you mean?"

"Katherine has been nothing but a burden in our lives. She has wasted precious time we could have been together and tried to take our happiness away. We have to put an end to her ability to destroy us."

"Are you saying that we should—?"

"You know this needs to happen. We will never be rid of the insufferable headache that she forces upon us unless we do this, Corey."

He steps forward, never taking his eyes off Katherine's desperate pleading face. "Unless we do what?"

I move in close to him and wrap my hands around Corey's back. "Unless we kill her together."

75

What's happening? I must be dreaming; caught in a nightmare I can't wake from. It's the only explanation my brain can make sense of as I witness Annette's attempt to convince Corey to help murder me. And to add to the chaos, I think he's considering what she has to say.

Corey stares right at me. Not once has he tried to stop Annette. The moment he walked in and saw me gagged and tied to a chair, he should have charged at Annette. He should have attacked her with every piece of strength he could muster. But instead, he remains motionless in the middle of this screwed-up room.

I try to yell through the gag in my mouth but it's no use. Annette stuffed a sock in there before wrapping a few layers of duct tape around my face. She then shoved me into this old wooden chair and bound my arms and legs to it with rope. I'm powerless to defend myself from whatever is about to happen.

"Are you sure this is the only way?" Corey asks Annette at his side. She holds up the now dirt-covered hunting knife from before in her fist and points it at me.

"We have to stop her from ruining our lives any further. She already tricked you into seeing past me more than six months ago. You married her when we could have been together from the start. We can't let Katherine waste another moment of our time."

Corey nods.

My eyes bulge as I struggle to comprehend what's unfolding before me. I feel like I'm witnessing my death in slow motion and can't do a thing to stop it. Surely my husband isn't about to kill me with my best friend's help. I shut my eyes and try to block out the world, but it's impossible to escape the anguish burning my insides.

Then I remember something through the haze of this severe concussion I am no doubt suffering from: Annette has Ava. I scream as loud as I can through the gag, begging them not to harm my daughter. They might kill me, but they won't do the same to my beautiful little girl, will they? No one is that disturbed.

"Help me do this," Annette says as she guides Corey's hand to her fingers clutching the handle of the sharp blade. There doesn't seem to be trust between them yet, but Annette wants Corey to be an equal part of this sick deed.

They take a step closer to me in unity. I writhe around and kick my legs, fighting back despite being bound with thick rope. But it's futile. There's nothing I can do now but plead to my husband with my eyes.

Corey has to see through the lies and brainwashing Annette has thrown upon him. Why can't he fight off her deception and repel the manipulation that is forcing him into doing the unthinkable?

"That's it," Annette says, encouraging Corey forward like a trained animal doing its master's bidding.

They both stop within striking distance and lower the knife down to my midsection. Corey shifts his focus to Annette.

"We can do this," she says. "It'll be over before we know it. Then we'll be free to move on and pretend none of this ever happened."

My nostrils flare as I fail to scream through the gag. The sound breaks through enough to draw Corey's attention away from Annette for a second, but she pulls him in again with her spare hand.

"Don't let her deceive you. It's what she's done from the start."

"I know; you're right. This has to happen, but I don't think I can go through with it."

Annette pauses. "I understand what you are saying, but we have to do this, together. It's the only way to secure our bond. It's the only way to break the hold she's had over you all this time."

Corey closes his eyes. There has to be doubt creeping into his mind. He doesn't want to kill me. He's not insane like Annette. Right or wrong, it's all I have to work with. Now I need him to wake up and realize where he is and what he's about to do.

"I need a minute," he says, releasing his grip on the knife and stepping off to the side.

"It's okay," Annette says as she too moves away from me. I get a moment to breathe as she follows Corey over to a workbench that is pressed against the wall. His head hangs low as he places both palms flat on the surface of the dusty table.

Annette walks over to him with the knife at her side, ignoring me like I can't hear a word she's saying. "Take a second to get your head straight but understand that if we are going to do this, time is against us."

"Okay, okay. I need a minute to think this through," Corey mutters with his back facing the room.

Annette paces over to him and places her arm on his shoulder. "There's nothing to think about. Follow my lead and help me put an end to this nightmare." She turns him around and guides him in my direction before stepping ahead with the knife up and ready.

Annette comes face to face with me and leers over my body with absolute control. Never have I seen such a demonic look in her eyes. She glances over her shoulder at Corey and says, "I'll do it. For us both."

He nods.

"I love you," she says. Her gaze locks on to his as she waits for a reply.

A tear trails from Annette's eye as a grin breaks through her determined face. She raises the blade up high and grabs me by the shoulder to steady her aim. "You brought this on yourself," she whispers with a sneer.

The knife comes down hard. I flinch and tense my core, but nothing hits me. When I open my eyes, I see Corey holding Annette's wrist with both hands as she tries to push the sharp metal into my chest. The hunting knife is only three inches from stabbing me.

"What the hell are you doing?" Annette asks my husband.

Corey's eyes stay locked on to mine as I try to plunge the knife into Katherine's body. He hasn't answered my question, so I remind him what's at stake. "You agreed to this."

"Put down the knife," Corey says.

"No. Not until she's dead. You know we have to end this."

Corey's nostrils flare. "It's not happening. Put down the damn knife."

My head snaps away from Corey's as my brain registers the extent of his reaction. Is this more than him having doubts? "What are you saying?"

"Let go of the knife. It's over."

My eyes close as a fear sweeps through my body, weakening my grip. "You can't mean that. This isn't you talking."

"Don't make me hurt you, Annette. I swear to God I'll..."

The dismay in my heart fades away, allowing my mind to accept what Corey has done. Katherine's power is still too much for him to break. My failing control of the situation disappears as an overpowering rage takes over every muscle in my body. I grab the hunting knife with both hands and push down. "She dies now."

"Stop!" Corey yells. He slams his shoulders hard into me and breaks my grip on the blade. I fall sideways and feel the weapon follow. The sharp edge of the metal cuts my arm before it topples to the floor. We both fall to our knees in the scuffle.

I lock eyes with Corey. As one, our focus drops to the knife sitting between us. Corey snaps at it first and scoops the weapon into his hands. Within a second, he jabs the blade out in my direction, leveling it at my throat.

"It's over, Annette."

"What?" I spit out at him.

"Come on. Did you really believe I would kill my wife just to be with you?"

I stare at him as I remain sitting on my knees while an external force rushes into my body and tears my soul apart. Blood leaks from my arm but I don't care. Has everything I've worked so hard for all been for nothing?

"Don't move from where you are. The police will be here soon."

I shake my lowered head. "When did you call the police?"

"Not long before I came here. You had me convinced that Katherine had lost it with all the hell you put us through, but you made one mistake."

"No, I didn't. I planned this all to perfection. You're lying."

"It was almost perfect, but you should have wiped the school's security footage when you left to go to your own house to mess with Katherine."

"What? No, I—"

"I only saw it by dumb luck. I requested a copy of any recordings made during the timeframe Katherine thought I was at your house terrorizing her. I wanted to have more evidence to prove to Katherine that I would never do such a horrible thing. The security company only emailed me the footage an hour ago.

You should have seen my face when I saw you sneaking out of school."

"No," I whisper.

"At first, I tried to tell myself you were only leaving work to go to the shops or something far less sinister, but you didn't walk up to your car the way a normal person would. You stayed down as low as you could to avoid the cameras."

"No, no, no. I was careful, dammit. I'm always careful."

"Maybe you thought you were, but what I saw got me thinking about you and everything that'd happened between Katherine and me. It didn't take long to piece it all together once I remembered our history. Why aren't you over me?"

"I will never be over you," I scream at Corey. "Don't you understand? I love you more than she ever could. All she brings you is disappointment. I can make you happy and show you perfection."

Corey shakes his head at me. "This thing you've imagined between us isn't going to happen. I'm sorry you feel otherwise, but I don't love you, Annette."

He might as well stab me in the heart with the knife. The pain in my chest feels like he has, but I remind myself of the truth. "You're lying," I say, "to protect Katherine."

"No. I'm not. And like I said, the police are on their way to arrest you for everything you've done to us."

"No. It's not true. I don't hear any sirens. You're testing me. Why else would you have kissed me before?"

"This isn't a test. That kiss wasn't real. I don't love you."

"Yes, you do. You—"

"I called the police straight after you rang me," Corey yells over the top of my voice. "I knew your story about Katherine running away with Ava wasn't true and that their lives were in danger. Why do you think I was trying to drag you away from the house?"

This isn't happening. Corey loves me. I saw it in his eyes when we kissed. You can't fake that.

"Like I said, Annette, this is over. Why don't you come with me upstairs and hand yourself in to the police?"

I chuckle. "You can drop the act, Corey. There's no need to spare Katherine's feelings anymore. God knows she deserves this. Do you have any idea how long I've had to sit by her side and be her inferior friend? All she ever does is take from me. Finally, that's over. We don't have to let her hold control over our lives. We can be together."

"You don't get it," Corey says as he walks over to me. "This isn't about Katherine's supposed control over me. I don't want you, Annette. I never called you back when we first kissed for a reason. There was no spark. No desire to be more than just your friend. Please understand we will never be together no matter what."

"Yes, we will!" I scream. I squeeze my eyes closed and feel the veins on my temples throb. "You don't mean any of that."

"It's the truth. You know I'm not lying, so get up and come with me." Corey steps over to within a few feet of me and offers a hand to help me up.

I stare up at Corey, feeling every muscle in my body tense at once. "Just tell me one thing and I'll do as you ask."

"Okay. Name it."

"Why?"

"Why what?"

"Why did you really choose her over me? And don't give me some line about us not having a connection."

Corey glances to Katherine tied and gagged in the chair and back to me. "Does it really matter?"

"Look around you. What do you think?"

Corey tries to dodge the question as his eyes move from one

corner of the room to the next. "Let's go before the police arrive. I came here ahead of them for a reason."

"No. Not until you answer me."

"There's no point."

"Tell me!" I yell, standing up. "I want this bitch to understand how she's tricked you. I want her to see again what she's done to me."

"Annette, please. Come with me and—"

I charge at Corey and reach for the knife. He turns his body sideways at the last second, forcing me to collide into him as he attempts to move the blade away from me. He isn't prepared for my advance and stumbles back, tripping over the plastic sheeting on the floor. Corey falls onto Katherine, hitting her torso with enough energy to topple over the chair I bound her to.

Within a heartbeat, I realize I've hurt Corey as I see a small amount of blood on his hands when he climbs off Katherine. What was I doing? I would never hurt him. He's under Katherine's control and doesn't know what he's saying to me. But before I can think of the words to say to Corey to help him forgive me, I notice something: the blood isn't his.

"Honey, I'm so sorry. Don't move," Corey says to Katherine as he stares at the knife handle sticking out of her chest.

Blood wets through Katherine's thin layer of clothing and spreads out wide as shock registers on her face. But that surprise soon fades along with her eyes.

"No, no, no. Baby, please. Stay with me." Corey holds Katherine's head in his hands, yanking her eyelids open as they give up their fight. With every second that passes, another piece of Katherine leaves her body.

I take a few steps toward the couple and hold my gaze on Katherine's dimming vision. I offer her one last smirk as she fades into oblivion. This is it. She can't lie her way out of death.

"Honey? Open your eyes. Stay with me, please. Don't do this."

"She's gone," I utter.

With his back facing me, Corey's body slumps to the sound of my voice. His knees buckle.

"You can drop the act now," I say to Corey. "Finally, we can be together."

A sigh escapes his lips. He half turns and glances at me over his shoulder. "You killed her."

"No, my love. We killed her. We had no choice."

"Police!" a man calls out from the top of the basement stairs. "Nobody move. We're coming down."

"We're free now," I say to Corey. "No longer can she keep us apart."

Corey doesn't say a word and continues to stare at me while he holds Katherine's head in his palms.

A commanding voice shouts out behind me, ordering me to my knees as more footsteps rush into the basement. I do as I'm asked while never letting Corey out of my gaze.

Corey's mine now. No longer will Katherine get in our way.

COREY

Katherine's gone. It sounds impossible to hear those words form in my mind, but the truth cannot be ignored. My wife is dead, and it's all my fault.

I have to keep reminding myself what has happened. On a loop, I blame myself for everything. If only I'd worked things out sooner. I should have seen Annette for the person she really was. Instead, I was off in my own self-centered world and kept doubting Katherine at every step, playing into Annette's hands exactly as she wanted me to. She used our weaknesses to her advantage with little effort, and Katherine paid the price.

It's been a week. Seven days of numb existence. I'm sitting in the living room of our rental watching Ava as she stares at the TV. I can see behind the despair in her eyes that she's not taking in anything on the screen. Not even the sound of the happy cartoon voices seems to make a difference.

When Katherine kicked me out, all I wanted to do was come back home, but not like this. Not to this empty soulless place. Now I have to continue on and somehow give Ava a decent childhood. How can I possibly do so when all I feel is misery and pain?

The nights have been the hardest. Ava struggles with me putting her to bed now more than ever. My heart snaps in two every time she wakes up after only a few hours to call out for her mommy.

My cell vibrates in my pocket. I pull it out to see a reminder I'd set earlier before telling me to prepare some food for Ava and me. It sounds absurd to do such a thing, but neither one of us wants to eat anymore. The three meals we're supposed to enjoy per day have joined the list of mundane tasks I have to achieve to keep us both in good health.

It's lunchtime, so I decide to make sandwiches. It's funny, my stomach used to churn the closer the time got to the next meal in the day and remind me to eat. Now, there's nothing. No expression. No animal instinct begging me to do what's necessary to survive. Just a void.

As I stand from the sofa, not pulling Ava's gaze from the droning screen in front of her eyes, a second reminder flashes up on my phone telling me to check the mail. I have an entire list of day-to-day jobs programmed into my cell to help keep this place afloat. If I didn't, I'd probably lie around all day long and stare at the nothingness until Ava said something.

Before I make lunch, I walk to the front door to check the mail. On a normal day, I'd only find an empty box when I came home from work. We email most things these days. But with Katherine gone, there's a mess of legal documents and proceedings being communicated to me the old-fashioned way through the mail.

I don't even know where to begin with it all. Katherine's funeral was hard enough to deal with. Why is it the second we lose a person we care about more than anything else in the world we're expected to have them honored and buried in the ground within a few days? There's no time to think or allow the shock of the truth to sink in.

Katherine's funeral didn't seem real. It was a bad dream my mind wouldn't release me from. I didn't shed a single tear until I had to get up in front of the crowd of family, friends, and coworkers to talk about my wife in the past tense. Only then did my brain accept that she was dead and would never come back. Never again would I hear her laugh or feel the warmth of her lips.

I run my hands through my unkempt hair to remind myself where I am and what I need to do. It's so easy to get bogged down in these horrible thoughts and fall into a spiraling stupor. All I can do is keep moving.

The cold ocean air doesn't register on my skin as I head down the driveway to the mailbox. Either I've gotten used to it, or I'm forgetting how to feel. It's hard to know which possibility is worse. Finally acclimatizing to the town after my wife dies seems cruel, while the latter is cause for concern.

I open the mailbox to see a new pile of legal hell to go through. Mixed in the stack are some handwritten notes I assume are condolence cards. They've been flowing in all week, each saying the same useless things I don't want to hear.

As I walk toward the house, I notice one of the letters is for Ava. So far, they've all been sent to my name. When I get back inside, I give Ava her letter, hoping it might be a note from a close relative. Maybe it will do her good to pull her head away from the TV for a minute or two.

"Ava, honey," I say once I shut the front door.

She doesn't react or show me any sign that she's heard me speak.

"Ava. There's a letter for you. Why don't we open it and give it a read?"

This time she turns toward me. "Okay," she mutters.

I sit down beside her, knowing that I'll need to help her read the words. The thought gets me thinking how badly all of this will affect her education. Losing your mom at the start of your schooling years can't be good.

Ava slowly tears open the envelope, leaving the paper a jagged mess. With rough hands, she slides out the letter and unfolds it upside down. I assist her to bring it the right way around and point my finger at the first line of the note then I read it to her.

"Dear Ava. I hope this letter finds you well. Words cannot express the pain your young heart must be feeling. Without a doubt, this will be one of the most trying times in your life. But I know you'll pull through to the other side, especially if you take the right path moving forward.

"By now, you and Corey will have been swamped with letters and care packages from family and friends who have all offered you their love and support. I'm not sending you a letter to add to the wave of empty promises. I have something more substantial to offer you."

I pull the letter away.

"Wait. We're not finished," Ava says.

"Sorry. Just a second." There's something off about the writing. Like it was never meant to be read by a child. Whoever wrote this shouldn't have sent it directly to Ava. I continue reading but to myself, not aloud.

Right now, you're being taken care of by the greatest man who ever lived, one your pathetic excuse of a mother never deserved. He may feel obligated to raise you and pay back a false debt his mind has generated, but the truth is Corey owes you nothing.

You came into this world against your will at the hands of a pair of contemptible lowlifes who didn't deserve the honor of creating life. I don't hold that against you, but if you think for one minute that I'll let you carry on the burden your mother forced upon Corey then you are gravely mistaken. You are not his problem. Considering you have a grandmother close by, there's no need for you to weigh Corey down.

"What the hell?" I blurt.

"What is it?" Ava asks.

"Nothing. You keep watching the TV, okay. This letter wasn't meant for you, sorry."

"But it says, 'Dear Ava' on it." She tries to point out her name on the paper.

I yank the screwed-up note away. "Watch your show, please," I say as I stand. I scoop up the envelope and realize there's no return address. How did Annette send this letter to me? She's supposed to be locked up tight at Oregon State Hospital, along-side hundreds of other criminally insane individuals. I continue reading her letter as a rage swells inside.

I don't want you to share the same fate as your mother, but I will do whatever it takes to get Corey back. No one, and I mean no one, will come between us ever again. As soon as I find a way out of the hellhole they've put me in, I will come for anyone who tries to impede our love. I will—

The letter continues on, devolving into nothing but a series of threatening rants, the handwriting becoming rougher and pressed so hard into the page there are holes throughout each line. It ends with a single line *'I love you, Corey. More than you can ever comprehend. Sincerely yours, A.'*

I read the words again and feel a shiver run down my spine with every word absorbed. My gaze slowly draws up to Ava sitting on the sofa. She is clueless to the threat Annette poses, and I aim to keep it that way.

I can't let Katherine's little girl live on in fear the way Katherine had to. But I also can't ignore a simple truth: Annette won't stop until she gets what she wants.

<<<<>>>>

ACKNOWLEDGMENTS

A big thank you to the hard-working team at Bloodhound for making this book happen.

As always, thanks must go to my wife for her loving support that gets me through the hundreds of hours spent writing. Another thank you to my young daughter for her constant inspiration.

And finally, thank you to anyone who has taken the time to read this book. Without you, none of this would be possible.